THE LI

Sam North has written four novels, the most recent being
By Desire. He won the 1990 Somerset Maugham Award
for *The Automatic Man*. He lives in London.

Sam North

THE LIE OF THE LAND

V

VINTAGE

Published by Vintage 1999

2 4 6 8 10 9 7 5 3 1

First published in Great Britain in 1998
by Secker & Warburg

Vintage
Random House, 20 Vauxhall Bridge Road,
London SW1V 2SA

Random House Australia (Pty) Limited
20 Alfred Street, Milsons Point, Sydney
New South Wales 2061, Australia

Random House New Zealand Limited
18 Poland Road, Glenfield,
Auckland 10, New Zealand

Random House South Africa (Pty) Limited
Endulini, 5A Jubilee Road, Parktown 2193,
South Africa

Random House UK Limited Reg. No. 954009

A CIP catalogue record for this book
is available from the British Library

ISBN 0 7493 9595 X

Papers used by Random House UK Ltd are natural,
recyclable products made from wood grown in sustain-
able forests. The manufacturing processes conform to the
environmental regulations of the country of origin

Printed and bound in Great Britain by
The Guernsey Press Co. Ltd, Guernsey, C.I.

To Annabelle

part one

There's the thrum of a car over the cattle-grid. She touches a wrist to her brow and thinks, the Enemy.

She stands, ducks her head, it's only a few steps from the kitchen to the hall. The door is cut from a single slice of a beech tree torn down by the hurricane of '87, swollen with a winter's worth of rain, closing the gaps. A tug at the handle; on the second try, it gives.

Outside, the wind has set the farm in motion: last year's leaves circle uselessly; the tops of the trees wave. She glimpses a splash of brilliant white through the wind-torn, tangled hedge surrounding the house.

This is him, his car, it's the routine, once-yearly visit, but she's anxious: *money*.

Her gait is a steady lope: the knees flexible, her hips square, she peers over the wicket gate leading from her neglected garden into the front yard.

The new man – she's not met him before – is strongly built, curly-haired, in his late thirties, smiling from the side window of the vehicle as he hops out to shake her hand. 'Michael Peddlar, hello, you must be Jane.'

'Yes.'

He's wearing a collar and tie, a rough woollen suit; clean shaven, a ready smile and an open face, unwritten on. He moves deftly to extract a briefcase, cheerfully slams the car door. The tie wriggles at his neck, caught by the wind.

3

He points out that cloud is piled on the horizon and there's the likelihood of rain to add to the March wind, so she reads it that he's trying hard for her and she tries hard for him – asks which he'd prefer, to come inside, or look over the place, first?

To think, he lifts his eyes skyward, then, politely, his gaze descends, he chooses.

He follows her down the narrow path towards the house; the rubbery clump of her wellingtons is the exact opposite to the *squish-squish* of his loafers on the soft earth.

It's a small circular garden planted with alpine varieties, overhung by an enormous, leafless beech tree, old enough to threaten the house with its limbs. It's an early Devon Longhouse, a low building dug into the side of a gentle slope, two storeys, built with granite walls three foot thick, roofed in tile, hunkered down against the weather. The joints in the stone are invisible – compressed by gravity for so long, each chiselled boulder has closed on its neighbour. Much of the surface has disappeared beneath a crust of mottled lichen, so it's a solid length of dark grey stone, cut with windows, the creepers have overgrown and dismantled the guttering, the window frames are freshly painted but the wood underneath bulges with damp; around the chimney the render has fallen off in patches, the slates are cracked, set awry.

Now – ahead of him, she ducks her head to walk through the low door.

He follows, looks for the mat to wipe his feet; there isn't one, he decides not to bother since she doesn't kick off her boots but walks straight into the kitchen, heads for the kettle.

'Old house,' he comments.

The windows are deep and small, the floors slope, the ceiling is low, the granite walls are unplastered, the naked stone visible, harsh to the touch, and against the upside wall

4

there's a bloom of green algae: it proves the incursion of damp.

With her back to him, Jane's setting out the cups. She agrees, there was a house here way before the Domesday Book, before history, even, not this exact one, but a hut circle or the like, similar to what you see on your way over the moor.

'Really?' He places his briefcase on the ground, his fingers fly to the knot of his tie, he sees cobwebs, electricity cables tacked to the walls, likewise the plumbing for the Rayburn, a clothes drier bolted to the ceiling, the floor muddy, a dog's basket snug against the stove.

This black and white dog isn't pedigree collie, he's a mongrel, with collie in the mix somewhere, called Roo, and although he's awake, he doesn't lift his muzzle from his paws; he merely fixes Michael Peddlar with a steady, questioning eye.

Michael Peddlar is amazed. 'To think of people living on this spot, then, for *thousands* of years.'

She steps to one side and then back with the kettle and the milk bottle; it's going to be powdered coffee. The kettle boils, now, and she suggests, 'Have a look around.'

So: he obeys, ducks his head to pass through the hall, to her living room, any man above six foot would be permanently stooped in here. There's a television, a mantel above a wood-burning stove, a chair with a dimple in the seat, plainly used more often than the others, and in three paces he's across the room and stands at the top of the steps. Now he can look down into a small, square space set four foot below, like an open cellar, which has been made into a bathroom. A roll of paper stands at the foot of the toilet, a single economy-size bottle of shampoo is parked on the side of the bath, a small mirror hangs over the sink. There's no evidence of medicines, soaps, or sprays.

He turns back and joins her in the kitchen.

She feels it, the burden of power on the man's shoulders, like an invisible edifice towering over him because the organisation he works for could stop her in her tracks, throw out her possessions, change the history of the house in a trice.

Meanwhile, she is putting a biscuit or two on a plate, which is ridiculous because normally she'd take them directly from the packet; so would he, no doubt.

He sits neatly, spreads his hands on the surface of the table, thanking her: 'Great.'

She drops into her normal seat, notices his smooth hands, white and unblemished, yet she might wish for their strength, and his nails are clean.

There's a brief pause, while the Enemy sips his drink.

HE REPLIES EASILY, as if it were not too grave a situation, something temporary, 'BSE put a lot of farmers on their back feet.'

He picks up a biscuit, then the instinct flies at him to put it back; he – his organisation – shouldn't take any *more* from her, but he daren't put it back, either.

She tells him, 'I'm not just on my back foot, I'm on the run.'

There's his discomfort.

She's guilty at sparring with him, he's only doing his job; she ought to thank him, maybe, the amount of letters he's sent; now he's here, in person, yet, for the moment, she can't remember his name.

'Beautiful, up here on the moor, isn't it; another world.'

'Different climate, anyway.' She indicates the direction from which the prevailing weather patterns arrive off the Atlantic coast to the south-west. Due to the proximity of the sea, the openness of the landscape – treeless and uninhabited for thirty miles to the west of here – and the extra five hundred feet of height, Dartmoor has a rougher winter and a cooler summer. There's been snow up here in late May – only last year she was cut off for three days by snow falling on the last weekend in April; spring comes a month or two later than it does just a mile away, downhill. Yes, the other side of the cattle-grid marks the boundary to a different country, it seems.

Then, she enquires about his work.

'Too many figures, for my liking!' he exclaims. 'Not so good with the maths, I'm not; luckily there's computers to do it for us.'

He likes to get out of the office and see how people live, arrive at an understanding of how a community knits together, and what they, the bank, can do to make life easier. He's steady, fluent – yes, she can see he's trying hard for her.

The paperwork drives him mad, he's saying, because he was brought up on a farm himself, he's only one generation away from the soil.

'But it's an office job and I suppose I'm an office worker, which is very different from what you're doing up here.'

She seldom looks him in the eye. Instead she watches his thick, strong hands coiling and uncoiling, the hurry in his voice betrays the guilt inherent in his position: he has the power to announce unpopular decisions. The bank can help, but it can withdraw help, it can never be seen to fail.

A pause in the conversation holds them; it rears up, impossible to break.

The eye of the black and white mongrel is fixed on Michael Peddlar.

Jane stares mutely downwards.

Suddenly her head lifts, she plants her hands on the table, a mirror-image of his gesture when he was first sitting down.

'Show you around then?'

'Yes,' he answers, keen, 'let's have a look.'

They stand, make their way outside.

THE WIND HAS risen. Finding the deepening low pressure, it tugs at their clothes even in the shelter of the house.

From the car he takes his boots and a Barbour waterproof; she notices the car's new while her Mini Cooper has a registration number from the last run around the alphabet.

She waits while he shrugs on the Barbour, puts his loafers in the boot, closes the lid.

'Set?'

'Yup, let's go.'

She takes him through the farm gate set between the Longhouse and the first in a line of low granite outbuildings, roofed with pig-iron, which reach behind it.

The sky is flannel grey, windblown, fast.

With her hand on the latch, she points back the way they came.

'I suppose the first thing I ought to say is, I've got planning permission for that.'

He turns to look beyond the cars to where a granite barn stands across the front yard. It's built squarer, taller than the Longhouse and there isn't the same impression of stones melding together with age. The pointing between the granite slabs is neat and emphatic, slates climb the roof evenly, the flashing has been relaid.

Yet it's blind, having no windows, only a blue-painted door big enough to drive a cart through.

'For a dwelling?' he asks.

She nods. 'I had an eye on converting it, moving in myself, when I first got the place, for the extra height of the ceilings, and the view, and so on, but if it came to the end of the road, I could always sell it, I suppose.'

'Right, excellent, noted.'

He follows Jane through the gate.

'What's the state of the interior at the moment?'

'Nothing there. It's an empty shell.'

They head through the stable yard: a mixture of breeze-block, granite and wood, roofed in pig-iron, frames three loose-boxes on either side while underfoot the concrete slopes to a drainage channel cut in the middle of the path to carry away water. Chickens pick at the ground, their feathers blown backwards. Behind the stables can be glimpsed hay and straw lodged to the height of the rafters.

'Horses, obviously.'

'How many d'you have?'

'Two.'

On cue, a brown muzzle appears, blows briefly, before withdrawing.

'This one's Lady, my number one horse.'

Lady wheels once around the stable, reappears, notices the stranger; her muzzle comes out again, points at him, gives a low snort of suspicion, the wind has spooked her.

Jane has her hand on Lady's chin, scratching the bony underside. 'Half thoroughbred, but with a sensible head, she's still all right for the moor. She knows how to look after herself, don't you? Eh, girl?'

'She's lovely.'

'Used to be a film star.'

9

'Huh . . .'

'Trained by whoever it was to lie down when you press somewhere on her neck.'

Michael Peddlar follows Jane's example and experiments: he dabs at the horse with the tips of his fingers. Lady looks surprised, rolls her eyes.

She doesn't lie down, though.

Michael Peddlar asks, 'Where?'

'I've never found out, but I was told, if you hit the spot, she'll just lie down.'

'Maybe she's forgotten.'

'Suppose so.'

They move on to the next stable. 'Tuppence is retired, she's over fifteen years old, she's just to keep Lady company.'

Tuppence is a grey cob flecked with pebble-shaped darker spots. Her backbone sags as if it were made of rope, her belly flares to a balloon shape, she rests a hind leg, doesn't want to move an inch.

Michael Peddlar asks, 'What d'you think is their value?'

She shrugs, 'Could trade down on Lady I suppose and realise a few thousand pounds, but I'm just as likely to go wrong with the replacement, end up having to buy another one.'

They walk on.

He repeats what was said to him once by another farmer on the edge of the moor: 'And you can't get very far around here without a horse.'

They reach the gate at the top of the yard. Here, the wind pushes them hard; they're in a funnel.

He fastens the collar of his coat.

She turns closer to him, shouts, 'I thought I'd take you up to the Top Field. You can see the whole place from there.'

He follows her steady trudge through a more open yard to

a further gateway. To the right there's an oak cattle crush, the strutwork grizzled with age, worn by the wind and the rain – but it looks serviceable. Ahead and to the left is a muck heap cut into the slope and with a network of planks arrowed over the surface, for the wheelbarrow. Parked next to it is the muck-spreader with its side open; chains hang from the drive shaft running down the middle.

Further ahead, there are two large slatted stock barns; the first contains six feeding traces, ring-shaped, a litter of wasted silage around them, dropped from the cows' mouths. He guesses the sheep facility is somewhere else altogether.

Adjacent, there's a levelled patch of open ground which has been surfaced with hardcore, designed for the bale mountain. Large-size silage bales are wrapped in PVC sheeting, piled on one another, so many circles give the impression the whole mass is going to trundle off.

This upper yard is flanked by a stand of beech trees which are bent, the wind presses their leafless branches when she opens the gate into the Top Field and holds it for Michael to pass through. The wind leans against him with a steady, uninterrupted strength like he's on a boat and the breath leaves his body, he has to tuck in his chin, turn aside to draw air that's racing past; his coat rips like a loose sail, it threatens to carry him off, the collar tapping an inconstant, staccato rhythm.

Ahead of him, she moves as steadily as before.

After some minutes, they gain the highest point on the farm; she continues purposefully towards the wall, so he follows – when's she going to stop?

She climbs on top of a matched pair of enclosed concrete vessels well tucked into the bank: they resemble the wartime gun emplacements you might see at the seaside.

She stamps her foot to signify what's in them and shouts,

'Spring water, for people and animals, gravity-fed to the roof of the house, and to all the drinking troughs.'

He follows, climbs up.

So: they stand with their backs to the wind; for a while neither speaks. Dartmoor is behind them, to the left and to the right. In front lie her enclosed fields, descending to a steep, invisible, wooded valley.

This farm is enveloped by the wilderness; others touch the moor with a tentative, single boundary but Latchworthy is shaped like a loop of string, with moorland enclosing it and the road – a ribbon of tarmac – the only way out.

'*Right* on the moor,' he says.

She points to their right, 'Caistor.'

It rises like a small volcano long since defunct, a plug of metamorphic rock, surrounded by a clitter of frost-shattered boulders.

She indicates the other side of the valley, which rises up as moorland to Scaur Hill, and in the V-shape made by Scaur Hill on one side and Caistor on the other sits a distant panorama: agricultural downlands, the mid-Devon plain, it rolls out as far as Exmoor, fifty miles away.

Jane turns into the wind. The long, walled-in side of the farm fends off a broader horizon counting five different tors which stand in a line, clear five miles distant. She names them, her finger bouncing along: 'Grey Weathers, Hound Tor, Sittaford ...'

The sky yawns, overbearing, the air rushing to fill the low pressure.

Jane turns out of the wind, her outstretched arm indicates the near side of the wall and she leans closer to shout, 'Ninety-eight acres, eleven fields in all, not counting the woods down there in the valley.'

'Which river?'

'Birthplace of the Teign.'

'Is that your only water?'

She swings around: 'There's a spring that rises from the bog there outside the corner stone.' Again, she stamps her foot. 'Feeds this water system, you'd have driven over the stream on the way up, before it runs down to the river.'

He nods, 'OK.'

They jump from the concrete tanks, head down the sloping field, across this last corner of cultivated land before the peat and granite outcrop and the sodden bogs take over to offer nothing but heather, gorse, sedge, hardly a tree except for the weird, stunted oaks of Wistman's Wood.

They descend, and the wind lessens, because this south-westerly side of the farm has been planted with a windbreak, a stand of conifers five deep, they're already forty foot high, these bristles crowded against the granite wall which marks the boundary. It allows only two gateways in its entire run down to the river; they head for the first.

Their boots swish through the wet grass. Otherwise, silence descends as they drop across the contour of the field.

They walk past the spot where Jane's father died: bent on one knee, facing the windbreak, his hand inside his jacket like he was reaching for a wallet, his head bowed, the figure motionless. Now it seems not a memory so much as a dream she had of water dripping from the brim of his hat, his face grey with strain; and he looked at her, but said nothing, rain splashed on his tilted face, his eyes fierce but distant, preoccupied with his own trouble, his teeth clenched, and as it turned out, never loosened. His stance, like that of a man at prayer or receiving a knighthood, faltered as Jane tried to help him to his feet.

He died in her arms, eight years ago.

Silently, they pass by.

The fenced-in track leading from the stock yard up to the gate is clogged with mud stirred up daily by the two hundred-odd head of cows walking in and out to get at the silage, it sucks at their boots.

The wind drops almost to nothing, this close to the windbreak. They could talk more easily, but don't, there's still this silence between them. Although anger nudges at Jane: she wants to ask for money, for the bank to let her off the hook or renegotiate terms, she thinks, *Fucking money*. No doubt it's impossible, it will be out of his control to negotiate anything different from what was previously agreed.

She wants to bite the hand that feeds the farm credit.

She can't even find a cheaper mortgage if she jumps ship, goes to a different bank; given her accounts for the last three years, the income would allow her about enough to buy out a quarter of her existing charge.

Beside him, she slogs along in the mud. Silence endures between her now and this nice man, just when they should be talking, trying to find answers, it's unbearable, what's not said, she with her debts, he with his enviable upper-body strength, only a percentage of which he uses, his fixed amount of money going into his account every month, with certainty he can bank on that.

They struggle through the mud up to the gate that leads to the moor; from this spot Jane lets the cattle in and out during the winter to feed on the silage for three hours precisely every morning. It's her most commonly used route on to the moor, she doesn't often have cause to ride down the front drive towards Caistor.

Here, on this occasion, she doesn't trouble herself with the gate but instead leans on the top bar in the classic pose of farmers in cartoons; she ought to have a piece of straw in her mouth.

14

The wind scoops her short hair, parts it neatly, first this side, then that, her scalp showing as straight white lines.

Next to her, his eyes stream.

A fan of paths wriggles out from the other side of the gateway – muddy tracks worn like miniature valleys into the hummocky ground. Two or three head downhill towards the river, some follow the contour line across to the bog, others climb to the higher ground on their left.

In this direction, uphill, twin tracks of standing stones are half buried, motionless as they have been since before Christ, yet seemingly on the march, over the closest horizon, all the way to the Langstone which leans at an angle, a giant menhir marking the end of the prehistoric stone row.

There's a belief that if the Langstone is touched and at the same time a wish is made, the wish will come true; she won't tell him how often she's touched it, marked the brief abrasion on her fingertips as she's ridden past, offered the usual demands: for animals' recovery, harvests, the banishment of insects, more income, trouble-free machinery.

'Cows.' She points to the herd of Belted Galloways – hairy, low to the ground and coloured either black or dun or roan, all with a belt of white around their middles. They're still bunched together: only let out an hour ago, they don't travel far in winter, they hang around to wait for the gate to open again the following morning.

'Slow finishers,' he comments.

'Yup,' Jane agrees cheerfully, in a good mood with her herd because this morning a perfect tan calf was born.

She summons the names of others due to birth soon: Betsy, Sunlight . . .

Her closest neighbours, the brother-and-sister partnership farming Wallistone, laugh at her for giving cows names – as if they were people or racehorses – but it makes for easier

15

stockmanship; otherwise to identify them she'd have to remember the numbers on their ear tags.

So: the banker and the farmer stand, look over the herd.

He says emphatically, 'They're very clean.'

'Yes.'

'Somehow cleaner than other cows I'm looking at down country.'

'They lead a cleaner life, have to use their muscles, actually walk, you know. In summer they travel for miles.'

'How many are there?'

'I'm up to my entitlement: two hundred-odd.'

'Could you not put a few more out on the moor without bothering the licence people?'

She replies, deadpan, 'I doubt the Duchy would notice, Prince Charles doesn't go round counting farmers' cows too often, after all, but either it's more capital to be laid out, and capital I haven't got, or it means keeping some heifers I've bred myself, but I can't afford not to sell them, every last one.'

She turns back and walks stodgily through the mud in the passageway.

He follows. The wind harries them until they've turned out of the fenced track and regained the shelter of the conifers.

They walk side by side in the unnatural quiet, the air turbulence twenty feet above, and the silence builds between them again.

Her debt, his job – it's as if they can't meet.

Downhill towards the furthermost reach of the farm, she has her hands in her pockets, she glances at the low-slung bellies of her ewes, reminds herself she's close enough to lambing. In the next few days she should load the temporary pens on to the flatbed trailer and haul them down here, one to each field . . .

The pastures are divided by stone walls but mature beech

trees are rooted every few yards in the granite: someone once decided to start off some beech hedges – was it the cheapest way to make the broken wall stock-proof? – yet for an unknown reason the saplings weren't trimmed, the branches not woven horizontal but instead allowed to continue growing vertically. It gives the farm these lines of trees atop the walls, sixty years later, a surprising graciousness, like a scene you'd find in a landscaped park.

The line of the windbreak, the steepening gradient, the cut of the river – this is the map.

The slope tips suddenly underfoot, now instead of pasture there's bracken and a litter of granite boulders, some marked with drill-holes in the face of the rock, from times when men shaped the stones here, long ago, to use as gravestones or for building mines.

It's the far edge of the farm, and as if the moor encroaches in an attempt to win back clean, cultivated acres and turn them into rough ground, every year it's a battle against nettles, thistles, bracken, gorse. She walks with a scythe, knocks the heads off thistles before they flower, squander their pollen.

A hundred yards further down, woodland colonises the steeper ground. Over a century ago, someone introduced rarities: a redwood and a monkey puzzle tower among the firs, pine, beech, silver birch. She has the only common oak to grow to full size on this eastern side of the moor.

The wood is unkempt, tangled with fallen boughs, left to its own devices, nothing except badgers, rabbits and occasional escaped sheep disturbs the process of decay and regeneration, the gradual slip of the land downhill.

Finally, wearing out the bottom of the valley is the uppermost stretch of the river Teign, baptised where the Wallabrook and the Wear come off the moor and join forces, it's not so much one mass of river as a collection of different threads of water stitched in and out of giant boulders, through rapids, quietened momentarily every now and again in a pool the water has dug for itself around a waterfall, before it breaks the edge of the stillness, hurries on.

Invisible in the woods, inaccessible, the river occasionally divides in two and patches of land stand as islands enclosed by the torrent. Jane's not sure, given that her boundary is the river, whether she owns these islands or not but the only time she has reason to go there is when she needs to rescue stranded sheep.

But she's not going to struggle through the woods with Michael Peddlar; she's only led him here to show him one thing pertinent to any discussion on the economics of the place – the hydroelectric plant.

They follow the boundary downhill and where the granite wall meets the river, the wind cuts past, finding the sudden disappearance of the windbreak, whipping around it in a fury.

They struggle for balance, crab over the elephantine boulders jumbled together in the river as though a giant had thrown them; they gain a position from where they can lean over to see the entrance to the pipe, visible as a shadow in the swirl of water.

She points, shouts, 'That's the start.'

A portion of the river is sidetracked, angrily, into this pool, where the pipe catches it; even in the drought of '76 the level didn't drop below the minimum required to fill the system.

Jane's father built it; when she was four years old they allowed her to think she helped mix the granite-chip and concrete composite, which looks like an organic part of the rock formation, now.

Michael Peddlar shouts, 'Must . . . have been . . . some piece . . . of work.'

18

She nods agreement and turns; the wind flattens against her back. From here the pipe aims out of the trap, straight as a die among the chaos of boulders, tree roots, into the depths of the wood, it tracks across the fall of the valley.

Michael Peddlar holds his collar to keep it from flapping against his chin and asks, 'Is it above ground all the way?'

'No, dips in and out, sometimes buried, sometimes not.'

'How far?'

'The generator's in a shed, about half a mile away.'

'Does it need repairing, on a regular basis?'

He remembers a letter – signed by the colleague who held the job before him – concerning an unauthorised overdraft last year for repairing the pipe. As usual, there was no reply from her logged into the file.

She replies, 'Occasionally the ground shifts downhill, pushes the joints open. The generator itself just seems to go on and on.'

'Massive saving, though, your own electricity.'

'But if I have to employ labour to work on the pipe, it'll cost me, plus, I'll have to mend it quick – the whole farm's powered off this system, if it goes out of action, so do I . . .'

She's hoarse from shouting above the sound of the wind and the water.

He calls back, 'Might be wise to think of setting up a repair fund, to save for that.'

'If I could afford it.' The wind blows away her words as she heads onwards.

He might point out that a repair fund is cheaper than an unauthorised overdraft.

Since they've reached the furthest extent of the farm, it's left to them to walk back a different way. They follow the seam between the bottom of the fields and the top of the wooded valley, a serviceable path, but overgrown; every time Jane uses it she determines to cut it back. On several occasions they have to clamber over trees blown down by the great storm of '87, the debris only partially cleared by successive trawls for firewood.

They pass under the belly of the farm.

On the way Michael Peddlar makes another money-spinning suggestion, 'How about, sell cow quota and buy sheep quota, there's quite a few who are still doing that – prices for lamb remain buoyant, compared to beef . . .'

She remains silent.

They climb up from the valley, approach the farm buildings from the downhill side.

Undaunted, Michael Peddlar prompts her with further plans to improve the farm's finances, but the timber can't be accessed without ripping the fields to shreds, and she hates tourism.

He offers other possibilities: build a cross-country event course, run a pheasant shoot, offer rights for the fishing in the lower reaches of the river where it might be possible to stock trout. Part and parcel of these initiatives would be to decide on somewhere unobtrusive for people to park their cars.

She lets him rattle on.

He wonders, would she be in breach of a planning restriction imposed by the Dartmoor National Park, that the property should only be used as a farm?

Finally, they approach the set of dilapidated, older sheds around the back here, thrown up out of old telegraph poles and pig-iron, one of which houses tractor implements, firewood, the belt-driven saw; the other garages her car when she can be bothered to drive it up through the yard instead of parking it outside the house.

Michael Peddlar stands in the middle of this shed with its uprights at sixes and sevens, part of its roof missing, currently stashed with long-forgotten timber and useless, rusting farm machinery, he's weatherbeaten from his excursion, his voice is suddenly loud, out of the wind, as he asks, 'Could this be rebuilt to house workshops?'

'What for?' she asks.

'Could you hire space to local artists, or craftspeople?'

She frowns, 'I don't want people up and down my yard.'

'Could you build a livery stable? If you can spare the grass, you could charge people to keep their horses up here, include minimal care and grooming? Must be some of the best riding in the country, out on the moor ... '

Anger rises again: she doesn't want to be hired out to look after other people's animals, at their beck and call, why can't this man understand? If she works all the hours God sends now, how can she take a second full-time job on top of that?

She replies, 'Worth thinking about, anyway ... '

He points at the caravan, which quietly disintegrates in its small, overgrown enclosure.

'Another possibility for developing tourism, of some sort,' he suggests.

Now, Jane doesn't answer.

So: they're left standing side by side in her vegetable garden, the full crop of his suggestions harvested, as it were. The scarecrow, made out of fencing posts and straw, is wearing her last year's coat. Does he realise, Jane wonders, that she wears out a waxed cotton coat every winter, costing seventy quid or more?

Meanwhile he continues, 'On the other side of the business coin, we should search for some possibilities for making savings in your outgoings ... '

She doesn't know whether to love him or hate him; the way he says 'we' as if sharing her predicament.

Bluntly, she mentions the figure allowed for her personal

spending; it's so low, it shames him into not exploring this avenue further, it barely amounts to his weekly budget for satellite TV, hiring videos.

She walks him around the vegetable garden and pulls off some leaves of spinach. 'Go on, take them home . . . I'll never eat them.'

He holds them awkwardly, it'd be rude to crush them in his pocket.

They head back; now it's a tacit agreement between them: they've covered the necessary ground.

When they arrive at the house he puts the spinach leaves on the back seat of his car.

Finally – can he come in and take down a few details on paper?

They sit at the same table, in the same chairs. The silence ticks away slower, here, out of the rush and hurry of the wind.

He's beginning to look damp, she thinks, like everything on Dartmoor, the water seeping into him, first of all it will make him clammy, useless, then with a few days of hard work he'll toughen.

She wonders at herself, wanting to save him from his desk job; that is her arrogance.

She notices, hunger.

Two hours have gone by – should she offer him something to eat?

Instead she watches his pen move across the paper. 'Your calf sale is?' he queries.

She replies, 'November.'

The pen moves again.

'We know already it's going to be a poor result, not as bad as before, when you couldn't sell a cow, not a steer or a heifer, at any price, but it still isn't up to where it was, plus I'm carrying extra costs on the overdraft.'

22

Another silence, except the marking of the pen.

He reassures her, 'It's like with salmonella in eggs, isn't it? That crisis blew over pretty quickly. There's only been a few cases of BSE in humans, the problem is going away, just a case of how quickly . . . '

In fifteen years, Michael Peddlar hasn't seen a farmer go bankrupt, there's too much capital sunk behind them: they can weather a storm or two, with so much collateral, the banks can afford to be lenient and renegotiate the length of time over which a loan might be repaid, yet, with the BSE crisis rumbling on, he believes he will see a farmer or two go under; those who were already standing on the edge might be pushed too far.

This woman could be one of them.

Suddenly she's looking directly at him, the blue eyes aren't wavering, the one on the left queered by the mole riding above it, he notices. Her face is long but well built and the mouth quite full, her eyes are a steady grey-blue: he can sense her persistence, obstinacy.

She's leaning forwards on the table, her hands intertwined like she's waiting for a meal in a restaurant, or about to say something . . . He stares at her, he doesn't know what to say, either.

The moment passes.

She's left with her anger, her scalp prickles, because the banks are allowed to pass on their trading difficulties. If their market rises, then they can go with it; if it drops, they can go with it, so they can always play both ends off against the middle, but she's stuck between a rock and a hard place: she can't control her prices, can't negotiate her charges, and she's gambling on one big sale a year, which she can't forecast.

She mentions with forced calm, 'I did my business plan all those years ago.'

23

He nods, 'Yes, which would have had a fail-safe, a get-out.'

'It did – selling my barn.'

He's about to point out this is the answer to her problems when she interrupts, 'But what was odd is that you took any notice of it, the business plan I mean, it's an impossible thing isn't it, you might have been better off if I'd been in trouble sooner, a quicker profit and then out. Christ, what daft bits of paper . . . '

'No – an indication the business was on a sound footing.'

'If you want a business on a sound footing, don't bury us in more debt.'

He puts down his biro. 'The trouble is, we have a duty to our investors, to maintain an acceptable level of return on their deposits.'

It's something he's said many times before; he tries not to make it sound too stiff and defensive – after all, it's the truth.

Now she mirrors his formal response: 'You've a duty to your customers as well, the people paying your wages, to keep them going.'

Yet, she can see his blindness, clear as day; she wants to get past this blank, formulaic approach, she wants to take that suit and tie off him and give him six months' hard labour, then he'd see life itself like a rank weed growing up in the cracks between the figures, the pluses and minuses, he'd see this place for what it is, its reality – not a threat to his organisation but a place that won't make him as much money as some, but equally one that won't lose him a bundle either.

She adds, 'You'll make more out of me, you understand, more money, in the long run, if you keep me as a customer instead of cutting me dead and taking a dive yourself.'

'A bank is not – '

She interrupts, 'I'll tell you what a bank is.' Then she stops –

he's too clean and distant to be drawn into this . . . hardship. She's guilty, not to have fed him. He's young enough to be enjoying his career, he's sticking to his guns. Perhaps that's to be admired.

So her anger subsides because he looks frightened, more so than she does.

In fact, he's embarrassed and he'd like to point out that much of the problem lies with her – her behaviour: she doesn't answer letters, she uses the bank like a tin of money on her shelf and incurs greater charges than she should, she doesn't talk to the bank, doesn't shoulder the responsibility early enough for finding a solution – all these things are doubly important because she's trading on the outer limits of viability anyway.

It's her responsibility, he can't tell her what to do.

Unable to say this, instead he swallows and nods, unsure of how things are going, whether she's crying for help or chasing him off her land, but his instinct is, he should allow her to lecture him; and then she'll let him go, so he waits.

Jane thinks, Out there, outside . . . and it's there again, a flash of unreasonable anger, like an explosive white, obscuring reason, thoughts burnt out, until reassembling in its wake . . . Christ, it can be bloody fucking tough, by herself especially, but what she's losing with one hand she's picking up with the other, and sometimes she's losing more, sometimes picking up more; that's life. Yet a letter from the bank – it's like a hand pulling her into her grave, dead, inhuman.

Meanwhile, it occurs to him that she's doing the man's job, while he's stuck in an office, surrounded by women.

Jane's not looking at him any more.

The entirety of her daily experience here – the land, the birth and death of animals, the sky bringing its load of weather – is a measurable force which buries her with work, but also uplifts her to a degree she never thought possible, it's like riding a rollercoaster; this is some trouble she's having with the farm's momentum.

Then, he begins tentatively, 'I know that an overdraft, on top of a mortgage, can seem impossible, I know, that's why I'm here, in person, to help.'

She unlaces her fingers and slaps her palms face down, 'I know, I'm sorry, let's have some help, great.'

She shakes her head and leans back in her chair.

He reaches for his briefcase and unsnaps the catches. He says, 'I'm going to report the circumstances to my boss, the head of the agricultural unit in Okehampton.' He fillets out a brochure from among the other papers in his briefcase. Then he adds, 'I'm going to sign you up for a consultation with the Devon and Cornwall Training and Enterprise Council.' He slides the fold-out sheet across to her. 'You won't have to pay for it, not the initial one anyway. So, we'll wait for their suggestions as to what you might do, then, after November, when we see what your sale actually does bring in, we can sit down and work out a way ahead ... '

She picks at the edge of the paper with her fingertips, 'Great.'

'We *don't* want to lose you as a customer.'

'Great.' And she's rising to her feet, so he's safe to do the same.

She's still avoiding his eye.

'OK,' she says finally. 'Thanks for coming out.'

He shakes his head. 'It's a beautiful place.' He wants to impress on her how much this place has struck him. 'Really beautiful.'

He leads the way out of the house and along the path to his

car. With the door open and one foot on the sill, he pauses and dabs a finger towards the barn and says cheerfully, 'Selling that is the obvious answer, that's all your worries over in a stroke.'

She nods politely.

He slides into his seat, 'And people are buying barns again, these days . . . '

Then he swings the car around, they exchange a wave goodbye.

IN HIS REAR mirror he has a brief view of her, only two or three movements: her hands go in her pockets, her shoulder turns, she steps towards the house.

He rolls down the drive in his new car. Next to him lies his coat, not worn enough to mark him out as a man of the soil, whereas her waxed cotton coat was frayed and the pockets were bulging and torn, stains blemished its surface; it must have seen years of work, he thinks.

These possessions of his – a new car, the little-used raincoat – they gather around to incriminate him, when he has to visit the poorer farms like this one, whereas in other circumstances he enjoys them.

Then, his foot squeezes on the brake pedal and he stops, curses, 'Goddamn', shakes his head, because, look at the beauty of this step of land rising in front of him on the other side of the stream, topped by the austere granite plug, Caistor.

And the *view* to his left – stunning.

He lets the car roll down the drive again, just as a thought rolls out, unbidden, in his head, to buy Jane's barn, himself.

He thinks, Call David Fowles, *today*, put his marker down.

AT THE SAME time, Jane goes to the five-gallon drum of cider and fills a tankard to the brim.

She doesn't want to sell the *fucking* barn. She won't sell, whatever.

She makes a sandwich, throwing open the lid of the bread bin and squeezing the loaf so hard her fingers break through the crust.

She thinks of Michael Peddlar pulling into a pub and ordering a meal, calling his office to say he might be late.

She hacks through the cheese. The sharp blade slides into her finger, the pain travelling quickly under her skin to her heart.

She swears and lifts the cut to her mouth, tasting blood.

MICHAEL PEDDLAR SITS at his desk in the Okehampton branch of Lloyds Bank. He's surrounded by a set of prefabricated, royal blue partitions; in front of him is the desk with a limed finish, oily to the touch and covered in papers.

He has this pride: he's the first in his family to have a job which requires him to wear a suit and slip-on shoes.

On his earliest farm visits he used to take off his tie, arrive open-necked, wearing something closer to working clothes, thinking it would fit him closer to his clients, but he learnt – his own father told him – it's important to do the exact opposite: emphasise the difference, not try and be one of them.

One of them . . .

He brings Jane Reeves to mind, his client at Latchworthy Farm: the outsize mole riding on the tail of her left eyebrow giving that side a questioning stance, the low-slung frame, working clothes, tousled black hair, strong, even features, her skin white, almost translucent, Celtic whiteness, washed clean by rain, her hair, yes, black with one or two lines of grey.

In front of him is the paperwork: how much is the barn conversion worth . . . with that view?

He scribbles a list – as it is now, as it will be – how much?

Imagining, he draws in windows, puts in bedrooms, installs himself and his family.

His eyes slide away, skid on the white notepaper, because Michael Peddlar has had this same idea lapping at him, all afternoon: *he wants it for himself.*

Yet, he should remind himself he's here – fiddling with this problem – as Jane Reeves' account manager, not as a prospective purchaser for her barn conversion.

He can picture the file containing the letters he and others before him have written concerning her arrears at Latchworthy, each one date-stamped – blue figures with a square red outline – marking when they were sent, filed in chronological order. Copies will be kept for a minimum of seven years.

There's none in reply from her.

He tries to work out what he might say that won't be patronising, that'll ask her in no uncertain terms to answer his letters and to attend more promptly to the paperwork, to change her personality, the way she irretrievably *is.*

It would suit her better, not having to manage a debt, merely remaining poor.

Yes, she should *sell the barn.*

The phone rings like an alarm, a warning. Nearby, the girl in a beige skirt, thickly made up, receives it. Michael Peddlar thinks she is probably the daughter of a farmer. Her heavy, bovine face easily carries the painted surface. Talking herself, she won't overhear him.

So: Michael Peddlar has a hand resting on his phone, but he knows something for certain: it's morally wrong to use his inside knowledge to manoeuvre himself into a superior position.

Nevertheless, he lifts the phone, taps in the number. The buttons are fluid under his fingers, as if hydraulically assisted. A girl's voice answers, the same chime as usual, 'Atkinson's', and he asks for David Fowles, Managing Director. A second later, another ringing tone engages, is immediately answered. He recognises David Fowles' quick, nervous voice.

They greet; formality prescribes a minute or two of chit-chat, polite, impervious. Michael Peddlar finds himself laughing, falsely, it's a nervous habit, he chastises himself: if there's nothing to laugh at, he shouldn't bother trying to make it seem like there is, it's a weakness. Most farmers – his own family included – wouldn't need to do it, their pulse rate is steadier, they're unaffected by a desire to please, they observe, they listen, they speak their minds; it's that simple and he should teach himself the same thing.

He moves on to the purpose of the phone call and for a while the available properties are discussed. Then, as if it were inconsequential, merely an afterthought, a prelude to the sequence of goodbye and thank you, Michael Peddlar advises David Fowles that the woman up at Latchworthy Farm will shortly be putting a barn up for sale and it should come to Atkinson's, since he's the only estate agent in Gidford.

In which case, asks Michael Peddlar, he wouldn't mind being informed of it, if possible before it goes on the open market?

So: NEWS OF the barn conversion passes from Michael Peddlar in Okehampton, maybe fifteen miles from Latchworthy Farm, to David Fowles in Gidford, only four miles away.

The town square is outside his window – often he's seen Jane Reeves pass by.

He doesn't know her personally, but David Fowles' manic brain picks at the scattered knowledge of her, available to Gidford society.

Her name's on the rota for voluntary work on the new sports ground bequeathed to the town. She has a long-standing reputation: her father lived up there on the moor, too.

Wasn't there an incident in her early childhood, when she badly hurt another child who was accused of bullying her?

When she was a teenager, she disappeared for years, then came back.

A pub person – she drinks pints of ale. Yes, she's in the pub, because there was the complaint against her driving.

A Mini Cooper, green, always parking very quickly, the arm inside pumping away, the heel of her hand turning the steering wheel one way, then the other.

A man, no, men – there've been no marriages that he's aware of, but there are various men she's been out with from around here.

Now it's towards the end of the working day and he needs to do some shopping.

He pulls on a coat, makes for the front desk and with a wave, a brief smile, he acknowledges his assistant, Karen.

He pulls the glass door, knocking the warning bell, and steps on to the narrow pavement surrounding Gidford town square.

David Fowles considers himself ostracised in this rural community for running an *office*. In the premises adjacent to his, they sell food. The next shop sells gifts, most of the window given over to the work of local craftsmen. Then there's the butcher's, a dairy, a baker's, a hardware store, an off-licence, the new vets' surgery. Four pubs fuel the area with alcohol.

He and the solicitor, Andrew Nixon, are the only two who run *offices* – not supplying anything, no crop, nothing but paperwork and bills. They're outside the norm and therefore, around Gidford town square, intent on his shopping, David Fowles hugs the walls, there's a shame attached to his trade. If someone were to speak to him, he would jerk to a stop, as if caught out.

No one does. He's left to dwell on the information given him by Michael Peddlar.

He counts the other houses he's sold over the years, on the road which winds up to Caistor: the Mill was the last one.

He'll send Jane Reeves the usual Atkinson's flyer, just as a prompt, no pressure.

Not to frighten her away, he commands himself, 'Wait, *wait.*'

LATCHWORTHY FARM: OLD, isolated and in debt.

Jane sleeps in the room above the kitchen, the stovepipe bursting through the floor, radiating heat.

There's a bed, a table, a chest of drawers; a single bulb hangs from the ceiling.

There are no lamps – the DC electricity made by the hydroelectric plant is too insistent: it will burn out the delicate mechanism of a lamp-switch.

There aren't any books, ornaments or pictures. The walls are plain, whitewashed.

The drawers in the chest stand half open, clothes hanging out like they've been rifled by a burglar.

Clothes also litter the floor. They're all the same: jeans, shirts and jerseys in dark blue and black.

The curtains remain pulled across. There's no reason to open them: it's dark when she awakes and dark when she comes to bed; she's outside as dawn rises and never sets foot upstairs during the day.

The dogs sleep in the room with her.

Roo, the mongrel, is too old to climb on the bed, his back legs fail him comically as he tries to walk up, all the bounce is gone. Instead he lies against the wall, legs thrown out, his front paws crossed decorously.

His place is marked by a thickening layer of hair; he's on a permanent moult.

Billy, the purebred collie, springs up easily and makes himself at home on the duvet; his long jaw with its rows of fine, brilliant white teeth lies on the pillow beside her.

He won't sleep anywhere else. When he rolls in foxes' dung and smells of aniseed, she sometimes asks him to sleep downstairs, but he steadily issues the single, high-pitched barks to call her, demand his usual privilege.

Jane and her two dogs breathe easily, sleep . . .

Time runs in a circle, brings the farm around to the same place, the same tasks as faced them last year, the rota changing by seasons, the circle always more deeply worn, entrenched.

Mostly, she doesn't think of the future or the past, only what's in front of her today, what her hand is put to now, this moment.

When lambing time comes, the bedroom degenerates further. The chest of drawers stands empty, the floor is ankle deep in detritus, the bed is a whirlpool of sheet and bedding which she half-heartedly straightens before climbing in.

After lambing, she gives the bedroom its once-yearly clean-out.

The floor is rediscovered, the clothes sorted into their drawers, the octagonal table has the dust wiped from it, Roo's spot is brushed clean.

The window is pegged open, ready for summer.

THE SINGLE-TRACK ROAD wriggles ahead of her, drenched with last night's dew and split by sunlight.

Both sides of the lorry touch the hedges, the roof scrapes the trees. The hydraulic steering and brakes and the automatic clutch of the Scania articulated lorry make it easier to drive, even, than the Mini Cooper. The cab rolls on six wheels and the trailer on twelve, yet she can throw it around like it's a toy.

The whole assembly blasts everything before it down the narrow lanes – no one asks her to reverse to find a gap. Maybe it's because Tim has the words BEAVER HUNTING printed on the sunstrip.

Over the quadraphonic sound system a female voice wails a tune, part happy, part sad, 'All I really need is a song in my heart, food in my belly, love in my famil-eeee.'

Behind her, three cows bang, jump, brace their legs against the sway of the vehicle, penned into a corner of its cavernous space.

A fox trots across; it's been on an early-morning raid. It disappears cleanly, as if switched off.

She has an impulse to drop a handful of gears – it wouldn't take more than a few flicks of her finger – and race crazily down this strip of tarmac.

The woman on the radio sings, 'And I need some clean air for breathing.'

She gums up Gidford town square, for a while, in her big lorry. Old folk wind their steering wheels, to get out of her way, a Renault is trapped in a parking space; in the vibrating panel of her door mirror Jane notices Eve, the spinster from the gift shop, caught in the cinch made by her vehicle as it cuts off the pavement, makes its corner.

Inches from the side of her vehicle, the walls of the new vets' surgery slide past.

On the other side of town and heading downhill, she makes for the sale ground, proud to be the only woman who farms by herself from around these parts, plus she can drive a truck this size: she's like a cowgirl riding in from hundreds of miles with a crowd of steers running in front of her.

Isn't it going to spoil the effect, when she drops the tailgate and lets out three cows?

They're part of her breeding stock and it's last ditch to sell them, because the debt is like a stone hanging around her neck.

Already the gateway to the parking area is a dustbowl with matting laid down so the heavy vehicles can make their way without causing too much dry erosion.

Inside, a local youth she recognises from a neighbouring pub darts team squints into the sun and shouts instructions. He holds out a slip of paper for her to take with a number on it.

She asks, 'Working, Graham?'

'Only for a bet,' the heavy-set, shaven-haired youth shouts. She notices the leather jacket he wears in winter has been left at home; instead he wears a white T-shirt and his skin is tanned. She tells herself: No more farm boys. She hasn't the inclination to think of people, men, any more, only of these sums of money, each becoming more familiar, little enemies which have grown to confront her.

She finds the empty pen and backs up the trailer, the going suddenly even easier; the steering wheel spins in her hand, light as air.

She leaves Roo seated demurely on the front seat, swings down from the cab and hunts around for someone to help.

Silently, she asks these people: where do they get their money, how come everyone else has a bit in their pockets, where's hers? It's unreasonable, but she wants someone to show her ...

There's the limping figure of Michael Grant from Thornton, his walking stick pushes forward and then is pulled back like he's levering himself along, his white shirt is brilliant in the sunlight. She calls his name.

Michael Grant stops and asks, 'How is it, up on the mountain?'

He lives not a mile and a half downcountry.

'You don't want to know.'

They drag the hurdles back from pen number 56, dress them close to the back of the lorry, then she steps up, pops the lever on the back, hauls on the tailgate rope.

'Lower the drawbridge,' calls Michael Grant and winks at her. 'That's what we'd say to the women in our day, when we were the young men of the county.'

He'll be in the pub before midday.

Jane hops into the trailer to untie the partition, then stands behind the cows, bangs the sides to encourage the bewitched animals to move.

Michael Grant inserts his stick through the slats in the side of the lorry, waves it up and down, clacks his tongue. The first, most inquisitive cow appears; then pushed from behind by its two companions, it scrambles down. They descend in a clatter, and it's done.

Jane follows them down the ramp, fixes the hurdles back in position, springs the tailgate shut.

'Pleased with your calving, so far, this year?' asks Michael Grant.

She notices he's not asking why she's selling adult cows – does he realise she's having to sell off breeders?

She shrugs. 'Well enough.'

'How many d'you lose?'

'Three, and an abortion, so far, if you're counting.'

He nods. 'Well done.'

Jane damps down on the glow of pleasure at his words, they're the only approbation she's had this year, because there's no one to recognise the work she does unless there is a God, after all. Certainly, there's less financial reward than before: last year she even paid out, herself, for the privilege of keeping her animals alive.

As well, no gratitude comes from the stock – why should they thank her, when she's selling calves for meat?

Because otherwise they wouldn't exist at all. Why does the fox eat the chicken, who eats the worm? Life is a line of hungry mouths and squandered sex: her animals can thank her, they ought to, for giving them a good life.

Michael Grant wanders off; a wave of his hand dismisses her thanks.

She climbs back into the lorry to park it a short distance away, then dismounts, lifts her arms, clicks her fingers, coaxes Roo so she can help him down.

He refuses, nervous of the drop, so she has to climb up, scoop him into her arms.

He wears a coy look.

When she puts him on the ground, his back legs stagger. Jane drops to her knees, takes his muzzle between her hands, says to him, 'You'll die this year.'

His clouded pupils slip sideways.

There's a sudden bolt of feeling which slides in her, fixes her to this old dog whom she's had for fifteen years.

She ties a length of orange baler twine to his collar, wanders towards the sale ring, surveys the scene. Pen after pen of bovines stand over half the field, ranks of lorries and other vehicles occupy the other half. Unlike the yearly shows, there isn't the same number of small, off-white tents selling tack, foodstuffs, tools, wet-weather gear, farm equipment. There's no refreshment tent – this is business only.

She's part of this – the people dress like her, they work at the same tasks, they have the same battles against the weather, sickness, pests, they quarry every spare moment to shore up buildings, mend gates, repair tractors, implements, yet, at the same time, she's separate, as alone now as on every working day when she pulls on her boots, heads out to start the feeding routine when it's still dark.

She'd guess it's the same for all the farmers who work the moor as opposed to the downland; there'd be this solitude that moves with them even in a crowd, excluding them yet protective.

Then again, she doesn't even have a wife, like most of them.

She moves on.

In the far corner the auctioneer has started to hatch prices in his shed which overlooks the ring. He hectors his buyers in the viewing gallery raked on all sides, while his assistant marks down the results. Market staff in dungarees drive the animals out pen by pen: each lot number trots through the passageway, into the sale ring through one gate, out through the other.

Jane notices only one other woman, perhaps twenty years old, anonymous in blue overalls with her blonde hair tucked under a cap, yet the auctioneers have given her the job of prodding the cows around the ring to encourage people to spend more, impress a pretty young woman, maybe.

So: the pair of white-coated, fast-talking men orchestrate the sale from the privacy of the shed. Meanwhile a knot of about forty men – buyers and sellers – are gathered in the lean-to. Although none looks like he's enjoying himself, this moment repeated three or four times a year is when the farmers sink or swim. Concentration is drawn on their faces.

The middle-men, the buyers, are more relaxed, they can play the market: if their prices drop, they can lower their bids, if their consciences can take it, they might send animals on illegal sea voyages to Greece.

Jane's cows move listlessly in the pen, her dog's at her side, she has one foot on the rail, while she waits for the team of overalled men to work towards her lot number 56.

There's the rattle of the auctioneer, as he climbs his figures, over and over.

She coaches herself to accept her fate, meanwhile examining her animals to compare them to the ones in adjacent pens.

She remembers how Michael Peddlar, the agricultural advisory person from the bank, described her animals as 'cleaner' because their coats are glossy, not stuck with mud and faeces like those from the downland farms, some of which will have been kept in pens or yards most of their lives. Her animals have a look in their eye, a wildness, an unfamiliarity with the business of farming which she knows counts in the quality of the meat. If they were slaughtered now and their bellies opened with a knife they'd have nothing but moorland grass in there, even in winter it would be the same – they eat silage cut off unfertilised pasture, treated only with manure. From here on the pollution begins: they'll be taken on, fed cake to bulk their weight, receive antibiotics as a matter of routine to prevent infection. Later, the meat will itself be injected with water carrying antibiotics to preserve the product for longer.

The staccato, excited voice of the auctioneer becomes louder.

Jane wonders if there isn't some way she can take her animals to a quality butcher, in London maybe, to win a premium price for her BSE-free herd, cut out the middle-men who lump her cows with everyone else's, however they've been reared, whatever they've been fed.

She thinks: Go organic, then.

Yet it sounds pathetic, weak. It won't make enough money, quickly enough.

She nods and smiles at the people she happens to know among the static crowd who are watching the auctioneers, bracing herself as pen number 56 is cleared out, her three cows are prodded into the ring.

The idea flips into her mind, to slaughter all her own animals herself. How would it be? She'd be wearing the heavy plastic apron, fire the humane killer in the top yard.

She'd step over the corpses, winch them into the barn, wield the knife, cut the skin to eviscerate them, dismember and parcel the joints.

A refrigeration unit . . .

For a moment she's blind to the scene in front of her; instead she runs with this imaginary one – she wants to hose the blood off herself, put on clean clothes, drive around in a refrigerated lorry, deliver the meat to people's freezers.

She curses inwardly: cook and serve the damned meat at their tables, then, as they pick up their knives and forks, *tell them the animal's name*.

Now the price rattles out over the backs of her three cows as they're walked around the ring by the young woman. Jane feels the rush of pride at the auctioneer's including the name of her farm in his description of the goods on offer, yet at the same time, pity that it's come to this, selling breeding stock, diminishing her capital worth.

The numbers climb fast to begin with, then move a notch at a time, up.

She watches the two men left in the bidding: one looks like a farmer who'll probably buy them to breed from, he's a short, wiry man in a flat cap, an army-surplus jersey. The second man wears a jacket and tie clumsily knotted, the remaining hair on his head stands in all directions, his mouth hangs open, a cigarette trails in his fingers; he is possibly a merchant or an agent for a merchant.

The auctioneer's voice slows from the fast, initial patter, coasts into the area where the sale might be expected to close.

She feels a rush of anger – *not enough!* It's unfair that her cows aren't going to sell for a bit more than anyone else's.

The price sticks fast, it's nearly over, she won't receive any premium. Without thinking, she finds her hand in the air.

The auctioneer clocks her; he knows she owns them already, nevertheless he has to accept the bid. The two men glance at this woman who's come from nowhere to start her bidding just as they were ready to close theirs.

She avoids their gaze.

They give way immediately, neither of them raise the stakes, they know something's going on but there's no need to play games, they'll buy the next pen, it won't matter to them that they've lost these three animals.

The auctioneer brings down his hammer, points it directly at Jane. The assistant has marked the price, the crowd's interest passes on. The animals are herded from the ring.

So: she's bought back her own cows.

She walks away with figures juggling in her head: she's lost the injection of cash but she'll telephone the Real Meat

Company, sell to them, as soon as they can qualify her as an organic herd.

She pauses and kicks the ground, feeling sudden confusion. Has she been stupid? She fights her way through the different factors: provenance is the big thing, the knowing of exactly where an animal comes from is worth a lot. Organic produce fetches a quarter more than non-organic, but it costs more to produce; how much of that extra fat will be left to her?

Roo wanders ahead, his orange baler twine drags on the ground behind him.

She calls, but he doesn't hear.

She shouts louder.

Roo pricks his ears but moves quicker in the same direction, he misreads the position of her voice. She has to run, catch him up.

Irritation at this deaf old dog mixes with her frustration – keep the farm going! – it's like a sharp stick, makes itself felt.

She turns him around, hauls on the string too hard.

She tells herself to calm down.

Her predicament surrounds her again. She asks herself, how is she going to make some effort, not pass through the same hoovering-up process of livestock that everybody else goes through, around the country?

She will have to develop the quality of her herd, sell at a premium.

Perhaps later this year she'll rent some grass, bring her calves on herself for another year, if necessary, ride the temporary loss of income, make back the cost of that and then some more on top, when she does sell, later on.

With the debt she carries she has to box clever, find a better price, take her animals further up the line to capture some of the money the middle-men garner on her stock.

She doesn't know quite how she's going to do it, but she's certain it can be done.

It has to be. A sweat of panic breaks on her brow.

Then, she wanders in the bright sun, pauses to talk to neighbouring farmers and others she knows from her dealings with dogs, horses, machinery.

She leaves the sale ground, walks the half-mile into Gidford and browses through one or two shops, again exchanges greetings with people she knows.

She's aware of strangers – visitors to Gidford – who look at the mole above her eyebrow and pity her, but she's past caring.

Roo noses ahead of her on his piece of string, but stops short when she turns to go into the Small Animals Surgery.

She has to go back, push his backside, bully him in.

Together, she and O'Bryan, the veterinarian on duty, lift Roo on to the examining table.

Jane explains – the dullness of his coat, his lack of energy?

O'Bryan is a thin, concerned man with a beaky nose, bright blue eyes, an educated accent. He scarcely looks at Jane, saves his eyes only for his patient and asks questions while his hands wander over Roo's body.

Roo stands, submits to the indignity.

'How old?'

She replies, 'Fifteen.'

'Kidneys are probably giving up the ghost, in which case, a diuretic, and his heart might be dodgy ... I'll take a blood sample now. And if you can get me a urine sample, we'll work out what needs to be done.'

A new hole opens in Jane's pocket. Money disappears, animals are like a drain.

She takes Roo off the table, holds on to the hope that he

43

won't cost too much, or the bill will be mislaid in the computer system: she needs some magic here.

She signs for the consultation at O'Bryan's desk, Roo at her feet, then she asks herself, incredulous, will she finally have to give in and *sell the barn, to pay for this old dog?*

It sounds ridiculous, can't be true.

A voice in her head says, have him put down ...

She heads out of the surgery, quickly. She's aware that she and O'Bryan have barely made contact, nor exchanged a glance, and her debt to the vets' practice is, yes, already one of the stones around her neck.

She winds up standing outside the Cross Keys, a pint of cider in her hand bought for her by the man who runs the artists' supplies shop, whose name she always confuses with that of his brother, they look so alike.

After covering the gossip which for two years has surrounded Gidford's new sports ground, they talk about bioengineering.

Roo stands patiently at her ankle. He doesn't enjoy the string around his neck, the crush of legs or the heat.

The estate agent, David Fowles, walks past, head down, a plastic bag straining from the weight of his shopping.

A while later, she returns to the sale ground and goes to the auctioneer's box to sign the sale slip while she laughs with them at the idea of buying her own cows.

She also books them to handle a farm sale for her: she has piles of old rubbish, assorted lots of timber, antique farm machinery, all of it from years back, three generations, someone will want to buy this stuff, won't they?

The auctioneer agrees, plus, it's a good time of year: in a month's time, around July and August, people become festive, they have time on their hands.

The auctioneer – who started off life as the son of Gidford's butcher – smiles. 'Good for the soul, a clear-out, plus it's some pocket money, isn't it?'

Jane bites back the familiar, restless anger, points out, 'Wish it was pocket money. It's all owed, I'll need as much as I can get for it.'

She went to school with this guy, her father caught him fishing their stretch of river one night, trying for the spawning sea trout, now he's become thickset, brazen, his Devon accent fills the shed as he reassures her they'll get rid of everything that's not tied down, they'll flog the clouds in the sky.

She tells him he's not joking, can they sell the sky as well, for her.

Then, Jane returns to her lorry and backs it up to pen number 56 to reload.

More sedately, she drives her old cows home to Latchworthy, unloads them in the same yard as she took them from only hours earlier.

It's almost funny. 'An outing!' she shouts to them as they wander up the yard into the field, dazed by the heat. 'An adventure! What's the matter with you?'

They crowd the trough, their jaws drip with water, they lower their heads, begin to graze.

She climbs back into the lorry, takes off to return it to Tim Caxton's, who lends it to her on the strength of their having been lovers once, plus, she used to work for him.

During the ten-minute drive her old dog is on the seat next to her. Every now and again she looks at him.

He used to sit up, ride the corners, watch the road keenly for wildlife. Now he's lying down, uninterested.

She feels a stab of annoyance. This dog is going to cost her, every day of his life now, she knows for sure, so is it the straw that breaks the camel's back; should she decide that she can't afford his life any longer?

Here's the list of her major creditors: Lloyds Bank, the Lydford Milling Company, the vet, the telephone . . . each one a stone.

Tears spill from her eyes, she swears, *'Fuck!'* She is bitterly angry because she'll have to sell the barn to set the place on an even keel, swallow the disappointment, keep the place afloat, *sell the barn*.

She advises herself, Grit your teeth, call the estate agency today, do it, all hands on deck.

In her mind's eye, she visits the old Milkvit box in which she files her letters because somewhere in there she stashed a flyer from Atkinson's, and she glimpses in her mind's eye the straining plastic handle of David Fowles' shopping bag.

The thought of selling any part of Latchworthy seems wrong, against the nature of the place.

At Tim Caxton's yard she picks up the Mini Cooper, drives it home. The setting sun gilds her insect-spattered windscreen, makes it difficult to see.

A BARN CONVERSION up at Latchworthy – it's a bit of poetry cupped in David Fowles' palm, at the moment, because now it's his turn: in his office in Gidford town square he picks at the telephone receiver, puts it down, taps it with a forefinger.

He starts to dial Michael Peddlar's number, yet halfway into the code for Okehampton he replaces the receiver.

He is struggling with a choice: Michael Peddlar, or Chris Gilbey?

He's conscious – as on former occasions when a rare property falls into his lap – there's a gift in his possession, something to give away, too valuable to put on the open market. To whom should he hand it?

At times like these he trades in favours, he owes and is owed.

It's true, Michael Peddlar tipped him off in March that the property might become available with a specific request that he should be informed, yet this debt isn't onerous. In all likelihood the barn would have come to him in any case, it's not a grand enough place to go to Savill's or Knight Frank and Rutley, Jane Reeves is the type who'd take the easiest path: just phone him, the local man in Gidford. Did she even notice the flyer he sent?

David Fowles tugs at the chrome buckle of his belt. He stands, pushes his chair back. Outside his window, Gidford town square is bright, already swollen with visitors shunting around the shops.

David Fowles loosens his belt, then tightens it. His fingers are thin, elegant, made for a musical instrument. With his other hand, he checks the position of his hearing aid.

Quickly, he leans forward, flips through a cardex which sits adjacent to his main log of names and addresses – he calls it 'the hot file'. These are people who, like himself, aim to make money out of dealing in property.

He rolls it through D, E, F, then stares at Chris Gilbey's name, various telephone numbers, a company address.

David Fowles is a good man, watches his children closely, loyal to his wife, he stays this side of the glass wall which in rural situations divides the professional classes from other people, he's indebted to no one, he's made his own way.

So: he's allowed to make money at his profession, and with Chris Gilbey there will be a payment due to him on both sides of the deal: a commission from Jane Reeves and a finder's fee from Chris Gilbey.

Yet, if he telephones Michael Peddlar, it's not so bad either: he'll make a quick sale with no uncomfortable complications.

Bank employees enjoy privileged interest rates, as low as 2 per cent for someone in Michael Peddlar's position, they find it easy to buy.

David Fowles sees the two men: one curly haired, local, in touch with farmers and their concerns, the other an outsider, wealthy, from the Home Counties.

He remembers Michael Peddlar at Okehampton Show last year, hanging on to a glossy black horse which, claimed a nearby display board, *'was the actual animal used in the advertisements for Lloyds Bank'*.

The reality was, as Michael Peddlar had told him, it's a franchise operation: all over the country, black horses are contracted to represent Lloyds Bank in the local area for this purpose.

The female employees of the bank's Okehampton branch, decorated with sashes, offered carrots to children so they might feed the irritable horse.

On the other hand, the last time he saw Chris Gilbey was at a church service hosted by a lodge of masons in Somerset. Chris Gilbey gave him that bright look, not curious but as though he, Chris Gilbey, held all the cards and David was lucky to know him, to hear his greeting, 'How's business?'

The words came to David Fowles muffled and indistinct because of his hearing problem when there's background noise. At the same time, the sun was burning through the stained glass window, of a blinding strength, so not only couldn't he hear Chris Gilbey properly but he couldn't see his face either.

His stammer came over him, he was afflicted by nerves, yet Chris Gilbey didn't for an instant swerve from treating him with respect.

Outside David Fowles' window, now, the bus to Exeter fills the narrow street, circles the Victorian hut built in the middle of Gidford town square and comes to a halt blocking the Atkinson's Estate Agency window. Tourists pour off, nod down the steps of the bus, aim straight for him. A moment before they might crash through the glass they turn off to the side, help their friends, struggle with backpacks, suitcases, arrange themselves on the narrow slip of pavement.

There is a confusing, bird-like chatter, the first calls of the high-season song of visitors in June.

David Fowles asks himself: Michael Peddlar, or Chris Gilbey, or both?

THE AIR IS fresh but it will heat through quickly; here and there, in the shadows of the walls that divide Jane's fields, glisten patches of spittle, from owls.

Jane climbs the stile at the bottom, threads down the steep pathway under the trees. She hears the tumult of the water, then sees the pitched roof of the little shed beneath her in the valley; the jet of water streams out of its underside, down to the river below.

She unlocks the door with the key hidden in the gutter under the low roof, goes in, picks up the old pair of gloves she keeps down here in order to perform the usual routine.

First, she closes off the inlet pipe; the rush of water quiets, dies, and the heavy flywheel begins to slow perceptibly. The mechanical hum drops in tone, note by note, while she unbolts and swings open the small, oval panel which lets into the elbow of the pipe as it addresses the generator wheel.

She reaches in, searches for any debris. Occasionally in here she finds a sea trout that has leapt over the metal grille, been carried down the pipe to be mangled at this point, but today there is virtually nothing.

49

She swings shut the oval panel and bolts it, but doesn't let the water through. Instead she moves to the business end of the machine, wheels the brake on to the flywheel, slows the heavy round of metal to a final halt within its safety casing.

Silence arrives, finally.

At the other end of the wire, in her house, any lights left on will have dimmed and gone out; the electric immersion heater will start to cool.

She greases the bearings, checks the electrical bushes for wear: this is the weekly service, done with now.

She releases the brake, unscrews the inlet valve so water hisses through the widening aperture, deepening in tone, hitting the cups on the wheel, turning the generator which builds to its steady, perfectly regulated hum.

She imagines the immersion heater in her bedroom cupboard ticking as it heats, the kettle coming to the boil, the lights brightening, her clothes drying out, the damp chased from the thick walls – power.

She checks the voltage and amperage: within acceptable limits. Time to go.

She locks the shed behind her.

Then, surprise hits her as she walks back up through the woods. She sees a figure ahead of her.

She stops.

A trespasser is standing not two hundred yards away, unaware.

Her first instinct is to call out, ask the person, has he lost his way? This is private property.

Then she checks her contempt. A slight fear overcomes her because the figure is strangely dressed – for hereabouts – in a light grey sports jacket and short, green wellington boots such as only townies wear.

Jane can only see his back as he stands by the stile. Is it

someone from the exclusive hotel which is hidden only a mile further down the valley?

Or, he's a bird-watcher.

She watches: the man places one hand on the stile, swings himself up. He moves with plenty of attack but he's unpractised; it's as if he were mounting a higher obstacle as he steps over the fence, turns towards her.

She can see his hair: sandy in colour, parted at the side. He has a suntanned complexion.

If he sees her, she'll walk towards him – she has a 'hello' ready.

He dismounts from the stile, turns away.

Quietly, she follows.

When she reaches the stile, the stranger is in the middle of the field; she judges, he's of medium height, moves confidently as though unaware or uncaring about trespass.

She waits with one foot resting on the step, watches him until he reaches the top of the field and unlatches the gate.

Casually, he disappears from sight: it's as if he owned the place.

She climbs the stile to follow. The electricity cable loops from pole to pole above her head. Then Jane hears the dogs' cry, which marks the trespasser's position as halfway down the bottom yard; she can picture him shying away from the door of their shed.

Billy, the younger dog, will be scratching at the woodwork.

She quickens, although still unsure whether she wants to talk to him or not, but when she reaches the bottom yard it's empty, there's no sign of him. Billy still barks, manically, with Roo's occasional contribution.

She unlatches the outdoor kennel, soothes Billy, lets him see everything's all right as he courses around, nose to the ground, still barking, his patchily coloured nose a black-and-white map drawn over his nostrils, which gives him this mad look. Then he stands alert, points towards the gate. Roo follows him, shifts his weight from side to side, before wandering off, unconcerned. His back legs, she notices, are worse, he is weak in the hips; she has to afford these drugs.

Safer with the dogs around, she continues down the yard to the gate that hangs between her house and the buildings. She looks for a car that might be parked here in the front yard, behind her own Mini Cooper, but there's none, which means he probably walked, or parked his car at the bottom of the drive where the National Park allows vehicles some fifty yards into the moor, but no further, the boundary marked with stones.

Her most likely guess is that it's someone who's heard the barn is for sale and she thinks, If that's true, it's incredible. The details – photographs and such – haven't been taken by the estate agent, no adverts have been published, yet already there's someone crawling over the place.

It's sad that she has to invite this invasion of her territory.

She goes through the gate, follows the path to her house, the dogs at her heels.

She sits in the kitchen.

Here, it's eerily quiet, the only sounds the breath of the younger dog, Billy, the click of his nails on the lino as he saunters around the kitchen, Roo's moan as he sinks into his basket by the stove.

She opens a can of baked beans which she eats cold, straight from the tin.

She takes a Mr Kipling apple pie to eat in front of the television. It's the build-up to the Grand Prix.

The day lingers, held in a quiet, sunlit somnolence; her blood cools, because she's stopped work.

She hankers after someone to talk to; where's Todd?

Her thoughts, as always, return to the work in front of her:

it's the month of the summer solstice, so the days are at their longest, she has plenty of time to do the afternoon chores, then fire up the petrol-driven screw, lift some barley into the grinder.

She thinks, the first crop of silage will have to be cut in a couple of weeks, she should be glad of this pause.

Later on, she wants to find out who was on her land so she calls Atkinson's; after four rings an answering machine clicks in, the message tells her yes, it's Atkinson's Estate Agency, please leave a message which they will respond to during office hours.

She realises, Of course, it's Sunday.

TODD'S UP HERE, wasting his time again; his mouth clamps shut on his cheese roll, he's suspicious, as if with this question she's signalled his imminent arrest.

Jane wipes her mouth, asks him again, 'Go on, what you doing here, really?'

Todd's lower jaw works away between the columns of ringlets; this long hair hangs on each side of his face. He swallows, looks perplexed.

She asks, 'You helping, anyway, this afternoon?'

'Could be, yes,' replies Todd. He tears at the bread again.

'I can't pay you.'

He nods. 'A'right.'

'I can maybe start paying you again in a couple of months, but not for now.'

'OK,' replies Todd, because what he's after, in total, is nothing short of starting up with her again.

She asks him, 'Feeding time at the zoo over, or ... ?'

He stays nodding.

That afternoon, of their own accord, tasks line up ahead of them.

First, they shear the seventeen lambs; there's the new shearing station to try out. To judge by the lambs' newly whitened backs, she and Todd agree they look less ragged, her shearing technique is improving.

They roll up the fleeces, store them.

One of the lambs is infested with maggots; they watch for a while – the grubs crawl blindly under the surface of the skin, eating – then, Jane takes a knife, Todd holds the lamb, turns away, while Jane cuts out the rotten flesh; nauseous at the sight and the smell, her stomach somersaults.

That evening, she meets up with Todd again down at the Cross Keys, he's wearing a black T-shirt with TANKED UP written across it, black jeans, plus the Harley-Davidson leather jacket stretched over his rounded shoulders.

She's always thinking his jeans will rub clean off his hips, fall to the ground.

She asks him, 'You're not following me around, then?'

'Hell no.'

She's stationed in her comfort zone, on the window seat parallel with the darts pitch. A pint of stout with a blackcurrant top is her drink, bought for her, more often than not, these days.

Todd harbours a glass of whisky in his sausage-fingered hand. He repeats, 'Hell no.'

He grins at her, the innocent, while between them a dart flies past.

She thinks: Like protection, I'm this side, he's the other, I don't want any more farm boys stuck as teenagers, still, even when they're middle-aged, dressed like Gothic bikers, wear their hair too long . . .

More than that, if she started out with him again now, it'd

be like she was bought, tempted to share his income, answer her troubles at a stroke.

She tells herself, No.

THE FOLLOWING DAY is overcast. Invisible, unexpected showers litter the landscape.

Jane hopes her newly shorn lambs won't be chilled.

A car engine strains in first gear: this is David Fowles' arrival, at the appointed time.

Jane takes the key to the barn from the hook by the door, goes out to greet him, her nerves tight because she doesn't want to go through with this; yet she has to, circumstances dictate.

She recognises David Fowles: one of those men whom she only sees when he's batting around Gidford town square, thin, shy, bespectacled, carrying that thin plastic shopping bag . . .

Now, for the first time, she has cause to speak to him.

They greet, while he takes equipment from the boot of his car – a camera on a tripod and a builder's measuring tape.

Jane is plumbed with disappointment because once this man leaves with his measurements and photographs, the sale of the barn will be unstoppable. She could blame Roo, the old man of the farm, or she could blame modern science, for making the drugs available . . .

She listens carefully to David Fowles' stutter, waits for the speech to clear a path.

For his part, David Fowles sees the woman in her early forties whom he's noticed most often parking the green Mini Cooper so adeptly in the town square: she's taller than he is, more strongly built, plus, she hasn't made an effort to tidy herself for this visit.

She points at the barn: 'There it is.'

David Fowles unsnaps the legs of the tripod, worries at the film in the camera, drops the tape measure. Words jumble and spill from him; he finishes, 'Right.'

Then he sets up his tripod and takes one or two photographs: first of the barn itself, then he turns to look at the view from this spot.

It halts him, literally, as if a hole had opened up in the earth beneath his feet: a clear fifty miles, through the V-shape, across the Devon plain, Exmoor a purple, smudged line on the horizon. It's possible to guess the world is flat, from this spot, the sense of space, of travel, is like a form of vertigo.

He struggles with his camera, but the photograph will flatten it, take away the true, third dimension.

Gidford is a toy on the elbow of a stream, there.

It's unique, to have the moor, yet also to have this view of the downcountry; he's represented properties in this area for ten years, but not seen the like.

They move the few short paces to the blue-painted door set into the granite.

David Fowles consults paperwork, mumbles several questions; behind his glasses, his eyes blink rapidly as he asks for clarification regarding the planning permission for the barn's conversion to a dwelling.

Jane says, 'It was granted originally for rebuilding the ruin.'

David Fowles looks here and there, as if hunted, then suddenly asks, 'Ruin?'

Jane stops, turns to point back to a spot downhill from her own house. 'When my father lived here, there was a big house on that piece of land there, down the bottom end.'

56

David Fowles suddenly remembers, 'Oh, yes, yes, wasn't it a ... a fire, er ... ?'

Jane confirms: 'Burnt down in 1962, it's a ruin now, I use the stones to fix my walls. The idea is one day to make it into a garden.'

David Fowles cranes his neck, but there's not much he can see from this point. 'A ruin, but, um, without planning permission, because it was transferred to the barn?'

'That's right.'

David Fowles frowns, asks, 'D'you mind ... could I have a look?'

Jane takes him along the front of her house and through the gap where a wicket gate once stood.

The ground is broken, unfertile, the foundations of the old house have been uncovered. Three walls remain standing, surrounding the rear portion of the manor house; within this area the floor is still intact, although rotten from long exposure to the weather.

Tenacious plantlife as well as many winters' worth of frost have left the walls ragged. Here and there are piles of stones, marking where the remaining, unsafe structures were demolished.

Jane shows him the old billiard table which stands there, blackened by the fire which engulfed it years ago.

David Fowles' bird-like scrutiny of the place takes in that the windows set into the walls are shaped in Gothic arches. He squints into the briefly apparent sun and says, 'Pity, great pity.'

Jane points into the sky: 'That was my room, there.'

'Of course, you lived here, yourself.'

'We were living in it when it burnt down.'

'I see!' and then, 'D'you, er, remember the fire, then?' he asks, intrigued.

'I remember more the next morning, seeing the damage.'

Jane explains that planning permission was originally granted to rebuild the big house. It was her father who had it transferred instead to his pet project: the conversion of the barn.

David Fowles is confused. 'Why the barn, why not rebuild here?'

'Wasn't the insurance, couldn't afford to rebuild.'

David Fowles is silent, shocked – not insured? It's out of his ken.

'Plus,' adds Jane, 'the barn has the superior view, anyway, in all directions.'

'So the planning permission was transferred.'

Jane reassures him: she herself renewed it shortly after arriving, seven years earlier. She's been diligent in keeping it up because she was looking forward to moving into the barn, herself.

They retrace their steps, back in front of Jane's house to follow the path out to the front yard.

David Fowles has this habit: he walks a pace or two behind her, Jane feels like she is shepherded.

The blue-painted door gives after some tricky back-and-forth with the key. They walk in.

David Fowles worries at the inside of the property with his camera and tape measure; occasionally Jane helps him.

David Fowles promises – it will sell quickly, no doubt, superb opportunity, an isolated, beautiful location on Dartmoor, the view ... the many problems in converting such a property will be well worth the effort.

Above all, he says, it's a beautiful place.

He murmurs, 'Um, it's that saying, isn't it, location, location, location.'

He doesn't tell her how easily it will sell because he's

embarrassed: there's Chris Gilbey up his sleeve, already set loose on the place, Michael Peddlar as a back-up.

So: it will take him unconscionably little effort to make his fee – two or three phone calls – and he feels a rush of shame. It quickens him; his thin frame becomes agitated, he wants to leave as soon as possible.

At the same time, Jane's heart sinks – the prospect of someone else, living here!

She remembers, she's hanging on by her fingernails. The money: her agreement will be bought.

David Fowles comes out of the barn and stops; just for a moment he's still, motionless, he murmurs, 'That view.'

His voice sounds odd, dreamy; she wonders, is he thinking of the property for himself?

Jane shakes hands with him, yet he seems reluctant to step into his car. He has the door open, but there's an uneasy silence, then, she watches his mouth work, a stutter interrupts him, 'I . . . I . . . this isn't going to be a problem, er, more of a problem . . . is who to choose, actually.'

Jane waits while he struggles on.

'I won't, er, need to put it on the open market, there's um, there's quite a few people, I have the details of quite a few people, who are looking for this type of thing.'

Now he's expecting her to comment.

'OK.'

'If, we can let them, have a look first, just to save you the time and the bother, of endless people looking around.'

Jane agrees. She has this instinct to help him, to latch on to the few words he can spit out, agree with him, make it all right.

'Right then, I won't put it on the open market, until we've, er, explored . . . ' he waves his hand, 'explored a few of these possibilities.'

'OK.'

'So you won't see any photographs tomorrow in our shop window, not yet.'

He's climbing into his car, patting his pockets, teasing out his car keys.

'No problem,' he adds; 'we'll sell it no problem.'

The car's engine ticks over; then his foot holds the engine to a high, unnecessary note before he releases the handbrake and the car jerks forward.

Jane thinks: Bad driver.

Yet, even as the Ford Fiesta disappears down the drive, she could kick herself because David Fowles' reaction to the barn's potential triggers Jane's realisation: *she's selling the wrong house.*

Why not: *she* should be moving into the barn herself, as she always intended to, and instead, *sell her own house.*

SHE STOPS AS the realisation hits her.

She stares at the Longhouse, the worn-out aluminium struts of its door frame, the small windows, the low roof.

A meadow pipit calls – a high, shrill warning from one of Dartmoor's summer visitors.

She works it out: a higher price, because she's selling a fully operational house with a bigger, mature garden.

Yet there'll have to be enough left over – she'll not only have to dissolve her debts, but convert the barn as well.

She curses – why didn't she think of it sooner? – but she's excited, immediately, to arrive back at her earliest, most optimistic plan – the one she thought she'd just been forced to give up.

She continues to walk up her path. These are the first steps on the road to doing this; she feels sure of it, she will *move into the barn herself*.

She's wasted David Fowles' time, he took the wrong photographs.

Suddenly it's a positive act of expansion, instead of a dreary necessity, to go through with this sale.

She opens her front door; now, all the things which she sees in their familiar places are just so many objects that have to be moved: the coats hanging on their pegs, the electric 'Cotto Oven' clothes drier, the gas-powered fridge.

So: she'll call Atkinson's, ask David Fowles to return . . .

Her head swims with plans. She's going to move into the barn. It's hers.

JANE'S OUT SHORTLY after dawn, riding Lady over the wakening moorland.

Field-glasses bump against her chest, a whip for opening the farm gates trails idly from the pommel of the saddle.

Ahead, Billy lowers his body, begins to stalk the distant group of sheep, runs on the line pointed by his patterned nose.

Seconds later, he gives up; it was just practice. Instead, he works diligently on the shoulder of the hill.

She's out this early to search for her cows, who wander for miles to take advantage of the lush summer keep at this time of year.

If she can return before 8.30 in the morning then she'll have avoided the heat, Lady won't have worked up to such a sweat, the flies won't have bothered them.

She climbs arduously, dips to the stream, staggers through the bog. Ahead of her, skylarks break cover, fleeing.

She comes across her cows in the bowl of land beyond Hay Tor. She draws close, walks among them, observant, calm, heated through, now, by the risen sun.

Billy lays up, settling on soft ground at the edge of the herd.

She's here to check if there are cows bulling. She calls out, 'Come on, anyone for AI?'

She stares, for a while, walks around to bump them against one another, then stands and waits. Lady pulls at the bit, asking to eat.

Jane folds her hands on the pommel; for ten minutes, she observes. The cows glance at her, not bothered, they know her; if it were someone else they'd be gone by now.

Her voice loud in the stillness, she asks, 'Anyone?'

None today: Jane wheels back, heads for home. Flies scribble madly around Lady's head; with the familiar jingle the horse shakes them off, taking an extra step to move through them, to be home quicker.

As they pass through water, dragonflies carry their long, coloured bodies like swords across the youthful stream.

A quarter of a mile from the farm, they hear Tuppence's lonely call and from underneath her, Lady calls back; Jane feels the deep, sonorous vibration through her knees.

Home.

Jane eats bread and cheese at nine while standing outside her front door, the hurry to sell the place and win some money causes her to rush her food.

This morning: weld a plate into the footwell of the Mini Cooper, run the tractor and scraper back and forth over the silage-barn floor, hose the concrete surface scrupulously clean for the first time since last year.

This afternoon: waste more time on the calf called Cocoa, a mysterious character who isn't ill, but for all the world depressed. She tries to encourage him to eat; Cocoa takes just a mouthful.

Then, when she returns to the house in the evening, Todd's there.

HE FACES BACKWARDS on his Harley-Davidson, throwing stones at a white, sunbleached sheep's skull.

She shouts at him like he's an intruder, 'What you doing here?'

He grins. 'Brought you a present.'

He dismounts from the Harley, ambles over, holds in front of him a slim, dark blue box.

If he can't go out with her, then he still wants to borrow a shed from someone.

She asks, incredulous, 'Chocolates?'

'What's wrong with that?'

She answers, 'Nothing, 'cept it means you want something.'

At that, he complains, 'No ... '

'Todd, what d'you want?'

'Borrow a shed for the winter.'

Jane rests the box of chocolates on the fence surrounding her garden.

Then, with a grunt, Todd folds at the knees, drops a hand behind to save himself, sits on the dusty ground of the front yard.

He paws the long ringlets clear either side of his face while, behind him, the Harley leans affectionately. It completes the picture of the kind-hearted Hell's Angel with a flair for machinery of all types, a rogue agricultural engineer, into heavy metal.

She warns him, 'I haven't got any beer.'

'Doesn't matter.'

Later, Jane says, 'Hang on.'

She ducks inside and fetches out her last two cans of Guinness Draught.

In the feedhouse, the task in hand is to soak sugarbeet cake in a bucket of water overnight.

The treacly nuts cling to her fingers and she remembers her childhood pony: a hump of brown fur, like a Thelwell cartoon, unshockable, a wooden neck, sulky mouth. A greedy pony, she broke into the feedhouse and stuffed herself with these nuts, only to find them swelling in her throat and gut; she was lucky to live.

Then, sudden noise erupts: a car rolls to a halt amid the din of the dogs' barking.

Jane wipes the dirt from her hands and ignores Lady and Tuppence who toss their heads at her reappearance from the feedhouse, in expectation of a meal.

She cuts through the yard to go and meet – she searches for the name and remembers – Mr Gilbey.

Light, feathery drops of rain touch her every few seconds. A summer storm is imminent.

As she passes through the gate, she calls off the dogs, swears at them to be quiet. Billy slinks off to watch from a short distance while Roo stands there; this is his old-man-of-the-farm act: he gives short, unenthusiastic barks every ten seconds as a matter of course, to show he can, because here in the front yard, the same sandy-haired man – whom she last saw climbing over the stile in her woods – stands by a large, dark green saloon.

She thinks, Yes, it's *him*.

Incongruously, he's wearing a double-breasted suit and tie.

She asks, 'Mr Gilbey?'

'Hello.' He moves instantly towards her, holds out his right hand: 'Chris Gilbey, you must be Jane.'

She answers, 'That's right.'

He shakes her hand firmly. 'And I've got to kick off with a craven apology for trespassing.'

'Don't worry.'

He smiles quickly. 'Hardly the way to endear yourself to a new neighbour.'

She shrugs.

His smile holds. 'And for my second apology, can I just mention that I know what an idiot I look' – he flips the lapels of his jacket forward – 'wearing this.'

She doesn't have time to think of an answer before he explains, 'I had a business meeting in Bristol, and leapt at the chance to hop a mile or two down the M5 and meet you, so either I offended *them*, by coming in clothes like *you* wear, or I make a fool of myself in front of *you*, by wearing the sort of clothes *they* wear.'

He looks pleased with himself.

She wonders, Is everything with this man a long journey two or three times around the block to arrive at the same place?

'Anyway, you're here,' she replies.

'Right!' He takes a summer raincoat from a hanger in the back of the car. 'Where do we start?'

She catches a flash of tartan lining inside the coat.

'This is it –' she points at her house. 'It *was* going to be that – ' she waves at the barn – 'but now it's *this*.'

He turns 180 degrees, twice, like a pantomime actor. 'I can see why you're hanging on to the barn instead,' he says. 'I would, if I were you.'

65

He fixes her with a look which lasts longer than it should, she can see him thinking – she can almost hear the clicks – and he says quietly, 'I'd like to say something.'

She waits. He's searching his pockets and meanwhile still pins her down with this look. 'I think,' he begins, in a low voice, 'that what you have here is one of the most beautiful situations I've ever seen in the south of England.'

He takes out an electronic pocket organiser and a leather-bound notebook, tossing them into the back of the car before shutting the door.

'I don't mind what you show me today,' he goes on. 'I just want you to understand there's enough to make me happy here, if you just sold me a half-acre of land with nothing but grass growing on it and guaranteed access.'

'OK.'

He smiles. 'I'd put up a deckchair and just come and sit in it for an hour or two, every now and again.'

She replies, 'I think I can offer you more than that.'

'Great . . . so, where do we start? I don't mind.'

He turns up the collar of his raincoat against the increasing frequency of the raindrops; the beech tree guarding the driveway shivers with the sudden air through its leaves.

'Inside?'

'OK.'

Jane shows him around her house: opens doors, closes doors; he ducks his head into each room and his eyes dart across all four walls and the ceiling. He switches from talking to listening, so she describes the defects of the house at length, cheerfully admits to being in trouble with the bank; perhaps she shouldn't reveal her position but a carelessness steals over her, either he wants it or he doesn't, the asking price stands as a marker, she won't negotiate, especially since he's the first to view it.

He nods, listens carefully, reads her face with an intent, searching look.

They walk outside to stand in the middle of the small, circular garden at the front while the dusk gathers quicker under the increasing cloud cover.

She watches as his gaze travels over the surface of the house, it snags here and there. His thin, sandy hair lifts with the slightest movement of air and he holds this look on his face, as if he's mentally adding up the cost of everything he wants to do, bit by bit. Her words don't reach him but instead wait in a holding pattern until he's ready to deal with them.

After a pause, he looks at her intently. He asks, 'Could we signify possible boundaries between you, in your new barn conversion, and me, here?'

'The fence here, around the garden – '

'Sorry,' interrupts Chris Gilbey, his tone implying that he has been stupid, 'let me start again and say what I meant to say.'

She waits for a moment, puzzled.

'If this yard here' – he points – 'which separates your barn conversion and my house, belongs to you, where will I get to park my car?'

He looks pleased with himself; this kind of talk, she recognises, passes for good humour.

'I don't know,' she joins in. 'We can paint some white lines and put up a parking meter, make you feel at home.'

He snorts, smiles broadly. 'You'd better believe it.'

Then he tilts his head on one side – a bird-like gesture – and nods beyond the house, downhill towards the ruin. He asks, 'Can we have a look at the end, there?'

Again, she's aware every phrase comes to her oddly made up – he asked could 'we' take a look, when plainly it is only he who wishes and needs to.

She guesses that in his work he negotiates with people, has his own way; these tricks which inhabit his everyday speech are a symptom of all the hidden paths down which he likes to nudge people, without their realising.

She should tell him she's immune.

They move off, pass along the front of the house, through the wicket gate which leads to the ruin.

They turn, come to a halt; he stares at the end wall of her house, he squints upwards, then he casts around as if he's lost something. 'None of this ground goes with it?' he asks, carelessly.

Jane shakes her head. 'No, sorry.'

He lingers, for a moment, then walks out a way; after thirty yards, he can take in the view that she will enjoy from her barn: the moorland sloping on both sides, holding this distant panorama, precious, exhilarating.

He glances at it, merely, before he turns to look at her farmhouse, for sale. He nods, OK.

They go around the other way to look briefly at the back of the house and Jane has to admit, it's not an inspiring sight: a windowless stretch of stonework, dug into the slope; the stable yard runs to within a couple of feet of the wall before plunging vertically into the gulley which runs along the bottom.

She admits, yes, after heavy rain, a small stream pours down there, abating an hour or so later.

'Same as the sides of the house, the back wall is the boundary,' she points out.

He sweeps the featureless expanse of granite with his calculating look, then wants to confirm: 'No land at the back, here, either?'

She apologises: 'It's part of the yard – it's where the lorries turn around, so I need this corner.'

'Right,' he replies, cautiously. 'Right.'

By now the light has dimmed, the clouds have intensified; it signals a proper summer storm and Jane's heart sinks with this interview – it's like he's checking her homework – because the first potential purchaser is perhaps slipping away from her, isn't he, she can sense his disappointment.

His earlier speech – a patch of ground being enough – comes back to reassure her, but then again, will he want to be squeezed between her future barn conversion and her stable yard, with its consequent loss of privacy? Maybe a patch of land is literally what he'd prefer.

He asks, 'If I have to site a Calor gas cylinder somewhere, could it be here, so I don't have to look at it in the front garden?'

She agrees, yes, she'll find him a spot for his cylinder, they'll have to take advice from the gas company because there'll be safety considerations – it will almost certainly have to be located at a prescribed distance from the house – but she undertakes to see it through.

'Right,' he says, cheerfully, 'I've come, I've seen, I shall make an offer.'

Again comes that smile and she feels a sudden lift, at the certainty in his voice.

He adds, 'Thank you for your time; I'll leave you only reluctantly, for the joys of the M5 and M4 motorways.'

They move towards the gate.

Roo stands, heavy, slow with age; he watches them balefully. Billy spares the stranger only a brief, curious glance.

As Jane turns to drop the latch on the gate to the front yard, she catches sight of Lady, tossing her head up and down, curious.

Chris Gilbey unbelts his raincoat. 'Glad I brought this, after all.'

He opens the rear car door, strings the coat on its hanger, then he looks at the sky, 'Worst is yet to come', and he tugs at his cuffs, steps forward. 'Goodbye and thank you.'

'Goodbye.'

He gives her hand a quick, additional shake, then releases his grip.

He tugs open the driver's door: the latch springs with a solid click, a red light illuminates the bottom of the door, the interior of the car is bathed in what looks like stage lighting. She's aware it's upholstered in leather.

Chris Gilbey folds at the waist, drops into the car, pulls the door shut. At the same time, the window is sliding down rapidly.

He cocks an elbow on the sill; again she's on the end of his concentrated focus – an intimacy with this man would grow quickly, she guesses.

'Listen,' he begins, 'you've found yourself a purchaser – ' he waves a hand. 'It's great, there's no way I'm not going to buy this, I just want you to know that, before we go into the hassle.'

'What hassle?'

'There's always hassle – someone else will come along and offer more than me, for a start.'

She answers, 'No one else has had a look at it yet.'

'No,' he continues, 'but seriously, there are always questions, surveys, drain reports, there's bits and pieces, wretched solicitors,' he emphasises; 'there just always are some niggling rows with these things, but what I want you to bear in mind is, if there's any argy-bargy, that it's all just a negotiation, it shouldn't affect you and me, we're going to be stuck up here together for a long time and I think it's going to be great.'

She feels a mixture of alarm and confidence; what should

she believe – that he's going to buy it, but he's going to make trouble?

Her reply is vague, good-humoured. 'Well, whatever happens, happens.'

Chris Gilbey smiles and his elbow comes off the door sill and his hand twists the key; the engine whispers, powerful headlights drench the front yard even though it's only dusk. He sweeps through a three-point turn, the front wheels change lock with impressive speed. As he faces down the driveway, he pauses, leans across the passenger seat to give her a final wave before slipping away.

It's a superior marque of car, but she can't find any badge on its rear end to tell her what it is.

With Chris Gilbey gone, Jane feels relief. The atmosphere of the place has been suspended during his visit, it was as though he brought his own aura with him, cloaked the trees and the buildings with it. His ferreting hands, his beady look, the way his front teeth peep from between his lips – he reminds her of a squirrel; even his colouring, the sandy hair, corresponds.

She can take that, though. In all, she liked him.

Roo wanders over, turns his rear end, sits on her feet – this is his habit when he needs reassurance.

She bends to comfort him. 'It's all right,' she croons, 'it's just Mr Gilbey, buying your house, we're going to make a new one . . .'

FROM HIS CAR, Chris Gilbey telephones David Fowles at home.

He doesn't give his name, or engage in any form of introduction, he simply and cheerfully says, 'Well done!' and

71

gives a snort.

David Fowles stands in the hallway of his modern-built, single-storey home on the outskirts of Gidford. He recognises the voice, pegs the fingers of his left hand into the pocket of his neatly creased blue jeans, shifts his weight from foot to foot. 'Oh, did you like it, then?'

Chris Gilbey's voice crackles, dips in volume, rides in and out of interference: 'Good location, dreadful house.'

'Yes.'

'But you're right, it's the ruin, that's the bit that has the potential, the view, incredible.'

David Fowles fidgets nervously. 'Remember, er, she doesn't want to sell the ruin.'

'I know she doesn't, not yet.' His voice is sprung with enthusiasm: 'But did you see that fucking view you'd get, if you could stand on that patch of ground just in front?'

'Yes ... er ... '

'That's where you'd build, you'd have your terrace, you know, take a breakfast out there ... so, perfect, well done.'

'Um, also remember, it doesn't have planning permission.'

Chris Gilbey repeats impatiently, 'I know.'

'So, should I say – '

Chris Gilbey interrupts, 'Make an offer on my behalf, the full asking price, on condition that she doesn't show it to anyone else, then we can sit back and persuade her about the ruin.'

'OK, so, not to mention the ruin.'

'Don't say a word, just offer the price she's asked for, see where we go from there.'

MOMENTS LATER, JANE is telephoned by David Fowles with

the news: they've received a formal offer for the house, precisely the sum asked for.

Jane is swept by a wave of relief – she can cancel the farm sale, now, her mortgage disappears. Her debts to the bank, to the Lydford Milling Co., to the Okehampton veterinary practice, to British Telecom, dissolve in the much larger figure she'll be receiving from Chris Gilbey.

She only begs him: Hurry up.

CHRIS GILBEY SWOOPS down to Gidford in his green saloon, the country fleet around him, as if it were the ground that was moving rather than the car.

He swings sharp left before he reaches the town centre, heads out on a different road which cuts lower in the valley, more or less following the river Teign upstream.

His hotel, the Teignhead Park, is an eight-mile journey from the farm by car, but to go out of the back of the hotel and walk upriver – as he did when he first heard about Latchworthy from David Fowles – it's only a distance of a single mile.

This hotel is perfect, almost. It's run by a pair of Americans, homosexuals, so it has the transatlantic excellence in service and attention to detail. It's a glorious Tudor manor house with manicured, terraced gardens stepping to the river, secluded, secretive, difficult to reach; most people don't know of its existence, let alone succeed in making a reservation.

There's only one thing it lacks – tucked into this valley, shrouded in rhododendrons and hard up against the birthplace of the Teign – and that's a view, but what gratifies Chris Gilbey, as he bowls up the long driveway in his luxury saloon and ignores the signs advising Caution, Drive Slowly, is the fact that when he was fourteen years old, over thirty years ago, he used to work here, it was his job to sweep up leaves and peel potatoes.

He sighs with pleasure because tonight he'll have another good-tempered but serious spat with that wine waiter.

JANE EATS A Battenburg cake, watches some television, potters back and forth with a screwdriver to fix the broken door latch.

Last thing, she goes out to check the stable yard. She straightens the horses' rugs, replenishes their hay and water for the night, counts the chickens on their roost.

It's dark, and the sound of animals eating is companionable; even though it's raining steadily, she's reluctant to go indoors, face an empty house.

So: she lingers, gentles Lady, watches her jaws move as the wisps of hay are lifted into her mouth.

She strokes her neck, presses her fingers into the muscle in various places in a half-hearted attempt to find the magic spot which will trigger Lady's memory of her old days as a film star. Lady merely grinds her teeth, carries on.

Then, Jane stands by Tuppence's stable door, puts her hand under his mouth, feeling his lips quiz for food initially; when he finds nothing he licks the salt from her palm, then he gives up. Yet, instead of taking his head away, he starts to rest on her hand, finds again the convenient pillow – for an elderly gentleman like he is – which she often gives him.

Jane waits.

By degrees, Tuppence relaxes further; soon she's holding the weight of his head and it's difficult to maintain. She puts her other arm around his neck, so she holds him in this embrace, his head against her breast, his eyes closed. His breathing sounds deeper, now, as he falls asleep in her arms.

It's a good feeling; she values his trust, because this horse carried her father around the farm for years.

Only when she can't hold out any longer does she relax a fraction; Tuppence's head suddenly jerks back to attention – his resting place taken away – so he licks his lips, uncomplaining, but wants to go back to sleep. These are his retirement years after all.

JANE TRACKS THE arrival of a high-pressure weather system on the long-distance weather forecast, waiting to make silage. It's like judging a high lob in a tennis match: wait for long enough, take into account all the variables, but strike it just right. She decides: start cutting – and hits it perfectly, it's warm and sunny, following a short dry period. Todd arrives with the four-wheel-drive Fiat tractor and mower, a massive machine, coloured brightly as a children's toy; the noise creates a sudden excitement.

Todd, heavy metal biker with straggly hair, thumbs a tape into the tractor's quadraphonic sound system, the music gees up his rounded, powerful body; now he can drive these large machines with manic concentration, precision accuracy.

The grass will be cut, then allowed to lie for just a day or two before it's rolled into large, circular bales which are then wrapped in plastic sheeting.

Jane provides her own tractor to power the mobile bale-wrapping machine, but from the start, she's fighting with her hydraulics: she's lost ten pints of fluid, the warm liquid like blood on her hands, where the overflow pipe for the engine oil exits.

Hydraulic oil mixes with engine oil ... She follows the

usual trail of analysis and now she can identify the problem: a broken seal.

She calls up, orders the hire of a tractor for tomorrow, plus the repair of her own; this sum of money from Chris Gilbey, even before it's in her account, gives her licence to work properly, do the job required, instantly.

It's like sudden freedom.

CHRIS GILBEY'S SECOND visit interrupts.

He wears casual trousers and an open shirt; on the bonnet of the car is a blue canvas holdall. Jane is pleased to see him – she hasn't blinked at the cost of the tractor repair, she's already enjoying the farm's new status, that of a going concern, viable, on a sound financial footing.

He insists she call him Chris, instead of Mr Gilbey.

He's fresh, full of energy, unworn by the journey, Jane thinks, whereas she is harassed by the heat and fury out there in the fields, and disappointed in her tractor.

She tells herself: Calm down, Todd's out there, circling the pasture, the tractor crisis is over, the sun is shining, there's no disaster.

Inside, the house is cool and still.

They enter into their first negotiation: the hydroelectric power.

Chris Gilbey wraps his hand around the plug in the living room to feel the warmth generated by the insistent power of the river, channelled through the house twenty-four hours a day. He says with a grin, 'I don't imagine you're going to let me keep it.'

Jane draws a breath, she's just about to answer that he's right, she won't, when he interrupts, 'I'm going to ask you to let me keep it, but it's only a formality, I don't expect you to agree.'

Jane decides she likes this man, he is sharp and straightforward, he would be effective in a crisis.

'I can't,' she apologises.

Chris Gilbey lifts his hands in surrender. 'I understand, sorted, don't let it bother us, I won't think about it again.'

'It's worth more than money,' Jane explains. 'Come winter, my clothes are always dry, hot water's always there . . . free of charge.'

Chris makes his usual dry whistle – she recognises it now: a brief exhalation through his rabbit-like teeth to show he's taking things in good humour. His eyes twinkle. 'Oh yeah, I get it and I'm the outsider who turns up in his air-conditioned car and hurries inside as quick as poss.'

'I'm not saying – ' Jane begins.

But he interrupts: 'Hold on, that reminds me . . . ' He's startled, critical of himself for forgetting: 'I brought something with me, damn.'

He ducks quickly back to the kitchen; she's left to follow.

Now he's squatting over the blue canvas bag on the kitchen floor.

'Somewhere . . . ' he murmurs, 'Ah yes.'

He withdraws a bottle-shaped parcel wrapped in tissue paper and a pink ribbon.

Jane thinks, Shop-wrapped.

He holds it out to her, an abrupt thrust of his arm. 'To celebrate, we're going to be neighbours.'

She's embarrassed. 'Thank you.'

Her hand steals out, closes on the heavy bottle. 'Have a drink, now,' she offers.

'It's just the right thing for hot weather, except it's not chilled enough, but never mind.' He grins.

Then he goes to the table, makes himself comfortable. 'Meanwhile, I can take a couple of notes on what I have to do about this electricity problem.'

He tugs the leather notebook from his holdall, dumps it on the table in front of him.

Meanwhile she looks on the draining board for a knife to cut the ribbon. She tears the paper to reveal a bottle of champagne.

'So-called black champagne, higher percentage of alcohol,' he puts in, as if this were a standard requirement.

'Cor, thanks,' she repeats, good-humoured; he couldn't know that she doesn't drink wine.

'Anyway, so let's think what I'm left with.' He draws a retractable pencil from his leather notebook. 'No heating, no hot water, no electric light, I'm cold, I'm damp, I'm in the dark; what do I do next?'

A blush of guilt rises up the back of Jane's neck.

'Go down the pub,' Chris answers himself with a cheerful snort.

Jane pops the cork off the bottle; she notices how broad the neck is, wide as an old penny piece.

She pours; then they tip their glasses together and the noise is a hard, brittle click.

'Cheers.'

He grins. 'Cheers.'

They sit for a moment; each tries to guess the other's thoughts; for that second or two it's an impossible task.

Yet, Jane likes him because he doesn't care about her worn-out clothes, the mole disfiguring her face, her isolated, unsociable life, he doesn't presume she's uneducated, or hasn't travelled; he talks to her as she imagines he might talk to anyone else.

Then Chris Gilbey points to the side of the kitchen, 'I'll put in an oil-fired Aga.'

He waves in the direction of the window, dabs a finger three or four times, 'I'll have you out there selling me logs for my living-room fire', and now he points above his head, 'plumb in gas fires in the bedrooms, or maybe radiators running off a back boiler in the Aga.'

She watches him, nods.

'That's everything I need ... except,' he snaps his fingers and points at her now, 'electric light.'

He holds her gaze. 'Fuck,' he adds, 'how am I going to see in the dark?'

Jane understands immediately: she'll have to give ground.

'Eat carrots,' he answers himself.

She says, 'I'll leave you a five-amp lighting ring.'

He waits for a moment.

Again, she can see him chew it over, although on the face of it what she's offered wouldn't seem to require much thought – more a simple thank you – but then, abruptly, he asks in a low voice, 'How many kilowatts does the hydroelectric dynamo give you?'

'Eleven.'

'Is it enough?'

'Enough for the hot water, four electric fires, the lighting, the kettle.'

He continues with his mental adding up, 'How many rooms are there?'

She counts from the top of the house to the bottom '... eight, nine, ten if you count the hall.'

'Eleven if you count the outside light.'

'Yes.'

He looks at her steadily. 'A hundred watts per room.'

She notices again his intense, predatory curiosity, this habit of showing he has knowledge of a subject, the way his teeth show over his bottom lip. 'Some of them are very small rooms,' she points out, 'and you won't be using all the lights all the time.'

'That's over one kilowatt,' he continues, as if she hadn't spoken, 'out of only eleven you've got available.'

'It's true, when the kettle's on, the lights dim to about half strength,' she tells him.

Again she waits while he thinks some more.

Then he reaches a conclusion: 'I'll have gas mantles.'

'You can't, can you?'

'Excellent quality of light actually, soft, slight noise to it, but never mind.' He tips his glass neatly.

'They don't smell too good,' she points out. 'Why don't you take the – '

'No, fuck it,' he says emphatically, 'I'm having gas lighting, I'm going for atmosphere, that's the way to look at it.'

Jane dislikes this shame she feels, like she's let him down already, but she agrees, 'OK.'

He takes the leather-bound notebook, flips it open; inside is a slim electronic personal organiser. He taps quickly at the miniature keyboard. 'Just put some of this in so I remember to get quotes for the work.'

He takes a further sip of champagne.

'Strip out wiring loom,' he mutters, 'install plumbing, gravity-fed central heating, mechanical boiler, gas fires, gas lighting . . . '

He pauses, squints at her.

It's like she ought to be helping him, they're in this together. 'What else?' he asks.

'We ought to talk about water.'

'Yes.'

80

He fixes her with his trademark stare, thoughts and reckonings tumble visibly behind his blue eyes. 'Water.'

'The source is on my land, but I can guarantee to supply you.'

'D'you have a cost in mind?'

She shrugs. 'No cost.'

He frowns. 'I'd expect to pay for repairs.'

'If something goes wrong, we can decide together how to fix it and how to pay for it.'

'OK by me, informal, I like it.'

His fingers stray over the pocket organiser again; he dabs at it three or four times. 'I'm all for keeping things simple.'

They have another glass each; with the drink loosening her tongue Jane teases his choice of this drink, 'More champers?'

But she confides in Chris Gilbey and he listens intently while she relates everything about the farm: how she came to inherit it, that she found herself in financial difficulties – but how, in fact, those same circumstances have led to her making progress: she'll pay off her debts, now, she'll finally put the place on a sound footing – plus, she can move into the barn.

He punctures her account, 'Great! Effing great!' or he murmurs, 'Incredible . . . '

So: she's encouraged to talk more, with her new neighbour, than she has done for ages, while outside in the sun Todd circles the fields in a cocoon of engine noise and heavy metal music.

It occurs to Jane that Chris Gilbey is feeding off the sense of this place already, the farm has gripped him in the same way as it does her, she feels a sympathy with him, across the distance; their being strangers, from different walks of life, only adds to the sense of their being kindred souls who recognise the value of this place.

81

Now he's closed the cover of his electronic organiser, folded it back into its leather holder.

They head outside to decide on where to position his oil and gas tanks.

The day remains bright and clear: it's the season for loving Dartmoor. She doesn't want to warn him how benign the atmosphere is now, in summer; she could say, wait until the weather tries to kill itself against the windbreak in the Top Field.

In the distance, Jane can hear the steady growl of Todd's tractor in the Lower Field, still cutting.

Chris Gilbey stands closer. 'This is where I have to admit to a problem,' he begins and he scans the ground beneath his feet as though something under there will solve it.

'What is it?' asks Jane. She is giddy from the champagne.

'These tanks are going to be a permanent installation, right?'

'Right.' She can feel the argument already passing her by. A carelessness steals over. She'd like to go and lie down.

'They're part and parcel of how the house will operate, given there's no electricity.'

She nods in agreement, not wanting to slur her words.

Chris Gilbey's unhappy. 'My solicitor's never going to allow me to go ahead without owning the ground they stand on, he's just never going to allow me to do that.'

'Why not?'

'I don't know, I can just smell it, I can see him saying it; if they are part of the infrastructure of the house, he'll want me to own the land they stand on and the land through which the supply pipes pass.'

She begins, 'Well . . . '

Then, it's like an idea he's had: 'Is there any chance of siting the tanks down the end, in the ruin?'

Jane frowns, perplexed, she has this impulse to give way.

After all, her problems are answered, she has everything she wants, they're getting on well . . .

There's this contemplative look from him and for a moment her mouth closes on the answer yes, before she remembers her idea for a garden – it will be her garden, that was always the plan, so she has to tell him about it, and then finally, say no.

SUDDENLY THE IMPETUS has gone from their meeting. Jane can't just be imagining it – it's as if a switch has been turned off.

He looks at his watch. 'Christ, I've taken enough of your time.'

He scurries towards the car: 'We can sort out the details in the contract, I've got all I need for now.'

He shakes her hand, throws his bag into the rear seat, ducks into the car.

Jane sways on her feet from the effect of champagne and too much sun on her empty stomach. There's one question she wants to ask, which remains at the front of her mind: what does he do for a living?

Yet, it seems inappropriate to go into it now.

Then, as a final confidence given her while he's halfway through the three-point turn, he says, 'Staying in the Teignhead Park Hotel, a night of luxury before I have to put my shoulder to the wheel.'

He grins; the two front teeth make their customary appearance over his lip.

She holds on to the good luck he's brought her; it could have been different. She wants to walk towards him in every sense, take on board his problems with siting the oil or gas tanks, because there's only one problem, really, *hurry up*.

Today it's 20 June; she imagines it's not out of the question they might have signed contracts, completed the sale, before September.

As he slides down the drive in the car, she finds she has a nickname for him – the Squirrel.

ROO KEEPS ONE eye on Jane, from his basket, but doesn't move.

She calls again, 'Roo!' and squeezes a corner off the cheese.

She takes the frusemide tablet, breaks it in half, drops one half back in the bottle, pushes the other half into the lump of cheese. She adds another tablet, a painkiller, Zenecarp, to the mixture, moulding the cheese around the tablets.

She leans over. 'Roo, Roo.'

He lifts his head, strains, tries to drag a front leg out from under him – a long struggle – then he's in a sitting position, his rear end planted in the basket, his front paws on the floor; his knees tremble.

He sniffs the lump of cheese, his mouth clicks open, she deftly chucks it to the back of his throat. As he swallows, his front paws slip on the linoleum and he gracefully sinks to the floor.

THE FAMILIAR FIGURE bends over the bicycle, her tousled head as low as the handlebars, almost. Her feet move steadily but slowly, walking the bike up the slope.

A woollen jumper is tied around her waist, the sack of mail, in modern red and blue livery, sits incongruously in the old wicker basket bolted to the front.

Then the Post Lady sees Jane and she tilts upright with some difficulty. Her face is heavily scored, weathered; she has the look of a farm labourer, which is what she has been for most of her life because this isn't a retirement job; for years she and her sister combined their running of a smallholding on the other side of Scaur Hill with delivering mail, then the younger sister died and this older one carried on.

Her round has become smaller; her wage, also, diminished as the vans encroached, yet she's left this one road, up to Latchworthy Farm.

She delivers to the people off to one side on her way up, to the other side when she freewheels down.

Miss Egan leans her bike against the fence, follows Jane indoors and it's the first sign of high summer when the Post Lady swaps her coffee for a cold drink.

On the kitchen table, Jane's mail is piled in the box marked Milkvit.

The Post Lady sits carefully in her usual seat, pulls her white Aertex shirt away from her skin; even this early, she is hot.

After a while, she takes the first letter, squints at the postmark, gives the date of departure. Her handling of the mail is delicate, practised, she likes to use a knife to fillet out the contents, so now she aims the tip of the blade into the corner of the envelope.

Miss Egan is Jane's reader, and she can't be hurried.

With perfectly judged irony, she reads a badly translated leaflet advertising the products of a German agricultural equipment manufacturer.

DURING THE WAR, Miss Egan was a Land Girl, then she

worked for Jane's father and mother. For a while, before she bought the smallholding with her sister, she was Jane's nanny.

She knows the farm and Jane equally and Jane likes to keep her tied to the place, in some way, like a mascot for its continuation, an emblem of endurance, fortitude, good humour.

So, since Jane doesn't like to open letters, they have this ritual: Miss Egan is in charge, she's the Post Lady, she does more than just *deliver*.

In return for this service, Jane gives her vegetables, which anyway would go to waste because Jane never eats them herself. Also, precisely halfway through her round in terms of distance but after she's climbed all the hills, the Post Lady rests, receives refreshment. Even if Jane isn't around, she comes inside to pour a drink, sit herself down, take five minutes.

Then, the old lady has this elegant way of launching the bike: standing on one pedal, pushing off, a controlled swing of the leg over the saddle, and she freewheels down the drive, brakes full on.

ON THE TUESDAY, a cow called Dimple aborts three weeks early out on the moor; the dead calf is full size. It's missing its eyes.

She isolates the mother in the top barn, ready for a brucellosis test; if it's confirmed, the herd will have to be tested, those infected destroyed.

The test proves negative.

Two days later Dimple smells badly from her rear end – not cleansed properly. Nowadays Jane finds it easy to shoulder the extra cost of the vet again but two days later she walks into the cow barn to find the foul smell stronger than ever. Dimple lies dead on the straw.

Then, just to ring a change, she saves a life: she has to sling the hand-powered winch around the post set in the corner of the calving pen to gain the necessary pull on the newborn, even though it's presenting OK, its nose lying on its hooves.

A boy.

Jane hasn't eaten for hours and the final, slithering run of the calf on to the straw draws a sense of nausea from the pit of her empty stomach.

THE SURVEYOR'S REPORT on Jane's house is a disaster – as might have been expected.

The report lists severe rising damp, wet rot in the timbers, the chimney stack weakened and in need of rebuilding, roof buckled, slates broken and missing, allowing the ingress of weather, gutters requiring to be replaced, no mains services provided, the water supply untested, window frames rotten.

Yet, Jane's solicitor reports, Chris Gilbey is undaunted: he doesn't ask to lower the price, as well he might have, and since he doesn't need to find a mortgage to complete the purchase, the reckoning on the value of the place rests entirely on his shoulders.

He's ready to move ahead.

Jane thinks, Success. She's found the right man, it's a privilege to have the Squirrel on her side, because Chris Gilbey understands, he sees what's on the ground, grasps the fact that people have lived here for hundreds of years and he looks forward to doing so himself, for all his city worldliness he fits in, it's a blessing that he's wealthy enough to ride out the contract on his own, whatever, as well as to effect any repairs.

Immediately, Jane telephones her solicitor and makes an unasked-for concession: Mr Gilbey can have the handkerchief of land behind the house so he can site his gas and oil tanks there.

She asks her solicitor to redraw the plot in red ink and her only request is that Mr Gilbey guarantee her right of access so she can turn vehicles.

There's one other thing she mentions: that the sale should be hurried through, her situation is urgent.

JANE'S IN A mood to celebrate, so she drives down to the Cross Keys.

She buys drinks, now.

She talks steadily in the company of several farmers she knows.

She wins at the dartboard, playing rounds of doubles.

Finally she drives home, having fended off several half-hearted offers from various of them, married or not.

Todd, she thinks, where are you when I need you? Now that she has been saved, financially, she's taken with the idea of going back out with him, it wouldn't be the same, it wouldn't be selling out, there wouldn't be any of that sense of sidling up to his income, they could go into it straight enough, now ...

She hares back the four miles in her Mini Cooper, singing loudly when she's not gabbing on the CB radio and crashing the gears.

In the front yard, she notices a scuff mark along the offside rear quarter of the Mini Cooper and remembers she did take a corner too sharply and she felt the hedge bump her back end round.

She books in the car for a repair, just like a normal person, and while she's about it, buys a new aerial for her CB.

JULY 7 IS hot, humid. The air stands in a column of heat over the sheep pens.

Jane hooks up both sets of clippers and enters this yearly race she has, to shear more ewes than Tony, the heavy-set, bald farm worker who travels around to farms in the area day in, day out, for a living, at this time of year.

By turns, they switch back the gate, pluck out a ewe by the horns, drag it to the clipping station, flip it on to its backside and bury the clippers under the fleece, stroking the wool away in one piece, more or less.

If the ewe's coat is waxy and young underneath, the clippers are gummed up, slowed to half the normal pace; one of them's swearing while the other pulls ahead.

Sweat drips from both Tony and Jane, the clatter of the electric shears mixes with the less constant calling of the ewes and time blurs, counted only in the number of strokes before a fleece drops clear, the number of sheep passing, held between their knees.

Billy gives up his nerve-racked pacing outside the sheep pens; he goes off to lie with Roo in the shade.

At the end of the day, it's 108 to Tony and 68 to Jane, not a bad score, this farm's doing OK now, it's on a roll.

TODD's NEXT GIFT to Jane is a single-barrel, 12-bore shotgun with a hollowed stock; it folds in half, head to tail – a poacher's weapon.

'What!?' she exclaims as he breaks the gun and hands it over.

'For you.'

Jane doesn't take it, instead spreads her arms. 'What for?'

'The mangy fox.' Todd shakes the gun once, in annoyance. 'Go on, have it, you had to sell yours.'

'I can't take that off you.'

'Well it isn't mine, now.'

Jane handles the weapon: hefts it, twice, then points it at the sky, brings her eye to the single barrel, 'Todd ... '

'What?'

'There's a family of mice living in here.'

'Needs cleaning,' he suggests.

Jane lowers the barrel, snaps the gun shut. The mechanism is stiff, unused.

'More than cleaning, it's rusted.'

Todd's careful black eyes scrutinise the gun, worried. 'Blow a few cartridges through it, that'll clean it out.' He adds, 'And a bit of oil.' He swipes at his hair. 'Got any cartridges? We could put a couple through now.'

She shakes her head.

He offers his hand. 'I'll take it back, then, clean it up for you, buy you a box of cartridges as well.'

She dumps the weapon back on him. 'Todd, you don't have to give me things, I'm lending you the shed anyway.'

'I know.'

'So is that all it's about, or what?'

Todd can't break through that question, it feels like he's being asked to tear out his own heart, and hand it over to her so she can trample on it if she wants to, so it feels daft, like there's too much to lose. He stays quiet for now, tells himself it'll happen in a day or two.

LATER, JANE WHEELS out the antique thoroughbred trials bike, the Husqvarna.

From stem to stern it's made of polished aluminium; it glitters in the late afternoon sunlight, high and light and ornamental, a silver flea next to the bumblebee of Todd's Harley.

Together she and Todd work to bring it out of winter storage: they empty the cylinder barrel of oil, clean the plug and the points, tighten the bucket of worn plates in the wet-clutch housing, take the chain out of its tin of grease and thread it, inflate the tyres.

After a few prods on the kick-start, the engine zips into life. Angry blue smoke pours from the exhaust, then clears.

Jane puts up her thumb.

Todd folds the rusty shotgun in half, stashes it inside his half-open jacket.

As he prepares to take off on the test drive he thinks, Christ, this woman is perfect: she's one of the boys, rides this little Husqvarna, she has her own farm, for God's sake, land given her on a plate, bloody *hell*, the unfairness of that – savage, isn't it – and she complains about money, cashflow, but how about if she took up with me, again, wouldn't it be the easy answer, my income from contracting, joined up with her farm, I'd park my machinery, free.

Two bikes, they'd have.

So: one big wish, granted him? He'd answer, that she'd have him back.

He settles on the Harley; with a touch of his right thumb the four-stroke engine double-thumps into life alongside the urgent clatter of the two-stroke.

Without helmets, they ride down to Gidford, overworked muscles calming at the thought of rest, drink, ease.

Jane's thinking, It's going OK. But of course, she shouldn't say that, because the minute she does, it's going to be the opposite, isn't it, and everything will fall apart.

THE SLANTING RAYS of sunlight comb through the beech tree and stripe the greenery which climbs this side of the house.

Jane and the Post Lady are sitting outside.

The words as they fall from the Post Lady's mouth carry the same weight; the West Country accent rounds the vowels, but Jane is wrong-footed.

She expected to hear that Chris Gilbey has signed the contract, that 10 per cent of the sale price is lodged with the solicitors as a non-returnable deposit.

Instead, her solicitors report that Chris Gilbey, at the eleventh hour, has asked *if he can include the ruin in his purchase.*

So the contract will need to be redrawn. Jane unfolds a detailed plan: the original plot is outlined in blue, the concession she offered him at the rear of the house is marked in red and now there's an additional outline, in heavy black, drawn around the bottom of the house, around the ruin, a surrounding patch of ground.

The Post Lady reads on: 'In recognition of this last-minute inconvenience to you, Mr Gilbey is prepared to offer a figure some measure over the anticipated valuation.'

Jane asks Miss Egan to read the letter again; she's hurt, angry, disbelieves it.

The older lady does so, unmoved; her steady voice calls out each word individually, without emphasis.

Jane can't believe it; she holds the plan, tries to decipher the meaning behind Chris Gilbey's demand, she's confused: how come, suddenly, after all this time, just at the moment when they're about to exchange contracts, he throws the whole thing up in the air?

Jane engages the Post Lady in a conversation, as if the other woman were involved, also.

'I always said how quickly we had to sell, that was part and parcel of going with him.'

The Post Lady, weathering the bad news, nods. 'I see.'

'I was definite as to what was on offer. Not the ruin, I said it again and again.'

Miss Egan waits.

'I even,' swears Jane, 'I even went as far as to give him the patch behind the house, you know.'

'Sounds like he's taking advantage.'

Jane repeats, 'He's throwing us back to the beginning, more bloody deeds, boundaries, surveys . . . '

Jane sits down again, her hands clenched in despair, an icy hatred steals over her – this *delay*, this *fucking-about*! Doesn't he know . . . he's toying with her whole life?

Even when the Post Lady rises to go, Jane continues to feel an unstoppable anger, irritation, at Chris Gilbey, and so Miss Egan's face shows uncertainty and Jane sees she might have infected the old lady with her own temper, it's like Miss Egan bears the blame for bringing the letter.

She takes a breath, then asks, 'What would you do?'

The Post Lady waits, stares at the ground, meanwhile Jane reads her familiar face: the large chin, slow and steady eyes, the stoop made for her, it seems, by too much cycling.

Miss Egan's gaze lifts from the floor, meets Jane's.

'Wouldn't have anything more to do with him; if he can take advantage once, he can do it again.' She adds, 'If you do sell to him, you might not have another chance of saying no.'

Then she's going, sets her bicycle in motion, her balance perilous on the broken, storm-washed surface of the driveway.

Jane tells herself, Don't shoot the messenger, put the letters away, go about your day's work ... She hardly sees her feet move in front of her, doesn't concentrate, she thinks only about Chris Gilbey and she becomes angry. She takes it out on the farm's infrastructure: she slams gates, shouts at the dumb beasts to move on.

All her debts arrive back, like the same stones arranged around her neck, heavier than before, they weigh her down, awful.

It's exactly like the money's been given to her, then taken away.

She tires herself out; to think about the disappointment is to try and wriggle out of it, escape ...

In fact, she succeeds. Suddenly she remembers: Chris Gilbey folding at the waist, dropping into the car and pulling the door shut, the window sliding down, the last thing he said, 'Listen, you've found yourself a purchaser ... I just want you to know that, before we go into the hassle ... '

She remembers how she felt – the mixture of alarm and confidence, that he was going to buy it, but he was going to make trouble.

She hears his voice again, '... going to be stuck up here together ... I think it's going to be great.'

Therefore, she ought to have known: Chris Gilbey is trying it on. For instance, when he asked for the electricity, he said, 'I don't expect you to agree ... '

An uncertain but welcome relief courses through her. She

94

understands, now, what's happened, yet the relief is tainted with dislike for him: Mr Gilbey tried to put one past her.

Yet, perhaps he underestimates how important this is, for Jane.

In any case, she's going to refuse. There is a simple answer, like with the electricity – no.

She tries to hang on to her earlier admiration for him, still allow herself to look forward to having him as a neighbour.

Maybe it would be possible if he'd actually been there – in front of her – to make his request for the ruin, then she might have understood it was no more than a reflex action, for him, an attempt at negotiation which he fully expects her to turn down, this is how he's made his money – the only difference, where she is concerned, is that he warned her first.

So: it puts them on a different footing. She knows in advance, he deliberately forewarned her, it's like an intimacy they share.

She goes inside her old house, picks up the telephone, to find there's no dialling tone, only an empty silence on the line.

She kicks a chair into position, slumps at the table. She's lost all respect for these rooms that she's about to move out of, that she's trying to sell, this house is just a nuisance, under her feet.

She deliberately shuts Chris Gilbey out of her mind, she doesn't want to decide whether she likes him or not, she doesn't want to picture him living here.

Instead, she concentrates hard on what she has to do: she jerks to her feet, goes outside, climbs into the Mini Cooper and drives down to the town square in Gidford.

She parks adjacent to the call box.

From there she telephones her solicitors to inform them she doesn't accept Mr Gilbey's request and could his solicitors please redraw the plan as it was before.

Then, staring out of the old-style phone box across the square, right into the front window of Atkinson's Estate Agency where Karen sits typing, receiving phone calls, she asks to be put through to David Fowles, Managing Director.

She watches Karen's fingers dabble at the switchboard . . .

Karen is no more than twenty, with a light Devon accent, and the long, overshot chin which characterises her family, she's Gidford's most powerful tennis player, she's a regular on the annual float for the Girl Guides' entry into Gidford carnival, a practically minded, good-tempered girl – but this is mad, to watch someone take your phone call.

Then she recognises David Fowles' voice, 'Hello?'

Jane rides on the annoyance which overtakes her. 'Mr Fowles, this is Jane Reeves from Latchworthy.'

'Oh, hello, is – '

She interrupts, swearing, 'Chris Gilbey is *fucking* me around.'

There's silence on the phone.

'Can you tell him there's a deadline on it now: contracts to be exchanged by the end of the week or we'll put the property back on the market . . . '

She slams down the receiver, drives home.

FIVE HOURS LATER David Fowles bounces back.

In the stable yard, Jane hears a car engine straining up the drive and she checks her watch: it's past nine o'clock. A summery dusk is turning to night.

She doesn't want an interruption, she was going to go and maybe watch some television, throw together a sandwich.

She retraces her steps, wondering – is it a neighbour with a

96

problem, some lost cattle broken away from the herd or a dog's been killing sheep?

She sees the light cast from the headlights swerve over the trees, then settle as the car jerks to a halt in the front yard. As she approaches, the engine dies and she hears the thump of the car door, sees the thin, slight figure looking at the face of the house, searching for a sign of life – David Fowles, Managing Director of Atkinson's; maybe he's earned his fee, after all.

He doesn't hear the latch on the farm gate, or the clump of her boots, so when she's standing behind him as he goes down the path, it gives him a jump. 'Ah,' he says quickly and pushes at his glasses, 'there you are.'

A wide smile breaks on his face but disappears just as quickly and she stands there, waiting for the news that Chris Gilbey has caved in.

Yet, before she can say a word he carries on, 'Um, um, your telephone wasn't working, but I wanted to come and discuss ... er, the slight change of plan, but only, maybe ... is there somewhere ... ?'

He looks around.

She's startled, because she expected to hear that the crisis had been resolved, but her anger at Chris Gilbey's ploy doesn't find the space to explode; instead she hears herself invite him inside.

David Fowles follows. He says something; she can't quite catch it, he might be talking to himself as he daintily picks his way.

They go into the kitchen; David Fowles has veered off the track, he apologises: 'Sorry for coming out so late ... er ... '

He makes a beeline for the table and in the light, now, she can see he's wearing the all-purpose lightweight Rodan clothing that has zipped pockets with the little pull-tabs stamped with the name of the manufacturer in miniature, yellow-metal lettering.

David Fowles finishes, 'And I was sorry to hear about the hiccup.'

'I won't change my mind,' states Jane flatly.

David Fowles is standing in front of her, his mouth open, slim frame bent in the middle. He leans one hand on the table, tucks his fingers in his back pockets, takes them out again. 'Fine,' he begins, 'I agree', and he wears this intent frown, as though they stand here together, shoulder to shoulder, at the outset of a plan which might provide an answer, 'Um . . . '

Yet, he suggests nothing.

Jane continues, 'I want this exchange of contracts signed and sealed. He's got everything he needs, as far as I can make out.'

'Ah, yes.'

His tone of voice, the fact he looks up, away from her, implies there's a problem.

'Doesn't he,' adds Jane.

'Um, I relayed your stance to Chris Gilbey immediately; he . . . er . . . he chose to withdraw his offer.'

David Fowles' eyes blink behind the spectacles as he fidgets at the table, he's waiting for something – a response. She fights on: 'So, so what you're saying is that I've wasted my time with Mr Gilbey, the deal's off?'

David Fowles replies, 'If you want, tomorrow morning, your house will be on the open market. It's about the quickest I can do, but . . . '

She is almost off balance from the disappointment, arguments whiz around her head, words spill from her lips but for a moment everything seems not to make sense, it's like she's been infected with his stutter, she struggles to catch up. 'Fine,' she replies. 'Put it back on the market.'

Then a blaze of anger catches her at the introduction made by this man David Fowles which has brought her to the brink of disaster, and she repeats, 'Put it back on the market.'

David Fowles stutters an apology. 'I'm afraid it's always the way, however close you are, until contracts are signed, you can never say, um ... '

Jane's scalp prickles with the heat of her feeling, over this; she wants to explain her exact position. 'I'll tell you what's going to happen,' she begins. 'We're finding another buyer.'

David Fowles' stutter is like so much debris or fallout from the conflict; somewhere in there is an apology and his hand comes out, palm down, like he's calming her. 'But I just want to know, um, for certain, that you understand, that if your house goes on the open market, it means we start again, surveys and so on ... '

'I understand that.'

'Fine,' repeats David Fowles. 'Whereas, if you choose to let go of the, ah, ruined bit, then we can sign contracts tomorrow.'

Jane shakes her head, slowly.

Some minutes later, after more toing and froing, David Fowles takes his leave, she watches him mutter and move jerkily down the path to his car; the shiny material of the Rodan clothing reflects the outside light which she switches on for him.

She trails after to see him off.

A moment later the car's engine breaks into an immediate start, the headlights come on which signals Billy to bark again, the rear end of the car jerks downwards against the springs so it's an automatic, he's just engaged the drive. Now the engine rises to the same ridiculously high note before he lets the handbrake off and the car kicks up the gravel, leaps forward.

She watches him through his four-point turn: the car bucks at each point, she thinks again, Yes, bad driver.

JANE IS A small figure outside a remote farmhouse, surrounded by moorland; this place is enormous; she is small next to it.

Above, the stars are a dense population crowding the night sky, the Milky Way is a sugary dust.

She walks forward, heading up to the yard to finish giving the horses their hay and water for the night; and euphoria takes over from the despair at today's news because she's trounced Chris Gilbey, she's rid of him, she saw him off, she *frightened* him, her acres of ground surround her still; look, her animals are fit, healthy, she's in charge of her destiny, money isn't everything.

She takes Tuppence's water bucket, fills it.

Roo stands in the yellow glow thrown by the 100-watt bulb while Billy courses around, idly.

She draws the bolt on Lady's stable, takes the half-empty water bucket, presses it into the thick, black water in the trough, the bucket's resistance dissipating as it quickly fills and she imagines, below in the valley, how the river Teign presses hard on the wheel, the generator thunders, water escapes, cascades back down to the river, its energy turned into electric light so she can see to fill the horses' water buckets.

Even with this solid, dependable machine working for her, night and day, she's struggling to pull both ends together, make them meet.

She tells herself to own up, she might be in trouble.

She draws the bucket and walks; the dogs watch carefully.

Billy pants, smiles, Roo wears his doleful expression. Are they proud, to have her as a mistress, because this is her success, isn't it?

Chris Gilbey won't be living here; ground won't be given. She can fight for her life, all right, it's clear what she has to do.

She separates a couple of sandwiches of hay from the bale, pulls it loose, fills Lady's hayrack.

Her mind fixes steadfastly on the path ahead: find another purchaser, quickly.

It's a smaller bite of hay, for Tuppence.

She's annoyed at the estate agent's manner, his behaviour, but she has to believe, given he found Chris Gilbey so quickly, there are plenty more people who'll want to buy. Meanwhile, she has to claw back on the money, quickly, stem the cashflow.

She searches for ideas – cancel Roo's prescription? No.

So: call it a day on saving the three cows until the Real Meat Company answers her request for an organic certificate. She'll sell them at the first available market – a lump to knock the top off the debt, stop it making more debt.

Plus, she'll rearrange with the auctioneers to conduct the farm sale, after all.

She could cry with frustration: one step forwards, then two steps back.

JANE WALKS INTO the house, tells herself, Confidence.

She won't ever run out on this place, she's tied to it, three generations.

The immensity, the pull of the stars above, the constant needing of the animals will hold her.

Lady and her retired companion, Tuppence, are safe in their

101

stables, the chickens are high on their roosting pole, out of the way of the foxes, all is well. Circumstances will swing in her favour, she repeats to herself.

She found a buyer quickly before – she can do it again.

So: maybe go and watch TV, in the company of her dogs.

Inside, she doesn't take her coat off, but, as if she's about to face an emergency, sits in the chair in the low-ceilinged sitting room with a cheese sandwich, moving her arms with some difficulty, squashed into her coat.

On TV is the featured example in a disaster reconstruction programme. While the accident is re-enacted for the screen, she remembers her conversation with David Fowles. A dread grips her, but she pushes it away.

At one moment, she harks back to Chris Gilbey's words, 'There's no way I'm not going to purchase this place' or something to that effect; she imagines him coming to beg her to retract, sell the house to him.

The next moment, in her mind's eye, she's found another purchaser.

When the programme's finished, she's sated with the idea of everyone – herself included – having to cope.

She goes outside again, decides just to look at the ruin, the patch of land she's refused to sell, that's cost her so dear. She takes the dogs with her, and doesn't have to shout at Roo, to encourage him out. It's an early sign that his expensive drugs might work, rejuvenate his old, slothful blood.

Outside her front door she turns left – as she hardly ever does – and walks down the seldom-used path in front of her house, through the gap where there was once a wicket gate, into the grounds of the ruin.

Here, she's surrounded by the darkened space formerly occupied by the old house, a ghostly presence: the remaining walls mark the outline of an old life.

Here, the Post Lady, Miss Egan, called for work.

For a while Jane wanders back and forth, retraces her childhood footsteps over the rotten flooring.

She imagines herself years hence, an old woman – she'll build a garden in here, among the gap-toothed, sheltering walls.

Then Miss Egan's face is suddenly there, lit by her imagination, and suddenly Jane feels optimistic: it'll happen, she hasn't been caught out yet.

Her experience with Chris Gilbey has been like stepping – with just one foot – on to a boat that has suddenly floated away: it didn't matter whether she pulled back or jumped forward, but if she hadn't made the decision quickly, she'd have fallen into the water and that's where she can't afford to be.

As usual, she risks losing everything because life offers her nothing but Jekyll and Hyde, good news and bad, which come towards her in waves; she has to ride them both.

She heads back to the house. The dogs are in front of her, their pushing through the overgrown path like a whisper in the silence.

She twists the handle to let herself back in – then stops when she hears a muffled thud, followed by three or four more, coming from the yard.

Billy's stock still, his ears alert; his black-and-white nose points in the direction of the noise.

Roo wanders indoors, unconcerned, deaf.

Jane waits.

She knows she has to check: what was that? She closes the door, heads off at a fast walk and ducks into the first shed to switch the lights on; when she hears another thud, she starts to run.

JANE REACHES THE stables to find Lady cast on her side, hard against the wall of the stable. Her neck strains, she's sopping with sweat, her eyes roll in their sockets, her stomach is bloated, abnormally round.

It's an unfamiliar view, the underneath of a horse; it gives no sense of its ability to run, the whole thing looks clumsily made, it shows the soft downy hair with a seam drawn down the middle like a zip.

Lady's legs kick, thrash, her neck lifts for a moment, before it sinks back down with a groan.

Jane goes immediately for a rope.

She re-enters the stable with the fleeting thought that she might not walk out alive. She has to avoid the thrashing legs, Lady's feet hammer the side of the stable at each cramping pain in her gut.

Jane reaches relative safety, tries to attach the rope to the head-collar but with Lady's head yawing and lifting unpredictably it takes several attempts to fix the clip on to the bronze ring.

The panic in Jane's breast rises.

'Get up,' she commands, hauling on the rope. 'Get up.'

She moves to Lady's rear quarters, begins to kick her rump: 'Get up!'

She kicks harder.

Then she makes a wide circle back to Lady's head, to haul on the rope again, shouting, 'Up!'

She wishes, more than anything else, for someone else to be there to help her, but by the time she might drive to a neighbour's phone, it would be too late.

She can see the inward focus of Lady's eye and knows she has to break through that, eclipse it, frighten Lady more than the internal pain frightens her, so she will get to her feet.

Yet with this beating and hauling, Lady's slowing down,

she lifts her head less often. To redouble her effort, Jane takes the whip from its perch outside the stable, thrashes Lady's hindquarters but it has no effect, she's losing.

Billy barks, wildly.

An idea occurs to her: she goes to let Billy in, takes him by the collar, guides him around to Lady's tail, keeping him out of reach of her hooves; she has the measure, now, of their strike, how to avoid them.

Jane lays into Lady again, kicks her, beats her with the whip as before, but this time she encourages Billy to attack because she wants the fear of the predator, the instinctive knowledge in Lady that a wild dog means death, to have its effect.

Billy gives sharp, hysterical cries and Jane notices energy flicker through Lady's stricken frame. Billy barks, dashes in closer still, inches away now, then he summons the courage to bite; Jane notices Lady's nerves jump, the surface of the skin judders – the message is getting through.

Jane redoubles her efforts, maintains a steady shouting and pulling at poor Lady.

Every few seconds now, Billy snaps at Lady's rear quarters; his jaw trembles with excitement.

With a lunge, Lady rolls on to her front, her legs tucked underneath at impossible angles. Jane keeps going, her voice hoarse, she's sweating herself now with the continual work, until Lady throws a front leg out and begins to test it for weight, then, with a groan, she struggles to her feet, stands there, soaked in sweat, shaking.

Jane feels a shiver of relief; love for the horse floods her, there's a sense of achievement, but she loses no time in hauling the animal around to face the door, each step won at some cost.

When they're finally walking along in the Top Field, slowly but surely, tears come to Jane's eyes and she soothes Lady with stroke after stroke on her plastered neck, explaining why such a beating had to happen. Billy trots alongside, a staring look in his eye, mouthing to evict Lady's hair from his tongue.

Jane cajoles Lady, tidies her mane, wipes the sweat from her eyes, tells her she's a film star, she's all right, she's better.

They return briefly to the stable yard, where Jane throws a rug over Lady, pushes dry straw underneath it to allow the sweat to dry off while she's kept warm, then she carries on, meanders around with this animal who has been, more than any other, her partner in the farm.

Jane keeps her moving: around and around the stable block, up the field, anywhere that's quite easy ground. In the early hours of the morning she remakes the stable for Lady and goes to bed herself, exhausted.

THE FOLLOWING DAY breaks hot and still: the whorl of high pressure is almost stationary, its centre holds steady over the south-west of England without any deep troughs of low pressure to the east to draw it away.

So: the air is from the north, cool at dawn but heating up the minute the sun starts to make its quick, summer ascent. The stillness suits the kind of day Jane wants: recovery, calm, growth.

She hardly wears anything: a pair of shorts, a T-shirt, boots.

She's perched on an upturned log outside the blue door of the barn, the sun hot on her face, waiting for her five tonnes of straw.

The view from here is a feast, in this weather. Her own valley – the one she owns every boulder and stick of, on this side of the river – channels the eye off the moor to the patchwork of downland fields, all different shades of green, which travel away from her, it seems for ever.

This view inspires her and the achievement of men and women in taming it to produce food, livelihoods ... yet, she knows every one of those farmers is caught in the snare of human society as it's arranged itself, the banks an overlording presence – she accepts it – so the quilt of fields becomes suddenly as if made not of mud and grass but of paper, the boundaries exactly *so*, financial agreements carefully stitched into place on the strength of those boundaries, the income they can generate, brooking no alteration except on demand from on high.

Yet, she receives EU subsidies: substantial payments per head of cattle and sheep to help the upland farms compete, this money isn't conjured out of thin air.

Also, she inherited this place from her father when he died eight years ago, yet immediately she had to shoulder a debt which he never had to: her mortgage was only to cover death duties, a man-made structure which the more she thinks of it seems designed to fracture the country, pull apart properties, people, and from that day she was headed for where she is now – having to divide the farm, dilute it – but she tells herself, by selling a small part of it, she'll hang on to the whole, she must only keep steady, find another buyer, meanwhile sell anything she can, to knock down the debt, realise some money, pay the Lydford Milling Company, have the phone reconnected, pay the vet ...

Her debts have come back with a vengeance, they have a particular stride, each one, the way they run towards her, always faster.

She ought to talk to Michael Peddlar.

She rises from her position seated on the upturned log, conjuring some determination.

Nothing of this sort is easy, without a phone.

ON 17 AUGUST Jane has an extraordinary ride on Lady. As early as seven in the morning she and Billy are bringing the Belted Galloway herd back from Ripator when they're surrounded by heavy thunder which bangs like artillery fire from the army range.

The lightning is close enough to scatter the cows in front of her. The rain is as if tipped from a bucket.

This summer storm is violent but local. She can see the outside wall of it: as if the storm has chosen them, which could be construed as godly, fateful.

She knows when to give up; she could waste hours chasing various strands of frightened cattle, it's enough they've been found and pointed back in the direction of the farm.

Lady frets, jounces on her hocks, naps, she tests for control of her own mouth, asks to be let go. Jane settles her weight forward in the saddle, relaxes the reins; it takes Lady some moments to forget her troubles, realise her mouth is free, then she gives an enormous jump, accelerates.

Like the cows – as wild – Jane and her horse scatter over the moor for a mile and a half, pull up only when they're out from under the storm.

She walks Lady, to cool her down, heading for home.

The cloud sits on that part of the horizon, a primeval concoction of electricity, water and air, maddening the wildlife.

JANE'S LONG OVERDUE account with the Lydford Milling Company attracts another penalty, crawls over the £750 minimum, which means they are legally entitled to lodge a petition for insolvency against her: a court hearing is set for 19 September.

The Insolvency Service, an executive agency within the Department of Trade and Industry, sends Jane a brochure. A number of questions on the facing page serves as its list of contents: 'Will I lose my home, when will the Official Receiver or trustee sell my home, can anything be done to stop the Official Receiver, what is meant by beneficial interest, what happens if someone wants to buy my beneficial interest, what happens if no one buys my beneficial interest, where can I obtain further advice?'

The phone company warns Jane that before she can be reconnected, her original bill must be paid, plus an additional cost will be incurred.

Michael Peddlar, from the agricultural advisory unit of Lloyds Bank, advises her that a charge is being added to her overdraft every day because the debt has risen above the prescribed figure.

Jane smarts at the unbelievable penalty.

Michael Peddlar points out that their scale of charges was laid out in leaflets given her when she first arranged the refinancing of the farm six years ago and sent to her periodically, as and when they've been adjusted; he requests that he be brought up to date *vis-à-vis* the possibility of *selling the barn* in order to rectify her financial position because if she decides to release this capital sum, he'll be pleased to expand her credit limit, remove the daily penalty, reduce the interest charge to its former low rate.

Under separate cover, a pro-forma letter informs her that the bank has cancelled her current account facility; any cheques she writes will attract a charge to cover the bank's costs in refusing to honour them.

Jane has to admit it: now it's a struggle to survive, she must find a new purchaser, *quickly*.

As she walks up the yard, she screws her willpower to a

further sticking point, it's all she has left: her strength, deployed as potently as she can, yet will it be enough – 19 September, in court?

She must beat the figures back, inoculate against debt. Most important of all – find someone to buy the house.

The innumerable pieces of paper – every day, every hour, she has to work against the rub of these figures.

IN SUMMER, SECTIONS of the road to Gidford are like tunnels of greenery. So: the cyclist flits in and out of shadow, slowly, the brakes on all the way down; her hands ache with the effort.

Miss Egan realises it won't be long before she has to walk downhill as well as up, with the strength gone from her hands.

The number of lines marking her skin, their depth, the work performed, the toiling up this hill every day at her age, carrying the mail ... it'll end, no doubt soon.

She's seen people come and go, over the years, in the properties up and down this road. There are some who've stayed on, and through terrible times, others who go.

The people who sell up, who move – she can tell them from the start: they're fidgety, already, before any problems are presented.

The people who'll stay ...

Her hands in their fingerless gloves pull mercilessly at the brake levers; otherwise the humpbacked figure is motionless, feet stationary on the pedals.

Every day she makes this slow descent to Gidford from Latchworthy, but it's the first time Miss Egan wonders if this practice ought to stop – if Jane ought to read her own mail – yet somehow the habit has been going on for so many years, it's impossible . . . it's the insignia of their long involvement with each other.

Yet, she has this sense of discomfort, now, as she reads the letters.

THERE'S A BOWL of light; it hangs a few feet above what Jane believes is ground level, although the intense illumination burns everything else into darkness. She doesn't know where the Top Field starts and the night sky ends.

She guesses it's within her boundary wall, whatever it is, and she counts it as part of the magic which hangs over this place: the farm is held in a spell, a religious feeling has stolen over it, and its value, she thinks, transcends ownership.

She wriggles her bare toes against the plastic of her wellington boots. She's wearing nightclothes and a coat.

Has a spaceship landed in the Top Field?

She clips the lead on to Billy's collar, lifts the latch on the gate, careful not to make a sound. Billy walks at her heel, growling; the whimsical breeze comes from behind him so he can't find the scent.

Jane doesn't know what to expect – a crashed aircraft?

Some hundred yards from the incandescence, she's no closer to having any idea. Then they hear a voice, 'Hello?'

Immediately Billy starts up his frantic cry; the lead whips tight in Jane's hand.

She shouts in reply, 'Hello?'

The silhouette moves against the light source. Jane stops, uncertain, working the leather of Billy's lead; it's slippery with the sweat from the palms of her hands.

Now she can hear the swish of boots through the grass. A tourist on a camping expedition?

Yet she can't think of a piece of camping equipment that might explain the orb of light.

Moments later, she thinks, Army, and she knows she's right because the man is dressed in camouflage, his face is blacked up. Sure enough he comes out of the light to introduce himself, 'Captain Hargreaves, Royal Berkshires.'

She can see his thin, axe-like face capped with a beret, his demeanour troubled. He squats, lets Billy indulge in his frantic begging for friendship, and now a crowd of around fifty young men are visible at the perimeter of the throw of light: their faces blacked out and yet cast in this brilliant phosphorescence, they resemble badly made-up extras waiting for a crowd sequence in a film drama. All of them are lost, they've failed to connect with their rendezvous.

Jane's angry, an aggrieved woman, dressed incoherently in a dressing gown, coat and boots, because it wasn't magic, just the army going astray on a night-time sortie. She tells herself, Come down to earth.

But then, it was magic after all.

On the following day, Jane finds two long canvas bags in the middle of Oak Field.

She pulls a drawstring, opens one bag to reveal a quantity of plain, off-white packages of different shapes and sizes, although of unvarying style. Each sachet of freeze-dried rations has its contents written on it in plain capital letters: SALT, PORRIDGE OATS, DRINKING CHOCOLATE, SOUP, MEAT, RICE, POTATO, BISCUITS, EGG, MIXED VEGETABLES.

This is a gift.

Jane looks up at the sky which today is as blue as would have been drawn by a child with a crayon and she thinks, Yes, it's a gift, out of an azure sky. She gives thanks, because she won't have to waste good money at the mini-supermarket in Gidford for however long, maybe months.

It isn't much, but she's closed a hand on the debt which is bleeding, she's pressing harder now.

She fetches the tractor, squares up to the consignment, heaves with all her strength and lands the two bags in the linkbox.

She wonders how long this stuff will last – until a new purchaser is found, put through the hoops, signed up . . . ?

Hurry.

Later, Jane picks up her spoon, presses it into a dun-coloured liquid. Fragments of vegetable rush to the middle. These are her rations.

She thinks, September, autumn, start to buckle down.

JANE HAS THIS idea of the sum of money, the amount she can expect from the sale of the house, as a disloyal presence, it was once in her grasp but now refuses to come forwards, instead stands a short way off, shadowy, uncommunicative.

It taunts her.

BUT THEN, AMONG others, Jane's account manager, Michael Peddlar, and his wife want to look at the house with a view to purchasing it for themselves.

Violently, she doesn't want them here, but can't think of a reason to stop them. *The bank manager . . .?*

They turn up; she remembers the strongly built, curly-haired man in his middle thirties, as he hops out to shake her hand.

'Hello again!' He's wearing a collar and tie, linen trousers, but no jacket; as before, he's scrupulously clean-shaven, with the same ready smile on the open face.

Michael Peddlar is embarrassed, so, keen to make her laugh at such a turn of events, 'Thought we'd come to help you out, ourselves!' he exclaims. 'Taking it seriously, you see, my duty to put my clients in the black, perhaps!'

He introduces Jane to his wife, a bosomy American woman with a pretty smile.

Jane is taken by a wave of unfairness: the idea of selling to the farm's account manager . . . it's ignominious. Worse, it's to admit to his face, to his *advantage*, that he was right: back in March, he advised her how to answer the problem, now he pops up, he is the answer.

Since March, she thinks, the same monthly salary has been electronically transferred into his account, which will enable him to make an offer to buy, yet at the same time, more and more has been automatically added to her overdraft, which presses her harder to sell.

For a moment, she could believe her bank charges are siphoned off directly into his account; the truth of it is there, anyway – what tiny fraction of her bank charge goes to him?

She bites back on her impatience to have Michael Peddlar and his wife go, leave the premises.

She asks, 'D'you want, just to poke around, by yourselves?'

Michael Peddlar hesitates, 'Er . . . '

His wife gives her brilliant smile, replies, 'That would be great, if you don't mind.'

Jane waves, 'Go ahead.'

She returns to her chore: trawling through every nook and cranny on the farm to organise the lots in the Top Field, ready for the farm sale on 16 September. Todd helps; his payment is a share of the proceeds.

So: in the calm of a September afternoon, while Jane and

Todd work in an uncomfortable, dispirited silence, Michael Peddlar's voice is a polite, interested echo, occasionally audible as he shows his wife around the garden.

An hour later, they've finished; Michael Peddlar seeks out Jane in the yard, calls her name.

She takes pleasure in seeing them off, she even warns them in advance that the survey will be bad news.

Michael Peddlar replies, 'Of course . . . '

Yet they make an offer, peg their hopes a small percentage below the asking price, but above the competing offer, from the Warwick family.

David Fowles keeps to the rules; Jane receives written details of all offers received.

Within two weeks, Jane feels a tentative security begin to steal over her, as before, but this time she tells herself, Don't allow it, don't let up for one moment on harbouring money, don't spend. Because she couldn't trust Chris Gilbey's money, she can't trust anyone's.

JANE PULLS ON the long plastic glove, then steadies herself at Puzzle's rear end. She plants her feet apart and leans her weight forwards. Delicately, she worms her hand into the cow's uterus; then she pushes hard.

Puzzle stamps her feet, sways from side to side in the crush.

O'Bryan, the vet, coaches her, 'Feel it?'

'Not yet.'

Jane pushes harder, she's in the cow's birth canal, up to her elbow.

Then, yes, in the soft innards of the cow, she feels ropes of harder tissue. She turns, looks at O'Bryan. He wears a boyish, intent expression: his eyebrows are permanently knitted, his eyes bright with enthusiasm, impossible that he should ever be uninvolved.

She nods. 'Feel it now, yes.'

Puzzle has scarred badly from the difficult calving last year, she has blocked tubes, she'll have to be culled.

As it happens, Todd passes by, trailing stuff for the farm sale. 'Morning Ms Reeves.' Then he asks, 'You lost something?'

SEPTEMBER 19, HER court date, looms large.

Jane watches another surveyor crawl over the house with a clipboard and an electrical meter which measures for damp.

Why couldn't they use the report by the other guy? It's all *wasted time*.

The surveyor erects a portable stepladder on her overgrown lawn, so he can see on to a small portion of flat roof at the side of the house, where it was formerly attached to the ruin.

She opens the trapdoor to let him into the cramped attic space.

Then, on the evidence of the survey, the mortgage company demands retentions of over 40 per cent of the sale price; the Warwicks lower their offer by exactly the same amount.

Jane has to refuse them.

She calls David Fowles, she offers to have more, different strangers traipsing over her house.

David Fowles is frustrated, he stutters, shouldn't they not show anyone around who doesn't have in cash at least 30 per cent of the purchase price to shore up the insecurities of the building societies, when they're reading survey reports?

Jane makes a decision: she will put the house with other

estate agents as well, swallow the extra percentage she'll have to pay for multi-agency representation.

She bites back her disappointment.

Anxious to whip this sale along faster, she also decides to give up, maybe, on moving into the barn. She will offer any potential purchaser a choice: the house, or the barn. Either, or.

The Warwicks boomerang back, to look around the barn.

The anxiety makes her shiver, sharp needles run down her arms to the tips of her fingers.

THE NIGHT BEFORE the farm sale, Jane dreams of her father.

The dream doesn't follow a sequence of events, but offers brief movements, like excerpts relayed to her from a home movie.

She sees him pick up his tobacco tin, his arm making an ostentatious swoop over the table, he bows over to open it, the unfastened jacket stands out like a skirt, strands of hair fall over his receding hairline, his thumb arches over the top of the tin and with a click the lid lifts clear, then the pipe is full, lit; periodically he holds it away from his mouth to stare into the bowl, as if something in there has surprised him.

In her dream, the smell of tobacco smoke hits her as a real, current sensation, rather than a memory.

By association, she sees him clasp the biscuit tin to his chest; his mouth straightens, compresses into a thin line, his elbow lifts an inch, the grooves channelled to the corners of his mouth deepen, momentarily, again the tin-lid comes off in his hand. There's money inside – he stirs it with a forefinger, then the tin dangles between his fingers, he puts it down on the table. Inside, the coins scrape against one another, settle.

She stirs in her sleep now at the sudden influx of worry.

She's clasping a plastic stable bucket to her chest, there's a weight in the bucket: something unknown.

The weight increases; she can barely hold it, the 'O' of the bucket in her arms begins to distort out of shape, from the strain; when she can no longer lift it, at the exact moment, the bucket becomes liquid, flows from her grasp, disappears.

She wants to know what was in it, but she'll never find out. Looking down to her lap, she sees a black, empty space.

Her eyelids flicker.

SHE SLEEPS ON her forearm, head tilted back to open the throat, allow for the easiest breathing, soundless time travel.

Next, she's wandering the ruin; it's the day after the fire has consumed the old house.

She arrives home, it's been raining, the wet air is filled with the smell of charcoal.

She walks around, a child in shock, her father ahead of her. Again she has this picture: his coat standing from his legs like a skirt.

Everywhere, she sees black. The charred strata of wood remind her of the belly of a beetle.

Everything is damp to the touch, there's no heat, yet evidence of its work is all around her, the ribs of the house have been exposed, the walls are stumps, a fireplace stands suspended halfway up a wall.

She measures the sky, to guess which cube of grey, damp air now occupies the space where her bedroom used to be.

A window has fallen out, lies there on the ground, the glass splintered but grouped, still, in symmetrical panes.

She's amazed to find the dining-room table in the garden, the surface of the wood has bubbled from the heat and on a cracked plate lies a piece of bread which has been burnt to a crisp: the fire made it into toast.

The sodden, debris-strewn floor.

She approaches the billiard table, it reaches almost as high as her.

She picks at the rubber seam which rings the inside of the table – it's come loose; she presses the surface of the green baize, cold water pools around the tips of her fingers.

SHE WAKES, CONFUSED, and part of her remains with the dream, is dragged back by it, she closes her eyes, tries to find it again, but she's disturbed by the difference of everything, then and now.

She opens her eyes. The room is dark but she can see the outline of Billy lying next to her: his ribcage rises, falls, a small, even rhythm; in sleep his breathing is different: deeper, effortless.

Out of her sense of dismay – directly as a consequence of her dream – a realisation comes to her; it's as though the words are spoken in her head by an unknown announcer: *she loves this place, Latchworthy Farm.*

On the heels of this realisation comes proof that it's true: why else would she be still here, all by herself?

She could sell up, pay off her debts, walk away a rich woman.

She's sitting upright, stung by tears, she has the feeling she ought not to be so involved.

She climbs from the bed, moves her limbs carefully so as not to disturb Billy.

Roo's tail moves back and forth once.

Then she finds Billy's wet nose in her hand, anyway.

119

She soothes them both, whispers idle nonsense to fight off the sense of foreboding brought by her dream.

She goes downstairs, tours the kitchen; she visits the lounge, the bathroom . . . Shadows stand motionless, conjured by moonlight from the uncurtained windows; her own shadow moves through them.

She climbs the stairs again, pokes her head around the spare-room door.

She continues up the stairs to her own bedroom.

All is as it was before.

She sits on the edge of the bed and tries to summon her father's ghost; at the same time she pushes it away, she has the sense she's floating, happiness only a stretch of the hand away . . .

She recognises how unusual this is, the inside of her head is normally occupied with a queue of things to do, often less than that, merely the task she's involved with at that moment, her hands' work, inches in front of her. Yet now she sees ghosts, reaches blindly for a sense of happiness, fulfilment.

She climbs into bed to find Billy's inert form, she puts an arm around him, the smell is familiar, even though they're both motionless she has the idea that she's riding on his back.

What day is it?

Then she remembers: 16 September, the farm sale.

She climbs from the bed, pulls on clothes, walks across the room, down the stairs, outside.

The weather is undecided: it won't be hot, sunny, but it won't rain; some leaves will fall, but only by themselves. There's no wind.

She passes through the front yard, acknowledging the barn

as always, even though in her mind it's already signed over to the Warwick family. She walks up the stable yard, escorted by the dogs.

One half of the Top Field will be given over to parking; on the other half she and Todd have laid out eighty-six lots of surplus material.

Lot 16 is a box of old iron hammer heads, lot 58 comprises four cuts of beech timber left over from the storm salvage of 1987 plus other pieces of scrap timber because they come from the one tree: the disease in the trunk makes the same delicate patterns through the beech. Lot 32 is a collection of old scythes, the blades sharpened, newly oiled, she can remember her father scything thistles in the end field where the wild fauna of the valley attempts to impinge on the farm's cultivated acreage; also, in those days, there was an annual crop of bracken, used as bedding for the horses, cut from a neighbour's pasture in the autumn when it had dried out, turned reddish gold.

So: marshalled in four long lines across the Top Field are the leftovers from two generations of farming practice, everything from an old polyurethane foot-bath to a pair of stable forks, because she doesn't need so many.

In addition, two of the stables are thrown open. Inside Lady's stall she's erected a table for refreshments complete with white cups and saucers – virtually unbreakable, she found, when she was setting them out. A hired tea urn stands at one end; there's room for people to congregate, if it's going to rain.

The second shed houses the auctioneers and their book.

Atkinson's have erected FOR SALE boards outside both the house and the barn because among the crowd who visit the farm sale might be another Mr Gilbey, someone with more than enough money, for whom she won't have to drop the purchase price of the house by a third, in which case she might choose to turn her back on the Warwicks, reclaim the barn for herself.

Jane trots indoors, runs a quick bath. She scoops her hair back into her father's racing hat – a jaunty touch, she thinks. She buttons on the coat she never wears, belonging to him also; it's not a coincidence that she wants to hide in his clothes, right now.

By 9.30 the first cars follow the signs provided by the auctioneers, through the yard to the parking area. The auctioneer pulls on his white coat, pumps himself up for the performance, promises that everything will go – he'll even sell the stones in the ground.

Jane suddenly has this knot tied in her stomach; she's on show, neighbours – many of whom remember her father – will know the farm's troubles, somehow, there's a smell that comes off a farm in debt, the whole neighbourhood recognises it, despite not catching sight of each other except for a moment or two in the town square or at the livestock sale or in vehicles squeezing past each other in the lanes, maybe because debt is a disease they all fight themselves, every day of the week, Sundays as well, there's no such thing as a day off from it.

By ten o'clock she's in the thick of it; the owners of more than forty cars browse up and down the lots. Crews of children drift off, entranced by the distant horizons, encouraged by their elder brothers and sisters.

Jane turns from one face to another, everyone cheerful in the autumn sunshine, talking business.

She feels drunk with goodwill, especially towards Mrs Stour, the wife somehow shared out between the two Stour brothers – no one knows quite what the deal is – because she's volunteered to provide a whole Land Rover full of buns, sausages, cakes, which she'll sell, she whispered, the money beyond her costs to be chucked into the sale total – no commission.

The nudge of the older woman's elbow brings sudden emotion to Jane's breast at this unexpected generosity, not broadcast to the world but neatly put in place without fuss.

She takes a turn up and down the lot numbers, to wear it off, recover.

Mr Robin Cook from Barton limps down the yard, ready to inform her what's wrong with her horses, meanwhile he'll mention the correct names for parts of the horse's anatomy – brisket, pastern, et cetera – but she has to tell him she's packed the pair of them off to a further field so they're not upset at the excitement, but if he isn't put off by a ten-minute walk, she'd love him to cast an eye over them.

The beak-nosed, self-invented aristocrat gazes into the distance, declines, but shakes her hand politely.

The Reardons turn up, the kindly, sensible family from the hardware emporium in town who've been in business for so long that a corner of their shop has been given over to a museum which displays the working implements and everyday domestic trivia used in the region in the past, in mint condition, presumably unsold by their forefathers; they'll be bidding for some of the antique tools.

For a while Jane talks to them about their plans to upgrade the museum. They recently travelled to York to see the famous Viking exhibition permanently on display there and from this experience they've had the idea of recreating 'scenes' from domestic or agricultural life, with the models of the people made perhaps as part of a school project they want to fund in association with Okehampton Comprehensive School.

As she listens, Jane makes a comparison between them and

herself: here they are, folk who have inherited a business, brought it on, just like she has – but their clothes are new, their children's clothes are fashionable, the vehicle they've parked in her top field is a Range Rover registered only last year, plus, they spread some money around for charity, to write their names larger in the local area, whereas she is sinking fast if the Warwicks can't be pressed on quicker, if their solicitors can't wade through this Agricultural Restriction Order they've dug up, attached to the planning permission.

The auctioneer and his assistant gather at the foot of the first row of lots for sale. He explains the terms: cash only or a cheque with a banker's card, commission payable by the vendor so nothing on top of the prices they put their hands up for, everything must go, no reserves, his assistant will make a note of names and addresses, moneys are payable in the stable set aside for the purpose.

Then he's off, with a slower, more holiday atmosphere than in the livestock sales because many of the bidders aren't used to it, he wants to encourage people to come forward, not feel ostracised by the sales patter.

Further up the field, various individuals dawdle near the items they're interested in, while a knot of people progresses steadily with the auctioneer from number to number like crows after a plough, drawn by the impetus of the sale, anxious to watch the money change hands, judge if someone's picked up a bargain.

So: it's an unfamiliar, crowded scene in her Top Field; Jane decides to head in the opposite direction, not to see the entrails of her family's livelihood pored over by strangers, friends, neighbours.

She retreats to the refreshment shed – Lady's stable. She still expects to see Todd at any moment: he's earned his share of this, yet he's not here.

Instead, she's hailed by the hard core of conversationalists, hangers-on who try to make one another laugh. After a while she joins in, describes the size of the sack she'll need to take the money away and count it.

Then Jamie, the stout, middle-aged son of the family who own the B&B which is also struggling down at Beaworthy, pipes up, asks her, 'All right, but how many hours d'you reckon it took to lay it all out?'

'What, the stuff?'

'Exactly, the digging it out, the cleaning it all up, the dragging it halfway across the field?'

Jane tells him she and Todd have been wasting odd hours at it for the last four weeks.

'Go on then, guess how many man-hours in total.'

'All right, I'd say maybe two weeks' actual work, as much as a hundred hours, maybe.'

'Now then, take that as being a hundred hours of work.'

He's won his audience now; no one is going to talk about anything else, instead they listen to him, not out of pleasure but because a serious, complaining tone has entered his voice, which insists.

'What d'you think,' he goes on, 'is the charge a solicitor makes, just for an hour's work, d'you say?'

A suggestion or two come: 'Too much to start with' and 'Half as much again.'

'Their pound of flesh, normally,' adds Mrs Stour from behind the urn.

Jane smiles, she wills the others to take over with more light-hearted banter, she wants Jamie to stop, but he persists, 'More 'an fifty quid an hour, though, isn't it, I bet you 'tis, but let's say fifty so what's a hundred times fifty quid, is that five thousand pounds?'

Blank faces wait for him to continue, to get it out of his system. 'So, if you was a solicitor, it's five thousand pounds is what you should be getting just for the *labour* alone, isn't it?'

'I hope she does get that,' replies the elder Pilkington – the 'play man' he's nicknamed for his habit of starting up amateur dramatics in the town, given half a chance.

'And that's not taking into account,' continues Jamie, 'she's a retailer, isn't she, she's selling something she's already paid for, or her old man did before her.'

Again, the audience wait. Jane senses their discomfort but can't think what to do: they're trapped now, Jamie's hijack of the camaraderie between the neighbours is complete, effective.

'So why the fuck can't we stand up together and tell the professions, back off, you so-and-sos, you're squeezing the bollocks out of us, you've got your hands round the fucking throat of the economy? Why can't we?'

Now, with the swearing, there's embarrassment all round. One or two make noises of discontent, move off.

'Because it's divide and rule, i'nt it, keep each of us in our little boxes, don't take off the lid, isn't that it?'

Jane hears herself saying, 'I'll put you back in your little box in a minute, if you don't keep quiet.'

There's a ripple of laughter which pleases her, but she senses Jamie's unhappy stare and she wonders if he's drunk, so she moves with her cup in her hand to the doorway to engage in a harmless conversation with the woman who runs the gift shop in town, Eve Crippen.

Then Jamie shoulders his way past, stomps up the yard towards the auction, and Jane only half listens to what Mrs Crippen is saying because she's watching Jamie's retreat and she thinks, He's right, the man is right, he cares about it, but I brushed him off, put him down, because I was scared of being seen to care, frightened to admit to people openly I'm in a shitload of trouble.

'D'you think you will?' the other woman is asking her.

Jane didn't hear the question so she has to ask, 'What?'

'Have another one?'

'What, this, another farm sale?'

'Yes.'

Jane looks up at the sky, then down to the round-faced, cheerful woman who stands next to her. 'I doubt it, for a while. It's taken a lot of years to build up this load of old rubbish, you know.'

THERE'S ENOUGH TO pay Todd his share, but not enough for Lydford Milling. She has to hope they'll take part-payment, and still cancel the court case.

Yes, hope: she's living on it, certainly she's holding her breath. Jane wants to drive over to Lydford now and leave that particular debt at their door, the bankruptcy hearing scares her, what it will mean.

Lydford Milling's office will be closed but she imagines she could push an envelope through the letterbox . . .

Instead she holds fast, prepares Roo's dinner, complete with drugs. She digs the tablets into the food, to hide them. Roo's daily prescription has three components now: a new wonder drug called Cardiovet has been added to the diuretic, frusemide, and the painkiller, Zenecarp.

For the same money she could buy a new pedigree collie every two months.

She watches him eat.

127

Roo's expression, she judges, has taken on an enlightened air, he's hungrier, spends not so many hours asleep, he walks about the place more.

Yet, it's not all good news: the diuretic makes him pee for so long that he can't keep his balance, he cocks his leg, the stream of urine arrives, continues for ages, so his remaining back leg gives way, he sits or falls sideways, the urine continues to express as he struggles back to his feet, walks on.

However, there's a gloss on his coat, he smiles often.

Jane goes outside to finish up the evening chores. Billy is full of life, he scatters wildly wherever he goes, pin-sharp dots of energy in the centre of each eye, reflected from the light in the yard.

Jane eats a tin of frankfurters in front of the television, it's an episode of *Animal Hospital* and Rolf Harris comforts a pensioner who's brought in her dog to be put down.

Tears course down the old lady's face; she's ashamed, tries to turn from the cameras. Her dog is white around the muzzle, blind, deaf, incontinent.

Jane's staved off Roo's death; it's been costly, but as she watches the gruelling scene on television, she finds words coming out loud: 'Don't die, Roo.'

Because this old dog's like an investment portfolio, now, in pharmaceuticals.

JANE FOLDS THE money into her coat pocket.

She asks, Will it be enough to fend them off?

She drives the Mini Cooper hard along the B3357, the only road which crosses the moor. As she steers, young Roo stands on the rear passenger seat, his nose at her shoulder, he likes to ride the corners, look out of the front screen, and he's immortal now, she realises, the presence of his nose being there, just behind her, will remain for ever.

She switches on the car radio to listen to the news on Radio 4 and hears a government statement from the Cabinet Working Group on BSE: 'The new scientific evidence now available means that further work is needed on appropriate culling strategies throughout Europe.'

It's the new scandal: that BSE can be passed from cow to calf, no one knows how, whether it's across the placenta, or through the milk, so another disaster looms for the dairy industry, this time.

She prays, Hold on, let no one die of BSE in the next ten years. The crisis is fading.

She listens to further extracts from the Commons statement, the minister's voice boring through the jeers of his adversaries: 'Meantime, the Government considers it right to provide significant new aid for the specialist beef sector in the UK. Accordingly, an additional £60 million will be provided in respect of cattle in the hills through the Hill Livestock Compensatory Allowance Scheme ... '

Jane takes both hands off the steering wheel and bangs them back. She exclaims, 'Ahhh!' because in the last few moments, as she listened to this news programme, it seemed as though first someone took a few thousand pounds out of her pocket but then moments later MAFF promised to write out a cheque to her personally for £60 million, if only she can wait that long.

She's used to the see-saw, swings-and-roundabouts feeling, it's what all farmers cope with, yet this mad cow disease crisis rumbling on exacerbates the effect, takes it to extremes.

It's not her strength, paperwork, subsidies, market trends; she wants to be left to do what she's good at: the stubborn slog of working the ground at Latchworthy, keeping the animals fit and healthy, the buildings upright, the tractor serviceable.

Instead, her main business this year is carving off a piece of her property.

She talks out loud: 'Come on, hurry up!'

The Warwicks' solicitor is advising them to take seriously the Agricultural Restriction Order attached to the planning permission for the barn, which insists it's used only by someone engaged in agriculture. So it will cancel them out, it looks like.

She might ask, what agricultural labourer is going to be able to afford to do it up?

So will there be no one who'll buy it?

If so, she's left with trying to find someone for the house, anyone but Michael Peddlar . . .

She shrugs off the thought of the bank manager, she doesn't want that sense of falling, the trap of failure closing over her, she hangs on to the idea that today's a good day, she's paying off debt, she'll sell the house even if she has to drop the price by 30 per cent, she will be all right, she'll survive, live in the barn like an animal for ten years.

She slows to navigate the switchback at Two Bridges, then, when she reaches Lydford, she slows to the urban speed limit and reads the wink of traffic lights.

If Lydford Milling will accept part-payment of the debt, she's escaped from a court case by the skin of her teeth, she tells Roo; this could so easily be a journey to Torquay, to hear the debt read out in the County Court.

She and Miss Egan, the Post Lady, learnt that the first two letters of the farm's postcode defined the court in which the petition against her would be heard; TQ – standing for

Torquay – pigeon-holed her case to be heard in that particular town. Isn't it sinister – all part of the conspiracy of letters which arrive, unbidden – that the secret code on the front of the envelopes should tie a line between herself and that courtroom; it's no wonder she doesn't want to open her mail.

She swings through the S-bend at the bottom of the town, makes the familiar right turn over the railway line. She marks the freshly painted, white post-and-rail fencing and the sign LYDFORD MILLING CO. She turns into the driveway.

Immediately she has to sneak on to the grass verge to let a bulk lorry past; the bearded driver gives her a cheerful wave from his position high up in the cab, he's on a wage.

A hundred yards further on is the mill itself: built in the thirties, it's a collection of tall silos holding soya and other grains, plus a machine room to mix the ingredients, bind them together.

She can hear the thunder of machinery within, stirring up the mixes, pressing out pellets of different sizes.

A high, narrow arch spans the gap between the mill itself and the office building, along which can be seen men walking their hydraulic pallet-hoists back and forth, fetching bags.

Jane runs the Mini through the tunnel; briefly the noise of the mill joins in concert with the reflected noise of the engine and then she's out the other side. She parks in the yard and climbs out, her hand in her pocket, folded round the assorted banknotes, thumbed over twice by the auctioneer, which nonetheless aren't enough, by any means.

Inside the office reception there's an immaculate, light blue carpet which stretches – a featureless expanse of colour – to all four corners of the room, tightly pinned into the seam between the skirting board and the floor. Jane walks across it, ducks, leans on the hatch marked RECEPTION, and asks for the woman whose name is on all the letters. She confesses to no appointment, but this woman will know what it's about.

Then she sits.

Beside the adjoining wall, there's another farmer who waits.

Jane looks at the carpet – imagine walking on this stuff all the time ...

Her thoughts are interrupted by the arrival of the woman, whom she doesn't recognise. She stands, shakes the woman's hand.

This is how an ad on the TV might be brought to life in front of her eyes: the woman is smartly coiffed, her hair in a brown coil on top of her head, she's dressed in a matching brown suit made of a tweed-like material, make-up is applied over the surface of her face. She is, Jane would guess, of her own age, in her mid-forties. Jane likes her immediately, without knowing why.

They greet each other and Jane mentions her debt ...

The woman frowns, hesitates, then for the sake of confidentiality invites Jane to follow her down a corridor.

On either side, doorways open into offices. The impression Jane has is of cleanliness: a sharp light covers everything, even the one or two people she glimpses – it doesn't allow shadow or indistinctness. She thinks, The weather isn't allowed in.

The woman leads them to the third office, invites her to sit down.

Jane is surprised at the size of the computer screen which blinks in the corner; the monitor is so large it requires its own workstation.

A desk is centred across the window and the woman now sits behind it.

Jane draws back her chair, faces up to her; the noise of the mill is a dull, repetitive rhythm carrying the business along.

'So, how can I help you?'

Jane can't remember the woman's name.

She draws the wodge of money from her pocket and picks at the elastic band around it. She starts, 'Well, I had a farm sale, so, I can pay off part of the debt ... I'm just hoping – what I'm asking you, is it enough, will you cancel the court case on a promise that – '

The other woman knits her hands together, frowns, interrupts, 'Hold on a minute.'

Jane stops, the money is heavy in her hands, she watches the woman rise and go to the computer. After a dozen keystrokes, a piece of A4 is fielded from the printer; the woman brings it back with her.

The woman – Jane fights with her memory, to find her name – pushes the sheet of paper towards her. 'Shall we just go over the sequence of events?'

Jane can make out a series of columns: Latchworthy Farm has an account, a file stored somewhere in the gigantic memory of the computer in the corner. Now the woman poses a finger neatly at the top of the sheet of paper. 'We made a statutory demand for payment of a sum owed us by the Latchworthy Farm account, we received no repayment from you and so, after twenty-one days, because the sum exceeded the minimum requirement, we made a petition for bankruptcy against you; the registrar confirmed that you are over eighteen, you aren't a foreign diplomat or a member of the Royal Family and so the petition was due to be heard at Torquay County Court on 19 September, two days' time, to describe the debt and ask the court to issue an order for bankruptcy against you.'

Jane thinks, The concerns voiced in this room, the procedures launched with paper and pen, computer and keyboard, have nothing to do with me, they arrive out of some other place, yet they're everything to do with me.

Jane looks at the woman's finger which rests on the sheet of paper: the nail is long, well manicured, Jane thinks they may be false nails. What intrigues her, however, is their colour.

She stares harder – barely hears what's being said – because the bottom halves of the woman's nails have been clear-lacquered, but then, starting with the crescent-shaped lines where the nails grow from the skin, and reaching to the neatly pointed tips, they've been painted a rich beige colour.

Jane frowns. This person, whatever her name is, has gone to all this effort to give herself two-tone nails.

The woman's voice continues, but Jane can only watch, entranced, as her finger follows the turn of events listed in front of her and a word jumps into Jane's head: talons.

The woman glances between Jane and the paper, her eyes travel back and forth.

Jane holds her breath because she realises she was asked a question.

'Your benefactor?' asks the woman.

In response to the woman's gaze, Jane nods her head; she lifts the bundle of cash, awkwardly, she holds it out for the woman to count.

Instead the woman asks, 'What's that for?'

Jane replies, 'It's well over half, but it's up to you, of course ... '

The woman taps the paper in front of her, 'That's what I'm saying, a chunk of it's been paid off already – yesterday.'

Jane still holds out the money, 'How d'you mean? Paid off already? Who paid it off?'

The woman ducks for a moment to check the name; then she pauses, her mouth hangs open briefly, before she continues, 'Mr Todd Baker.'

134

ANGER MIXES WITH amazement in Jane as she hurries out to the car park, skirts the Mini Cooper too quickly and catches her knee on the front bumper, curses.

She recovers, yanks the door open, pushes Roo out of the driving seat, jumps in, drives off, hell for leather.

So: Todd used the cash to pay off some of her debt? It's incredible. She swears at this debt, it's in the way of her friendships, it's fouling her life ... she has to get rid of it.

Jane drives directly to Gidford, she aims to reach the town before lunchtime when many of the shops – probably the estate agency as well – close for an hour.

It's not just Todd; everyone in Gidford knows her troubles, shopkeepers suddenly – all together now – won't take cheques from her.

She finds a parking space in the town square, climbs from the car, hurries towards Atkinson's, which is squeezed between the post office and the delicatessen. The door pings a warning; she pushes through.

Karen looks up. The few words of welcome die on her lips as Jane cuts in, 'Hello Karen, is David Fowles in?'

Karen reads the hurry in Jane's voice, she's already on her feet and replies with her own question, 'What's it concerning?'

'Tell him it's urgent.'

Karen says, 'Hold on a minute ... '

She disappears down a corridor which is flanked on one side by smoked-glass partitions erected to convert one room into a reception area plus two meeting rooms. On the other side of the smoked glass, blinds are drawn, to give additional privacy.

Jane walks forward: she can see Karen lean into the room at the end, her weight on one leg, the other lifted behind her. She hears the muted tone of Karen's voice as well as that of a man, presumably David Fowles.

135

When Karen returns she sidesteps Jane, who turns to follow her. Karen draws a breath and holds it, before saying, 'He's in a meeting, at the moment, I'm afraid.' She watches to see what effect it will have, then adds, 'He asks could I make you an appointment for as soon as possible, in half an hour or so.'

Jane insists, 'I only want to talk to him for a second or two.'

The girl blushes crimson; once more she steps from the safety of her desk to make the trip down the corridor.

Jane stares after her, she tries to hear the subdued words spoken in the room at the end of the corridor.

The door clicks; Karen walks back, still flushed. Behind her desk she adopts a formal pose, hands crossed in front of her, to announce, 'David Fowles asks could you wait for just a few moments while he finishes his meeting and then he can see you.'

This is her pleading with Jane to be easy and accept what she says. Karen is high on the list of youngsters who were put forward as needing the new sports ground, a keen tennis player, so she's aware of Jane's voluntary work clearing the field at the bottom of the hill.

Jane sits down on one of the chairs lined up against the window. She looks around at the photographs of properties, searches for her own place. With a start, she recognises the pictures of her house and the barn. She goes to stand in front of it and thinks, Looks nothing like it. Yet it's exactly her house.

Karen bows her head over imaginary paperwork, her fringe drops over her eyes, she shuffles drawers in and out, rises to consult files stored in a cabinet.

Jane can't wait any longer. She treads down the corridor: there'll be a cry of objection from Karen but she's prepared to ignore it.

This debt will be the undoing of her, it's unpicking her friendships. She has to tell David Fowles, now.

When she reaches the end she opens the door, leans around it. At an oblong table sit David Fowles, plus a couple in their late thirties and a small boy. The man is tall, fair-skinned, while the woman is shorter, darker in colour with bright blue eyes. The curly-haired toddler has matching features, sits on her knee. Between them is an array of papers, photographs.

'Sorry to interrupt, but I just wanted to say – '

David's fidgety voice interrupts: 'Yes, um, I said I'd be with you in a minute, I'd be quite happy' – he nods his head to emphasise it – 'to answer any amount of questions, er, after I've finished . . . ' He waves at the couple who frown, insulted at the interruption; the child's mouth lies open.

Jane continues, 'I just wanted to say, tell Chris Gilbey I'll accept his offer.'

David Fowles stops in his tracks, his hand flies to his hearing aid. 'OK, OK.'

OUTSIDE, JANE HARDLY sees the sunny town square, she forgets the list of things she needed from the ironmonger's, she doesn't think to go into the vets' surgery and pay off her account with the fold of money which bulks out her trouser pocket, still. Instead, she walks blindly back to her car.

Again she pushes Roo off the driver's seat, climbs into the Mini Cooper.

Having struggled through the snarl-up of cars, she hares back up to Latchworthy Farm.

Jane crashes the gears, swings the spirited little car around these corners which she knows like the back of her hand. As the hedges fly past, Jane can't decide whether to be more or less in favour of Todd, now, because underneath her anger and amazement and disbelief, she is flattered. She can't imagine the trouble he went to, to get there before she did.

Why? Did he feel a sense of responsibility for the trouble she was in? He didn't need to. Or was it just that he wanted to put himself in the frame, to buy a part of her? In which case, it was a wrong move. She won't be bought.

She drills the Mini over the final cattle-grid, bumps up the drive, home.

RAIN FILLED THE sky all night: a steady, windless torrent emptied out of low, heavy clouds.

Jane's hands are reddened and slippery with water: she turns the two forks into walking sticks and pulls herself through the mud and slurry in the passageway which leads to the feeding traces in the top yard. Underfoot is a sticky four inches, before her feet land on the chafed concrete.

October 12: she's gearing up for the winter feeding routine.

She passes into the stock barn. A cow – Porlock – nervously harbours her newborn calf.

The instant she's under cover, the direct assault of the rain lifts as if by magic: it's no more than a steady drumming on the high roof, echoing off the sides of the cavernous space.

Yet, it's no less unpleasant: she's still soaked to the skin from riding out to Stone Tor Cross this morning, to find her errant cows.

There's a rustle of straw: Porlock and her calf shimmy sideways, eye her suspiciously. She trudges over the litter to the corner where the water trough is raised on concrete blocks.

Nearby, Todd leans against the side of the barn, heavily patched with wet on his knees from riding through the rain. His leather jacket is still tightly zipped, a ruff of scarf pokes from the collar, his coal-black eyes regard her steadily.

Jane asks, 'Fork, or fork?'

'I'll take the fork, then, please.'

She hands him the implement.

There's a leak in the pipe which leads to the water trough in here, it's soaked the cows' bedding and turned this one spot into a mire; Jane aims to find and repair it.

Todd drives in the fork, levers out a hunk of bedding. Jane does the same from the other end; she tugs at the black plastic hose, frees it up as she goes.

There's no conversation between them, yet, silently, in her own head, Jane asks: Why the sulk? Likewise, Todd wants to repeat, Look, come on, don't do it. He could swear at her, What's wrong with taking me on? The extra income would save her, because she shouldn't sell a bit of this place, it isn't designed to be cut up, parcelled off, he's mad about it.

None of this is said; yet the inside of one is known by the other. As their heads work near, bent over in the search for this leak, there's no question put that hasn't been answered before.

Jane heaves on the buried pipe, a foot or two jumps clear of the litter, a dribble of water clings to the pipe before it spirals from the lowest point to the ground.

'Gotcha.' Jane takes the pipe, twists it to find the puncture. She holds her thumbnail against the place, pulls a penknife from her pocket, hands it to Todd who unclasps the knife, hands it back to her, handle first. She holds the blade to the pipe, saws briefly to mark the spot, then lets it drop to the ground.

Then she trudges through the mud, back down the yard, to

139

turn off the supply. With the rain a steady curtain all around her, she feels the onset of winter, the emergence of the silage-feeding routine.

She grips the knurled, red-painted tap, turns it once, twice – and it's like a falling – *yes, it's true, she'll have to let Chris Gilbey back in.*

Three times – and the water pressure is halted at this point. *It's done, the decision's made.*

She walks back up the yard to the stock barn.

Todd is already sawing into the pipe with the knife. She picks up the other end, holds it taut.

Then, with a sudden give, the hose is cut between them.

LATER, SHE PAUSES in front of the barn to catch the distant panorama: Dartmoor slopes from both sides, in the middle the Devon plain rolls out.

She remembers the nickname she gave Chris Gilbey – the Squirrel – because of his sandy hair and the front teeth which peep over his lip . . .

A picture of him springs up in front of her as clearly as if she were holding a photograph.

ON SATURDAY MORNING, 22 November, rain walks in columns across the fields.

Jane abandons any idea of muck-spreading; instead she walks into the house to find the contract has arrived, left by Miss Egan just inside the door.

Jane drapes her streaming coat over the clothes drier, kicks off her boots, walks into the kitchen. She takes the envelope,

140

pulls it open. Inside there are several pieces of paper, including a coloured plan; the boundaries between herself and Chris Gilbey have been decided and marked on the ground. A line is drawn around the house, the handkerchief of land at the back, the ruin, a surrounding two-acre plot.

So: Jane will be rich.

Yet she dreads her first sight of Chris Gilbey, after all this.

She tells herself the fight is over, she won't have to panic about money, any more, *ever*.

The irony is, it feels like a mistake, in her bones. She should remember, she can still back out.

THE RAIN AND wind continue for the rest of the day. Roo stays indoors.

Jane and Billy move forty-eight ewes on to the moor, each one newly covered, rubbed with a dash of colour from the ram's harness.

She backs up the tractor to the cows' feeding traces, forks a helping of silage into the linkbox, drives it steadily through the Sheltered Field where the remaining ewes wait to be covered.

They follow the tractor, glad of the easy food in the bad weather.

Now, the afternoon chores, but she stands for a moment in the yard; next to her, a stream of water falls from the end of the guttering, chatters constantly into the water butt. She looks around her, at the soaked rooves of the stables, the trees dripping, the sluice of water running down the middle of the yard.

Lady and Tuppence are warm and dry in their stables, the

chickens have retired early, Roo and Billy are side by side, seated under cover of the feedhouse, waiting to be fed.

She asks, Are we all safe, now?

Later, indoors, she looks at this contract. She picks at the sheets of paper pinned together, reading bits and pieces, but her eye wanders in the legal jargon; she'll trust her solicitors to have protected her.

She makes toasted cheese, settles Roo and Billy on a dry towel.

Then she wonders, will she have to find someone to witness her signature? No.

Nonetheless, she wants a drink, to mark the occasion, talk to other people, run what's happening past someone else. So in the early evening, she drives down to Gidford.

On the way, she pulls into the parking area at the top of Manton Cleave. She aims for her usual place, on the rough ground where lovers go on Friday nights.

The surface is worn friable and stony by the cars, over the years; this evening the indentations are filled with grey water.

She circles the Mini Cooper, splashes through the puddles until she's parked overlooking the town; then she kills the engine, listens to the rain tick against the little car's roof.

The sound is at once eerie and intimate.

She looks down on Gidford, below her; yellow street lights mark the three roads which converge on the town square, a sprinkling of lighted windows shows the extent of the housing estate newly built on its eastern slope.

Next to her, on the passenger seat, lies the contract: a promise to sell. It remains unsigned, the choice is still open to her: she could go along with it, or refuse.

She tugs a pewter flask from her pocket, takes a drink of Boots home-brew; it's cheaper, to kick-start being drunk, before arriving at the pub.

The square of paper waits for her.

She thinks, Sign it in the pub, lift a glass – hell, buy a round, pay back all the good souls who've bought for me this year.

She wonders, will Todd be there, looking for her, because she offered to lend him the shed, over the winter, to house his Infernal Machine: she has given him something in return.

She steps out of her car, runs to jack up the new aerial, then climbs back in. Her fingers stray over the tuning dial of the CB radio.

Her code-name is 'Ring-ding-ding' because the Mini Cooper used to make a noise similar to that, on overrun, before she mended the manifold.

She finds the local CB frequency and listens to a driver from Gregory's Transport talk about his illegal sleeping arrangements in a lay-by on the A30.

A woman answers him with monosyllables, each word – 'Yeah?' 'No' 'What?' – coming over in a dreamlike, hopeful tone of voice.

CB radio conversation is to be chewed on not only for its meaning, but also for itself, just to *be* there, to prove these two people exist via the radio; for them, the conversation is a sort of fame.

The Gregory's Transport driver and his lady friend talk back and forth, so Jane loses track of her own life, becomes immersed in the concerns of this unknown pair, she floats, shares their intimacy – it's an unearthly medium, radio.

For Jane, this is a brief hiatus: the pressure on her to make a final decision on this contract lifts for a half-hour . . .

Then she switches off the radio, turns on the engine, bumps over the rough ground.

Rain channels along both sides of the road as she chases the narrow ribbon of tarmac into Gidford.

The soaked hedges whip past, catching at the nimble car

with long tentacles of bramble; she thinks, Someone's late, trimming.

She finds a spot downhill from the Cross Keys and hurries back up to the town square; the contract for the house she holds under her coat.

In Gidford's cornershop newsagent, Jane is surprised to see a queue, even though it's beyond normal opening hours. Then she remembers: the National Lottery, these are the last-minute gamblers.

She'd never win, herself.

Yet, almost by default, she ducks in to join the queue, which includes one or two people she recognises, because if she did win, then she wouldn't have to sign the contract.

So: she's among the flood of people who clamour at the gates of the Saturday jackpot.

It'll never happen. What are the odds? Sixteen million to one – she's more likely to be knocked over by a London bus.

'Our turn, Jane, isn't it!' cries Maisie from the bakery in the square, flapping a damp umbrella, 'it's our turn this week, I'm sure of it.'

Her eyes are bright, addicted.

'It's my turn, Maisie, I don't know about you,' Jane answers cheerfully, cottoned on by now to the daft optimism of the competition, so many others are making fools of themselves, to the tune of a pound or two.

'If I win, I'll share fifty-fifty with you,' begins Maisie.

'OK,' interrupts Jane, seeing what's coming.

'And if you win, you share with me.'

'No, that's not part of the deal.'

Maisie points a finger good-naturedly. 'Hey, there's witnesses.'

Jane's nerves settle; she can relax, her financial crisis is over, anyway.

144

She catches on that while queuing up she has to strike out her chosen numbers on the slip of paper provided for the purpose at a portable mini-bar by the counter. An idea for the selection arrives: her birthday.

The sense of the numbers – their importance at the moment – is a ridiculous play at good fortune and she thinks it's never been her thing, to pick winning tickets, she's never even won a bottle of whisky in a raffle.

She takes the slip of paper, fills in the numbers; the sales assistant registers her choice and Jane pays for the gamble, folds the ticket into her pocket, then heads out of the shop.

She runs across the road to the Cross Keys, but on the way notices that Todd's Harley isn't parked under the sign, its usual spot.

Inside the porch, she's faced with two doors – the lounge bar and the public bar. She hears the noise of the television, which reminds her to choose the public bar.

She orders a pint of Kilkenny's ale for a change; also she puts in a long-overdue round for Bob Worth, the alcoholic scrap-metal man and smallholder, who congratulates her on her surviving these cussed times in hill farming. His flushed, cheerful face, with its Dickensian spread of whiskers, listens in awe as she describes her visit to the lottery till.

They drink steadily until 8 p.m.

Jane explains her pact, concerning the sale: if she doesn't win the lottery she'll sign the contract, if she does win, she'll tear up the contract and buy everyone drinks all night.

Bob Worth takes his responsibility as her adviser seriously. He inspects the document, no, he says, he wouldn't sign anything as long as that, it feels like a deal too much work. Best win the lottery, then.

Jane opens the document to the appropriate page, asks the barman for a pen.

Bob Worth's spending the prize money for her: wild ideas spill into the public bar.

Their gazes fix steadfastly on the television screen.

Jane rubs the ticket in her fingers.

The guest star is welcomed on to the stage, the name of the machine is chosen, the guest star is asked to press the button which starts the balls tumbling. Just for a moment Jane forgets everything outside this oblong tunnel of space between her and the effortful entertainment on the television: she and Bob Worth soak it up.

When the first number is called, it's not hers; when the second one doesn't correspond, they grimace; she hasn't won any kind of jackpot.

The next few numbers fall out of Jane's reach and she's left with nothing, not a single correct guess, the numerology of her birthday, now, is a chastising statistic, the outside world arrives back, arranges itself around them: this room with its square windows which are set low to accommodate the window seats, the crackling fire, the beaten copper pans hanging from the ceiling, the polished bar.

Jane turns to where her elbow rests on the swatch of printed paper and, with good grace, she picks up the biro loaned by the barman, signs her name, Jane Reeves, Latchworthy.

ON CHRISTMAS DAY, Jane rides out of the front gate, which makes a change – because this isn't work, it's pleasure.

She points Lady up the hill to Caistor, gives her a few hundred yards at a fast walk to open her lungs, to warm up her tendons, before she presses her to a canter, spurs her up to the tor and circles it before taking off down the gentle slope heading to the long-abandoned homestead called Cleave Farm, which is slowly giving itself back to the moorland.

To begin with both Billy and Roo keep alongside her, the black and white of their coats fitting among the granite boulders, then Roo quickly flags, drops back to a trot, he will stand, watch for a while, before making his own way home; it's amazing that he came at all.

Meanwhile, Billy runs full pelt beside her.

This gentle slope is relatively free from hazards and Jane feels the excitement mount as Lady's stride lengthens, her feet hammer harder and quicker into the ground.

Jane stands in the stirrups, tucks herself out of the wind to decrease her profile, her cheek almost against Lady's shoulder.

Beneath her, the ground blurs.

She marvels, watching Lady's leading foot strike out to its full extent, punch the ground and disappear – all in a moment, because they're galloping now and even at this speed Lady judges carefully where to place her feet: whether to drop short to avoid a tussock or an indentation or an occasional stone glimpsing through, or instead to overreach . . .

They cover acres of ground effortlessly, the lines of hills change by the moment, define their position, woman and horse, as together they slip over the nearest horizon to discover a wealth of further horizons, dipping again and jumping the ditches and small stream before slowing on the uphill slope.

Lady herself knows from past experience that the gallop ends here, where the first stone wall interrupts their progress.

Through the gate, Jane presses Lady on again and willingly the horse jumps forward: they canter steadily for the whole

147

two miles to the abandoned homestead which stands, a granite ruin, in the lee of Grey Weathers.

Billy pants heavily; nevertheless he follows scents, busy with his own ideas.

Jane clatters Lady through the stream, hardly breaks pace, gains the upside of the derelict property, then she gentles Lady to a walk, drops the reins and gives her her head so she can catch her breath unhindered by the bit, but the run has heated her blood, she's reluctant to go slowly. Every now and again she bursts into a trot, reaching for a canter again, but Jane soothes her and momentarily picks up the reins to remind her she's there, the gallop is over.

She looks back for Billy, he's way back, on the opposite hill, stopped – and checking with the field-glasses Jane can observe he's busy with carrion of some description.

She picks her way carefully among the pattern of walls, heading for her usual spot, in what must have been the inhabitants' living quarters however many years ago, because set into the remains of the chimney is what was obviously a cooking oven.

In this roofless place, sheltered, tumbledown, she dismounts, takes a short rest.

Billy catches up, he knows where to find her.

She tries to picture what her own property would look like, abandoned as this one is, and in her mind's eye she's in her house, but she casts off the roof, disappears the woodwork, the furniture, she whisks the animals from the fields, breaks down the walls, she invades the farm with furze and sedge.

It wouldn't look so different from this.

Now the sweat is cold on Lady's flanks, so she remounts and sets off, climbing the sharp scree to Grey Weathers. From this isolated, windswept vantage point she can see not only clear across mid-Devon to Exmoor, but also south-west to the last parapets of Dartmoor on that side. The rump of Corsand Beacon is the only rounded shape – everywhere else are the distinctive tors and scree slopes which give the landscape its unique impact. The place is littered with stone circles, kistvaens, cumuli, stone rows: it's like an ancient, inland sea, shored by cultivated fields.

Her own silage barn roof is the only sign of habitation; for this reason whenever there is a human disaster on this side of the moor – an injured hiker or someone lost or in trouble – people head for that barn roof; she's been interrupted from her chores to deal with various emergencies. Quite apart from this year's case of hypothermia, she's called out the helicopter twice in the last five years: once for an attempted suicide, the other time for a man with a broken back, who'd fallen from his horse on to a boulder in the middle of a stream. Once, an escaped prisoner was trapped by police dogs in the shelter of her End Field.

Now, homewards. Of the many possible routes, she chooses to go via Sittaford Down.

On the way, she finds a clutch of her sheep, identifiable by the two black bars painted across their backs. She checks Lady's impatience to be home, in order to herd the sheep back with her to join the main body of the flock; as she pushes the strays ahead of her, she counts the cost of their being away from food, in terms of their condition. They are listless, dull-eyed.

She watches as they mingle with the rest of the ewes and silently she tells them, Stay there.

Then she lets Lady have her head and take her home, the only difference being she turns towards the front entrance again, for the novelty and because she wants to miss out on the mud stirred up by the cows making their daily pilgrimage in and out of the back gate.

Finally home, Jane wipes Lady down, leaves her to cool off in a vest with straw pushed under it. She carries the tack down the yard, meanwhile noticing that everything is hungry: the chickens hang around the entrance to their enclosure, Lady and Tuppence toss their heads, irritated by their empty stomachs, Billy circles the feed bin anxiously.

It seems to Jane that the farm itself has a renewed hunger, a looking-forward, occasioned by the imminent injection of funds.

She is happy, out of danger, crisis resolved.

Yet, Todd's absence is like a hand – which until now has been constantly pushing her. Suddenly taken away, it makes her feel off balance, alone.

She wishes herself a happy Christmas but more emphatically, a prosperous new year.

part two

David Fowles consults the mirror. He checks himself from the toes up: black leather moccasins, a beige suit with a 20 per cent wool twist, a black belt with a chrome buckle, a plain blue tie – smarter than usual.

He looks at his watch – twelve o'clock – and touches his hearing aid, adjusts the volume, seeks normal.

He can hear his children playing in the open-plan living/dining room, further down the corridor; the Christmas holidays aren't over yet.

A pang of hunger cramps his empty stomach, he didn't have much breakfast, because he'll eat a three-course lunch.

He pulls on a raincoat, mumbles to his family, lifts a hand briefly, twice, to signal goodbye. Outside, he flinches at the weather; from this man-made promontory which holds aloft his single-storey, modern-built house he can see the wind blow the rain carelessly over the fields, across hedges. The bungalow's downpipes gurgle behind him as he hurries for the car, a Ford Fiesta, three years old; it could be a Rolls-Royce but he has the Jewish fear of possessions which are too heavy, visible, on the ground.

The car splashes through Gidford, out the other side where the road dips sharply, finds the river, hugs its left bank, heads upstream. Along this obscure, narrow lane are some of the area's most exclusive residences, several of which he's sold himself, over the years; he might say his income is mapped out along the pathways hereabouts.

The public road ends at the entrance to the Teignhead Park Hotel's driveway; the tarmac narrows, rhododendrons screen the hotel from view, the fences are new, tight. Signs warn against trespass – there is a deliberate air of exclusion.

David Fowles drives on. The thin, elegant fingers of his left hand stray needlessly to the knob of the automatic gearshift and, as so often, he thinks of his children, watches them in his mind's eye.

In the hotel car park he unconsciously veers from the smarter marques of car, eschews the showiness. Instead he finds his corner, parks abruptly, catapults from the Fiesta, screws up his face against the rain.

The inside of the Teignhead Park Hotel, he remembers, is like a private house: there are no uniforms, no reception desk, if you don't know your way around – if this isn't your regular haunt – then you probably haven't managed to make a reservation anyway.

David Fowles has eaten here before, always at Chris Gilbey's expense; he knows to take off his coat and hang it on a peg as if he owned the place; now, he should just make his own way.

He pushes at his glasses, wonders whether to head first for the bar or the dining room, then he sees Cheryl, one of the prettier daughters of Gidford, carry a tray down the oak-panelled staircase. He blinks rapidly, exchanges greetings and asks for Chris Gilbey by name.

She smiles, points him towards the bar.

In this comfortably upholstered room the fire is well and truly alight: the suck of the open-hearth chimney drags flames off the gigantic logs, these tall swords of light give off a fierce heat. At first David Fowles thinks the bar is empty, then he

154

turns to see Chris Gilbey has chosen the seating area tucked into the alcove, while beside him rain clatters against the window and beyond it soaks the grey-green lawn, swells the river at the bottom; the trees are heavy, dripping.

Chris Gilbey is surrounded by papers – on the sofa next to him, on the low table, scattered over the floor.

An oasis among the business files, a drink floats a slice of lemon, flower-like, in a thick, crystal glass.

It's an expression of excitement when Chris Gilbey exclaims, 'David!' yet he doesn't pause in his mechanical sorting of his work.

David Fowles smiles, hovers above the table. 'Chris!' he answers, matching the other man's ebullient tone, then he waits for a more comprehensive greeting – like, Happy New Year.

'With you in a tick, mate, just let me clear up.'

So: David Fowles settles on the other side of the table; the matching sofa buoys up his thin frame.

The other man's sorting of the papers lasts for a minute; time drags interminably because David Fowles isn't looked after: no drink is offered, not a word to recognise it's made any difference, his arrival.

David Fowles leafs through a copy of the hotel's brochure mounted on a stand to one side. He reads, 'The hotel is tucked under the shoulder of Dartmoor, with its ancient, unchanged landscape, its stone circles and notorious mists . . . '

Then, Chris Gilbey plumps the papers, squares them, throws them on the floor. 'Sorry!' he exclaims in the same congratulatory tone.

'No, don't worry, er . . . ' It's as if David Fowles is trying to hush the matter, keep it secret, the absence of a generous greeting.

'Right,' continues Chris Gilbey, 'Latchworthy Farm.'

155

David Fowles nods. 'Yes.'

'The ruin.'

'Yes.'

'Where are we?' asks Chris Gilbey, then, straight away, he answers himself: 'We've exchanged contracts but haven't completed yet, which is when – the middle of this month?'

'I understood, er, 15 January.'

'So, in the normal run of circumstances, your finder's fee is due.'

David Fowles pushes at his glasses. 'Yes.' He bounces once on the sprung seat.

'Except, isn't it illegal?'

David Fowles feels a lurch in his hungry stomach. 'Um, technically ... '

'Technically,' interrupts Chris Gilbey, 'you can carve yourself a finder's fee as well as a sales commission only as long as the property doesn't go on the open market. As soon as it *does* go on the open market, you're bound by the rules of your august trade body, not to say the law, aren't you?'

'True, that's true,' fumbles David Fowles.

'Which demands you can only take from one side of the deal, not both sides.'

David Fowles can't speak, he's imprisoned in his stammer, his throat burns.

'After all, Latchworthy went on the open market.' Chris Gilbey's eyes open wide, he enjoys the other man's discomfort. 'It wasn't to begin with, when you and I first spoke, but it went on the open market, then came back to me.'

'Ahhh ... '

'So, hands up, I can't pay you!' Chris Gilbey makes a gesture of surrender. 'In your own interests, I can't pay you, not even if I wanted to!'

Yet at the same time he tugs at the inside pocket of his

jacket, takes out an envelope, dashes it on the table between them and he repeats, 'I can't pay you!'

David Fowles reads the glimmer of humour in the other man's eye: he looks at the envelope, then back at Chris Gilbey. He's still caught; indecision plagues him . . . is there money in the envelope, or not?

'What I can do, however,' Chris Gilbey continues, 'is pay you for a little consultancy work.'

David Fowles is hooked, torn between doubt, shame at his greed, expectation of payment, anxiety to keep in with this man.

'What about, if I ask you a couple of questions, just while you sit here, then I pay you the same amount as you'd have earned as a finder's fee? Sound all right?'

Now David Fowles understands: he's being teased, partly, but also, Chris Gilbey always watches his back, scouts the sides of any deal, the legal nooks and crannies in events, which carry a disproportionate weight as to how they turn out.

David Fowles doesn't touch the envelope. 'A couple of questions, sure, sure.'

Chris Gilbey waits a moment, reads the other man carefully, then he says, 'The Dartmoor National Park.'

'Yes.'

'Our local regulatory authority, at Latchworthy, as far as planning goes.'

'Yes.'

'Know anyone on it?'

David Fowles shakes his head, he lies, 'No.'

'There are planning authorities and planning authorities,' continues Chris Gilbey. 'In Leicester, there's a bastard who puts up his mistress in one of my one-bedroom flats', and the breath hisses between his teeth, his eyes twinkle in amusement.

'I don't think they're corrupt, here,' begins David Fowles; his voice suddenly works. 'Rather the opposite.'

'What's their favourite turn-down?' asks Chris Gilbey.

'They're very keen on keeping things as they are, or restoring things to what they were.'

Chris Gilbey nods, sniffs, his gaze continues to bear critically on David Fowles.

'They're not keen on traffic, they hate cars.'

'OK.'

'They favour agricultural use over tourism.'

'Of course.'

Silence descends. It's turned out to be, David Fowles realises, a tense preamble to the lunch and he waits, uncomfortable, tries to think of something to add.

Chris Gilbey breaks the spell. 'That's it, then!' he cries. Leaning forwards, he pushes the envelope into David's lap. 'Thanks a million, mate, send me an invoice, consultancy, a few typewritten pages, say what you've just said, et cetera', then he slumps back in his sofa, his hands tie behind his head, his knee wags. 'Know what, I'm haemorrhaging, fuck, a lot of money, all over this, but I tell you, the nicest thing about having a bit of disposable cash lying around is' – and he jerks forward again – 'you can afford to fall in love with an idea.' He leans on his knees. 'Falling in love with an idea,' he emphasises, 'and having the means to bring it about – that's fucking luxury.'

'Right, right,' nods David Fowles; he holds the envelope delicately between the tips of his fingers.

Chris Gilbey rises, shakes out the legs of his trousers.

David Fowles stands also – glad, now it's lunchtime, it was

as well to have the business done with first, he feels a sudden hollowness – hunger!

At the same time he hears the impertinent tone of a mobile phone.

Chris Gilbey reaches into the blue canvas holdall at his feet, drags out the phone by its ear, but then he holds out the other hand to David Fowles: 'Listen, this might be a long call, so I'll say well done, thanks for coming out here, I'll let you know how I get on.'

This is goodbye?

David Fowles nods, dumbly, his empty stomach howls, his hand is shaken.

In a confidential whisper Chris Gilbey finishes, 'Cheers.' He prods his phone, waves at the same time.

David Fowles backs away, shocked, he's humiliated, as he retraces his steps. The Teignhead Park Hotel, made over as someone else's home, it's like he's stealing through it, with his envelope.

He climbs into the Fiesta, drives back to Gidford, starving.

A LOAD OF muck flies from the spreader – black bits hurled against a grey sky.

Jane wears gloves; under her coat she's packed out with two sweaters. She's driving the tractor, sitting still, so it doesn't allow her blood to quicken, it's cold.

She unwinds a can of sardines for lunch.

In the afternoon she takes her toolbox, a roll of dustbin bags, a bucket full of cleaning equipment and accompanied by Roo and Billy she walks up the stable yard, turns right through the gate, past the grain store, the pair of ramshackle sheds on her left, in front of the lean-to where the tractor is parked.

A few yards further on, hard against the wall and fenced off in its own patch of land, sits the caravan, last used two years ago, for visitors, but soon, after vacating her house and before moving into the barn, Jane will live in here.

She pushes with her foot at the gate, feels the rot in it; sure enough it gives with a wet, tearing sound, comes away at the hinges.

She drops everything to tug it clear, she drags it back, throws it on top of the wood pile.

Billy and Roo meander, pick up strange scents in this corner of the farm, seldom visited.

Jane walks back through the gap in the fence but before she can get to the caravan she faces a wilderness. In summer, this is a sunny, sheltered spot so it's quickly become overgrown.

She stands at the edge, hands on hips, kicks at the ground to determine what's under the turf and sure enough, a couple of inches down, her boot skids against concrete: she was right, there's the path.

She returns to the shed, collects a spade.

So: squaring up to the undergrowth, she pushes until the blade hits the concrete underneath, then she lodges the handle in her stomach, walks forward, bulldozes the weeds standing in their thin layer of sediment, clears a path to the door of the caravan, levers the spoil off to either side. The weeds fall on their neighbours with a light rustling sound but mostly, she can hear her own breath.

She tests the standpipe which guards the entrance to the caravan: with a squeak the tap opens, the water coughs, splutters, but it's adequate.

She climbs on the slab of granite laid down as a doorstep, tries the handle. The caravan door refuses to give and at first she thinks it's locked, she tries to remember the last time anyone used the key, then she pulls again, the lug at the bottom comes free from the hinge and with an hysterical *honk!* the door opens.

Immediately, there's the smell of stale linoleum, overlaid with the bitter tang of damp and Calor gas. Billy hops up ahead of her; she herself climbs in.

Inside, she finds a lost world.

On her right is the little kitchenette: the kettle sits on the stove, a cobweb strung in its Bakelite handle, there's a collection of chipped mugs; lightweight tin saucepans are jumbled together on the surface, a Calor gas cylinder sits on a pair of bricks.

Jane ducks her head to peer through the window above the miniature sink and alongside the caravan. Under the leafless branches of the beech trees, the granite wall runs down the slope of the Stable Field to meet the valley below. On the other side of the wall she can see Lady and Tuppence in their waterproof rugs; they pick idly at the wet grass.

She turns to see Roo with his front paws on the step, half in, half out of the caravan, he's smiling.

She pats her thigh: 'Come on.' With a lunge, Roo jumps into the caravan, she didn't have to help him, so he's better, isn't he, and she congratulates her old dog, feels the silkier pelt, notices the renewed distinction between black and white in his coat, in the last few months he's become rejuvenated. She thinks, Expensive old man.

She walks down the length of the caravan, counts five paces before she comes up against the dining-room table. Her footfalls sound hollow; the floor might be rotten.

The dining area is surrounded on three sides by windows; in the aluminium runnels which seal them to the body of the caravan there's a quarter-inch-wide rim of moss and silt, soaked, now, in winter. She picks at it with an exploratory finger, it comes away marked by the black, fertile sludge.

The seats around the dining table convert to beds, she remembers.

Over the back window, an electric heater is wired into the farm's electricity; Jane clunks the switch and moments later the element reddens, there's a smell of burning dust, it still works and she thinks, I'll need another one, maybe, plus the *Cotto Oven* clothes drier, a kettle to run off the Calor gas.

She leaves the fire switched on and continues her inspection.

In the middle section of the caravan is a cupboard for storing clothes; she pulls it open to find a deflated football and a pair of old gardening gloves. On the other side, square to the clothes cupboard, stands a blank wall – apparently – but its function is given away by the chrome-plated arm which has worn a mark into the plywood surface.

Jane experiments with this fiddly handle, twists it, and the wall jumps an inch towards her. She reaches to the top, her fingers seek the indentation provided to pull down the double bed, then a breath of musty air swirls around her.

Jane pushes at the mattress; it feels damp.

Billy's claws click against the linoleum; both dogs stare at her, uncertain what's happening, while she sits for a while on the mattress which, she decides, she will drag out, burn.

Roo comes to perch on her boots; she takes his ears in her hands, squeezes them affectionately: 'Welcome home.'

JANE CAN RELAX, now, when she spends money, it's like a side of herself has been given back, a restoration.

The first small sums go into the pockets of the Reardons'

seventeen-year-old son and Mrs Stanton's nephew; they were lucky enough to have stood closest to her in the Cross Keys when she asked for two hands to help her sack the house.

A week before 15 January, a slow-moving high-pressure weather system dawdles in from the Atlantic; Jane takes advantage of it, marks out two days.

She mends the floor of the flatbed trailer, patches the holes with planks torn from an old sheep-feeder, then hitches it up and with a flourish from the vertical exhaust, the tractor hauls it down to her front gate.

She and the two young men fetch and carry; furniture is walked out of the house, they push, shove, lift, manoeuvre around the narrow corners.

Together they work out the puzzle: how to fit the pieces together to make the load.

They unwind the industrial-size roll of black plastic sheeting left over from silage-making and then hold down these great lengths of black sail, to blanket the trailer. Jane throws loops of rope three times around the short axis of the trailer, once down its length, until the load is parcelled from top to tail, then she drives it up to the barn, reverses the flatbed smartly into the shed vacated by the detritus she sold off in the farm sale. She tweaks the hydraulics, drops the hitch on to an old tractor tyre and the load sits, ominously black, shiny.

This thought excites her: when she next moves the trailer, she'll be a good way into converting the barn.

Then, Dartmoor is shrouded in dense fog.

The farm is invisible, buildings float, often turn up unexpectedly; hedges, trees drift in a wet grey smoke, the yard, the fields, the animals themselves hold no colour because the light is miasmic, held in the moisture, there are no reflections, only a grey wool.

It suits his purpose, because for the second time, Chris Gilbey is trespassing.

He stands in the middle of the ruin – which technically isn't his own until two days' time.

Underfoot, the soaked wooden floor is slippery as a seaside rock; he holds on to the old billiard table, glad to have something to tell him where he is, because the ruined walls, just a few feet away, are practically gone, a thickening in the mist, merely.

So: these unused walls, the ground beneath him, his two acres, the ramshackle Devon Longhouse attached to it, all this passes to his name the day after tomorrow.

The strangeness of the territory he recognises is special, virginal, fleet – foreign ground – because as he becomes immersed in his idea for the place, he'll grow familiar with each corner, how the place as a whole fits into the jigsaw of land and society around it.

It's difficult to focus: the impenetrable grey light around him confuses any sense of distance and he thinks, It's fitting for the place to be shrouded in fog: like a painting at auction, before the sheet is pulled away to reveal . . .

He compares himself to the vendor, Jane Reeves, who will know every inch of the canvas, she's worked on it for years and he remembers her story: three generations of this soil, always less money to keep the place, her duty, finally, to square the circle, salvage the economics.

He has some envy of her, for those three generations: they're like bolts fixing her to the ground, and he thinks, My turn!

So: he's hired an architect in Exeter, Elizabeth Jennings – *rule number one, use an architect who's been passed by the*

164

Dartmoor National Park many times before – and now he imagines her dragging an electronic pen to tease the building into existence, as if to uncover what already exists in her computer's memory, because soon the fog won't be allowed in here; in his mind's eye he takes a pencil, draws the walls around him, the roof over his head, a cellar underneath his feet.

He thinks, *Castles in the air*. The elation rushes to his head like a breath of madness: the power, the belief inspired by ownership. The day after tomorrow, he takes possession.

He relaxes his grip on the side of the derelict billiard table, walks around it, once, his hand trails its oblong edge, it locks him into the geography of the place, given he can't see more than a few feet in any direction.

He presses the surface of the green baize, feels cold water around the tips of his fingers.

Blanketed by fog, the place is utterly silent, yet it talks to him, he can hear ...

IN THE SAME fog, on the same day, Tibby is lost.

He's a Dorset cross, a bold ram with a black face, a Roman curve to his nose, and it nags Jane, but isn't it against all common sense, to look for a small grey animal in a dense grey fog?

She veers from filling the muck-spreader, nonetheless, to lose an hour, search for him.

The trick is, he'll hear the rattle of a bucket so she chooses a metal one, puts a noisy handful of cake in the bottom, climbs over the section of her boundary wall which is most in need of repair – possibly he escaped from this point.

She walks outwards, calls his name, shakes the bucket.

She knows the ground out here, every tuft, hummock and rock, there's no chance she'll be lost.

She stops, checks her watch – just half an hour, she tells herself; she'll sweep a large semicircle, safe because ahead of her is the bog, behind her, the wall, to her right is the Wallabrook, to her left the land rises in a double loop to Caistor.

Her boots pass over the soaked ground, there's little else she can see. She maintains a steady rattle of the bucket, bounces the nuts on every other stride and every half-minute or so, she calls his name.

It's more bewildering than darkness – plenty of light, yet it's carried in this grey soup. If she wasn't utterly familiar with this ground, she'd already be lost.

She treads the right-hand sweep; then notices clumps of rushes underfoot, instead of gorse and heather, so she's reached the mire and she makes the left turn, to walk up the side of the bog.

'Tibby!' She rattles the cake.

Then, mysteriously, a gang of ewes appear at her feet, butting, asking for a second feed; she stops, lets them drift in and out of the small arena which she occupies, but she can't find Tibby among them.

Ten minutes later, she marks the slight increase in the gradient, the first rump of land which rises to Caistor, and just then she hears – unmistakably – Lady's call. It comes from her right-hand side, when the farm should, by rights, be on her left.

She turns around, faces the other way; she's right: the land slopes downhill, now, so it must be the sound which misinforms her, she judges that noise can be reflected by fog, just as it can bounce off buildings.

A quarter of an hour later, she makes her left turn to head

back for the farm; however, instead of a gentle downhill she finds herself taken upwards and the ground looks unfamiliar, this stretch should be grassy.

She stops, smiles, exclaims, 'God!' in a tone of awe, she can't believe she's fallen for it – the Dartmoor fog claims its next victim, only a few paces from her own back gate!

She trusts the gradient more than her sense of direction, so she turns back.

She's lost interest in Tibby but automatically, of its own accord, her right arm continues to shake the metal bucket.

She hears Lady call again – this time from behind. Where is she?

Helpless laughter overtakes her.

The fog separates, allows her through, then closes behind her; yet somehow at the same time it can turn her around, rotate the ground beneath her feet. She can't believe it, for half an hour she walks, clueless, and tries to keep to a straight line so she might run into a landmark, a patch of ground she knows beyond doubt, yet experience tells her she's probably walking in circles.

Is there a trick to this, she wonders, and she racks her brains, stares hard into the fog; will it clear, to give her a glimpse, allow her to take bearings . . . ?

For a moment, only, panic grips her. She imagines when the fog lifts, the farm will be gone, lost to her; she'll be somewhere else altogether.

Then, in a circle of peat worn bare by the occasional flow of surface water, she finds her own boot print and she thinks, I give up.

She's deep in the wilderness, there's nothing for miles around, the farm doesn't exist any more, she's doomed.

Then she swaps exasperation for laughter again.

It's ten minutes before she comes across a stone she

recognises, nose-shaped, twisted, with a bowl weathered into the end of it, as if given for the birds as a drinking table. She knows for certain it's only a few minutes' walk from her front gate, so she takes a bearing from the stone, strikes out; yet even now she's not confident, she stares hard at the few yards in front of her feet.

Then she hits the path which leads from the outside corner of the farm down to the front entrance – she's safe.

She thinks, This is a story for the pub; in her mind, she begins to tell everyone.

While she was lost outside her own back gate for an hour, Tibby was strolling in the woods.

JANE WAKES WITH a start. Her scrambled dreams flee in an instant. She sits up; the first thing she sees is the square, orange glow from one of the electric bar-fires she's hung on the walls. A burst of wind rocks the caravan, rain squalls against the windows, a drip sounds, somewhere.

Then with her hand on Billy's flank she remembers: she's in the fold-down double bed in the caravan and tomorrow – today? – Chris Gilbey will arrive.

The heat is oppressive; she's not used to a warm bedroom. She throws the bedcovers aside, her feet thud on the floor – an unfamiliar hollowness – as she walks to the bar heater, pulls the plug from the socket; blue sparks leap from the fitting as she does so, like lightning, to accompany the storm outside.

Roo, she notices, has climbed on to one of the upholstered seats which run underneath the windows; thanks to the drugs, he has been dialled back in time, years younger.

She courses through the dark, looks for the drip, her feet find it first: a patch of wet. She switches on the electric light to see where the ceiling bleeds drops of water, then goes to the sink to find a pan, position it on the floor. As she does so, the wind bursts again; the overhead branches suddenly thrash the caravan's roof, make her jump, the leak makes a worse sound, *blip*.

She fetches a towel, drapes it over the pan to deaden the noise, then returns to her unfamiliar bed, climbs under the covers. The bed flexes, a corner nods downwards: one of its fold-out legs is broken, she's made do with a pair of upended concrete blocks.

She lies back, but her eyes remain open. The caravan roof is patterned with grey mould; she guesses caused by condensation. In her mind, the new order of things challenges her, sets up rows of tasks which have to be accomplished quickly, in the right order. Her fear is, she won't finish the first stage in converting the barn before lambing time, only three and a half months away.

She ticks off the list: drains, electricity, plumbing. She sees, in her mind's eye, the fat blanket of fibreglass insulation between the new internal skin and the outer granite wall, she imagines what it will be like in the barn, to find herself living there, walking to and fro, running a bath in the featureless interior, she puts her bedroom in different corners, to see where she might best position it.

Most of all, she imagines herself in front of a pair of new windows cut into the thick granite walls – the view from this spot the same, almost, as from the concrete water tanks set into the Top Field.

These new thoughts are interrupted, barged aside by the farm, because it's mid-January: winter timetable as usual, plus pregnancy tests on a clutch of cows, fill in the hole dug by a fox under the wire fence around the chicken compound ... For a few minutes she's back in her own head, she's the person she used to be, still is: a farmer with this work always in front of her, what's done quickly forgotten.

Then, closer to sleep, she dreams again of her new life: walking out of the front door of the barn, waving hello to Chris Gilbey, who climbs into the green saloon.

There's dread at the prospect, mixed with a determination to make it all right, it'll be her job to rub along with him, but she's lost the old way of life, hasn't she, her head is filled with new concerns, whereas for years it's always been the lack of money.

She mustn't let her concentration slip, she's still in her circle of time here, wearing herself deeper into this place, with hardly a conscious thought in her head, beyond the manipulation of her hands, the feed in animals' mouths, the flesh on their bones – but she's invaded by worry, time is carrying her on a line now, a trip of people, of events, it's not the same.

THE CLOUD IS a high, grey curtain, evenly discoloured; Jane tugs at her woollen gloves, pulls her fingers into her palms, to warm them.

The Scots sheep are a crowd of grey fleeces traipsing ahead of her through runnels of mud. Billy weaves back and forth behind the flock, he picks delicately over the sticky terrain, his snout pointed, held level, his gaze intent. Roo wanders, disinterested, he keeps to one side to avoid the sludge.

Together Jane and Billy push the sheep out of the gate, on to the moor.

The air is still; her pull on the gate, the movement, is like an interruption. She drops the latch, turns back and immediately she sees Chris Gilbey: a figure coming towards her over the

Top Field, his shoulders hunched, his arm aloft, now, in greeting and she thinks, the Enemy.

Billy sets up his hysterical cry, runs for him, while Roo waits, uncertain. Jane waves a response, slogs towards him over the field. The earth is soft underfoot, forgiving; her breath clouds in front of her, she walks into the cloud, breathes another.

When Chris Gilbey is still thirty yards away, he holds up both arms in a gesture of surrender and she remembers the first glimpse she had of him, last June as he climbed over the fence, his back retreating, slow moving, as he tracked the loop of the electricity cable suspended on poles over the field.

The difference is, now he's walking towards her.

He keeps his arms lifted, as if she were holding a gun on him; she can make out his grin, the top teeth peep over his bottom lip, the sandy hair is parted at the side.

When he arrives, 'I'm here,' he says. 'Apologies for seeking you out, I felt I had to come and say hello, I still feel like a visitor.'

She swallows her dislike. This is the man who nearly pushed her over the edge, last year, for what he wanted.

They start to walk back, fall in step, and she notices again: he wears the short type of wellington boot.

Today, she thinks, suddenly surprised, she is rich, the figures are added up, subtracted, the specified amount – lying in wait – has changed hands. They walk down through the yard, by unspoken agreement, head for the house.

In the front yard she remarks, 'Different car', because a black Saab convertible has taken the place of the mysterious, unmarked green saloon.

'Yes.'

Then Billy pushes past her, suddenly he's crying again, trotting around the car, to see in. Answering barks come from within, the car moves slightly on its springs and through the oblong panel of glass set into the flexible material of the car's roof, the shadows of two dogs mix back and forth.

Jane curses inwardly, *Dogs*.

Yet, why shouldn't he have them?

She calls, 'Billy!'

Billy stands on his hind legs, props one delicate paw against the driver's door, his black-and-white nose wrinkles, his ears are cocked.

Inside the car, a pair of red setters are going haywire. Chris Gilbey asks, 'Shall we let them get used to each other?'

She calls again, 'Billy!'

Chris Gilbey heads for the driver's door, a set of keys in his hand.

Jane is incredulous, she asks herself, He locked his car? and suddenly she reads the difference in their lives.

Chris Gilbey unlocks the driver's door, swings it open, at the same time he calls, 'Joey, Max . . . ' A blanket of red silk flows from the car: a pair of setters, long-legged, goofy, beautiful, they perform a graceful dance, run circles around Billy and he tails them; hostility burns brightly in his narrowed eyes.

Roo stands with his ears pricked.

'Lovely dogs,' comments Jane.

'My babies,' answers Chris Gilbey.

For a while, they watch as the dogs circle; Billy growls continually, a low hum comes from his throat, despite himself, it seems.

In the still, cold air, Jane is also aware of slight noises in Chris Gilbey's throat: a variation in the pitch of his breath, a sniff, a slight click, the prelude to a cough.

She notices, as well, that he's always moving: a hand fidgets in his pocket, or an elbow nudges spasmodically, he shifts his weight from one foot to another.

She thinks, Nervous energy.

Chris Gilbey explains what's going to happen: he won't start work on the place for a few weeks, there's various planning applications he'll make to improve the property and, as he points out, the regulatory authority is the Dartmoor National Park. He huffs, 'Tighter than a duck's arse, as far as permissions go.'

So: she won't see much of him – he'll only come down to show various contractors over the house.

She agrees, it'll be a slow process for her as well.

He tilts his head sideways, his teeth peep through his grin: 'Race you.'

She asks, 'What?'

'Race you, seriously, my house or your barn, who moves in first.' He holds out his hand to shake on it, his stare ambitious, but in good humour.

Jane distrusts him, she always will.

'All right.'

'Bottle of champagne for the winner, courtesy of the loser.'

'Done.' She thinks, Keep him in his box, remember – although it's her job to get on with this man, for her own sake.

He shakes himself, as though ready to run the race right now. 'That's it then, we're neighbours.'

JANE RISES AN hour earlier, bashes Lady around the block, just to the stream, around Caistor, back, instead of the usual hour's exercise. She forks up the silage around the feeders, dropped from the cows' mouths, then lets them out through the muddy passageway on to the moor, but stops short of

173

raking out the calving pens.

So: she earns a couple of hours to wander around the barn, think about how to make it habitable quickly – certainly before lambing time.

She scrapes back the blue door, goes inside; it's a cold, featureless interior: concrete floor, A-frame roof timbers, granite walls half rendered on the inside, water trough, single electric lightbulb crowned with dust.

In one corner, the pedigree silver Husqvarna trials bike is laid up, for the winter.

The only signal of the barn's future use is the incongruous presence of a brand new telephone-cum-answering-machine on the floor and she enjoys the sight of this phone, it's a measure of the difference in her position: last year the phone was cut off, now she can afford to install a new one in an empty barn, so she's confident, optimism renewed by her triumph last year over the financial struggle.

She likes the boost given to her, by this packet of new wealth: it supports her, a cushion, a whole side of her can rest, it's that valuable, she wants to keep it rather than spend it.

Plans knock around her head: the aim is to move quickly, she won't have time to commission drawings, do the whole works in one go.

So, she asks herself, What are the basics?

Heat, light, a place to sleep, a bathroom, cooking facility . . .

Then the building will slowly evolve – over four or five years, she guesses – before it's completed.

For now, she tells herself, make life practicable, start at the end and work backwards.

It will squeeze her schedule, because it's the wrong season, the middle of winter, this is summer work and she judges that for the next few months the fences will go unmended, the muck-spreader will be parked up, empty.

Then she picks up a stone, walks to the front wall and scratches into the soft render more or less the position of the two big, double-glazed windows she'll cut out, one each side of the blue door.

This done, she pulls open the door – and the view is there.

On the right, the slope of land from Caistor is drawn over by the patterns of stones, from when this was a crowded upland, the remains of hut circles made before history began, plus the ancient iron foundry.

From the left side, the ground running downhill from Scaur Hill is marked by the leat built to take water from the mine workings.

In the middle, directly in front of her, there's nothing but distance: the countryside unfolds over the Devon plain to Exmoor.

Except, like a gun-sight trained on this far horizon is the figure of Chris Gilbey, who stands in the grounds of his ruin.

She remarks on his posture. His feet are together, he looks down at his toes, it's like he's at the edge of a diving board and has to decide whether or not to jump.

CHRIS GILBEY STANDS in the grounds of his ruin, looks down at his toes.

He thinks, Yes, build out to *here*.

Take in the view.

IN THE AFTERNOON, Jane drives Talacre into the cattle crush, pulls the brace tight against her neck. She watches as O'Bryan, the vet, pushes a needle directly into the cow's opaque eye.

This time she doesn't wince, she counts it as an achievement.

By the minute, it's colder; she pulls on heavy gloves to haul stones on to the broken section of her boundary wall.

Then darkness comes over the place quickly, a blanket so pitch black that the stars are thousands upon millions, a sugary dust sprinkled through a sky of impenetrable depth.

She eats Mr Kipling Farmhouse Cake in the caravan, then drives down to the Cross Keys.

While she drinks and eats she talks to other farm workers, drops her plans in people's ears, posts the new telephone number behind the bar.

Even if they aren't in that night, the usual suspects call her up within a day or two to offer their services. This time, she notices how things move quickly, effortlessly, there's no juggling of dates or favours, because she's paying, this is what it's like to be rich, things happen.

A SOUTHWESTERLY OVER the moor turns the landscape into a seascape: the hills roll like waves, everything is in flux, the boundary between the ground and the sky blurs, disappears, reappears. Jane stands on the edge of her valley and watches a buzzard cling to the top branches of a thorn tree; it looks too heavy, impossible that it's held up. The bird lifts with a lazy stretch of its wings, immediately it's caught and blown downwind, rolling and twisting, as fast as if shot from a gun, in two moments it's travelled the valley, disappeared.

TODD AND PATRICK are ready to go.

At one end of the barn they build a platform for a bed, drill into the soft render that faces the inside walls. Pegs of wood are hammered in, as giant rawlplugs.

For a temporary cooking facility she buys a Calor gas stove fuelled by two 50-kilo bottles; she keeps the pair of cylinders outside to minimise the danger from fire, drills a hole through the rear door frame of the barn to take the thin, malleable copper tubing.

She disconnects the water supply, removes the trough from the corner; she replaces it with an old ceramic sink in which she meant to grow mint, never used, needless to say. Now the sink is mounted on a wooden frame, plumbed in, she'll use it to brush her teeth and for the washing up.

So her new money dribbles out, fitfully; she gives a good account of herself, she thinks, doing so much of the work even though there's enough to pay someone else.

It will be difficult not to worry about money any more.

She employs Kevin – waves cash under his nose to tear him from his motorcycle repair business – and he installs the essential plumbing: for maximum speed and economy, he advises a 100-gallon, plastic cold-water tank to stand on a plinth, the hot-water cylinder adjacent and below, with the pipework and the wiring tacked to the wall.

She buys a bathroom suite from the MFI on Exeter trading estate; when she can afford to do the interior properly, she'll use these bits and pieces in their places, but for now the bathroom, the kitchen, the living room, her bedroom are all open plan.

She determines, from this corner she'll take the drains outside, by the back door she'll mount the main fusebox, from here run a cable to the shed housing the electricity supply. At the moment the power is capped; the governers work overtime, with only the farm lights and a single cable strung back along the poles, tacked to a tree, then looped into the caravan.

Next, she concentrates on trenches: she has to hook up to the soakaway sewage system that serves her old house, so an eight-inch pipe will have to run across the yard that separates her from Chris Gilbey; it was agreed in the contract, she'll have to break into the manhole cover outside his kitchen.

The other trench she marks out for the powercable.

She goes down to the pub to collar Mick, who works for the National Park.

'Come on then, what you after?' he asks before he's even taken a sip.

'Nothing,' she replies, ironically.

After his second pint he says, 'Right, you can tell me now, what 'tis?'

She waits.

After four pints, a grin is worn on his face almost all the time, so she puts it to him and he agrees to bring up the JCB digger from where they're doing the forestry work in the valley.

So: in a few hours on a Sunday the massive hydraulic tool does the lion's share of the work for a minimal sum; with a pick and shovel, she dreads to think how long it would have taken.

There's damage done to a retaining wall and the fence which surrounds Chris Gilbey's garden is broken through in two sections, which will have to be put right – but she'll do this after she's laid the pipe, dismantled the manhole to accommodate the new inlet.

She thinks, There's some life breathed into the place, now, it's the start towards a long-held ambition, good progress, the barn is alive, suddenly.

SHE REMINDS HERSELF: tell Chris Gilbey about the damage to his garden fence, he will expect that courtesy, contract or no.

Yet, she has no telephone number for him, nor an address.

IN MID-FEBRUARY, Jane stops, exhausted, tells herself to concentrate on her animals. Her impetus is suddenly suspended.

Her hands are chafed, broken, because of the extra work; she has to lather them in cold cream twice a day, a penalty for the amount she's accomplished.

As well, she must keep her stock gathered, up to the mark. She notices that Lady holds the door of her stable between her teeth, doesn't chew it but squeezes, uses the back pressure in her throat to belch, every now and again, she's bored, because Jane's had less time to give her favourite horse the usual exercise.

In addition, the bad weather means both Lady and Tuppence spend more time in their stables; Tuppence has an accepting nature, he contentedly spends the time with one leg cocked, his ears at half mast, a thoughtless calm reads on his face, but Lady, even on reduced rations, isn't impressed, she entertains herself with this belching.

Jane asks her, 'Fed up, huh?'

THEN, LADY IS overworked, if anything, because for five days, rain leaks under Jane's collar, seeps under her cuffs, somehow percolates under her waterproof trousers; her skin goes soft, moisturised for hour upon hour, her dark eyelashes work constantly to blink away water, she changes her coat, her

179

waterproof trousers and the first layer underneath every four hours. By the time she comes into the caravan again the clothes drier has stiffened the last set of clothes and when she puts them on, they're hot to the touch.

Too many of the Scots sheep are missing, scattered by the weather: she spends the whole day riding Lady – accompanied by Billy – in a search: she tacks herself to the horizon here, there, to look inwards, searching the great basin of moorland which undulates around the farm.

As the hummocky, rock-strewn, boggy landscape speeds past in the twin circles of her binoculars, it's as drenched as she's ever seen it, the water level is so high that the two streams which meet at the foot of her land have joined forces earlier, two hundred yards upstream.

Uncomplaining, Lady breasts the tide, walks solidly through it, the usual pathways lost under this new estuary of water.

Billy has to tunnel a further distance upstream along the new bank, until he reaches a point he can swim across without being carried away; Jane watches him, brave dog, battle with the current, lurch over the unseen boulders underneath, the water pulling at him as he drags himself across.

In scattered groups, Jane pulls together around forty of the missing Scots ewes, brings them back to join the main flock.

They're thin, bedraggled, shot through with the weather, undernourished, their legs like black sticks which might be too meagre to hold up the fluffs of dirty grey wool and unhappy, downcast faces.

She feels a twinge of pity for her favourite breed of sheep; at the same time she knows they're hardy enough, if you were to part the wool all the way down to the skin, there wouldn't be a drop of moisture underneath, the temperature would be constant.

Lady's coat, on the other hand, is sleek with water; Jane leans forward to pat her neck, to give her a thank you for the hard work and the surface is wet, naked muscle.

In the stable, Jane uses a rubber to stroke the water from her flanks. The steam from Jane's breath mixes with the fog pouring off Lady's sides; she thinks, Lady is a trouper, more than Billy or Roo. Lady is her partner in this farm.

After these few days of hard going, when the warm front has passed, leaving behind it a dry spell, Jane gives Lady a reward.

She switches back the bolt on the stable door; with a click of her tongue she encourages Lady to step out, then takes her around the back of the feedhouse where the chickens have their fortified enclosure.

She drags back the wire netting, steps through, turns around to guide Lady; there's only an inch to spare on each side. With a snort Lady dashes towards her, eyes and ears reading the narrow gap.

Then Jane leaves her to get on with it.

Lady doesn't waste time: her nose drops to within an inch of the ground, she adopts the uncomfortable, rolling gait of a stallion out to stalk mares . . .

The difference is, it's Lady's game to herd the chickens. They oblige by trotting a few feet ahead; with a burst she catches up. They jump, squawk, the clatter of their wings startles Lady; she lifts her nose, stops.

Her ears flick back and forth.

Jane wonders what the chickens think of this game: an oversize animal comes into their enclosure, uselessly pursues them.

Moments later, the predatory stance comes over Lady again, she's after the chickens with a vengeance: her ears are pinned back, her feet slide in the mud, she squeals with pleasure.

ON 20 FEBRUARY there's a flurry of activity, vehicles come and go; carried by the clean, cold air, the sound of engines – in and out of gear – comes to her in her caravan as they're drilled back and forth in Chris Gilbey's front garden.

At the end of the day, the overgrown patch of land in front of her old house has been swept aside.

She worried about knocking down the fence to lay her drain, but she needn't have: the fence, the earth under it, everything growing in her old garden has been pushed downhill towards the ruin.

It makes a heap; the frost still coats the timbers of the fence, the earth is rich, wet, revealed, and whereas before the house had been set into a gentle slope, now the ground in front has been levelled, written over by a tracked vehicle.

It would have been polite, wouldn't it, if he'd told her what was to happen?

She shrugs off the loss.

She tells herself, forget it, it's not hers any more, that patch of ground, the house she lived in, she sold it off to enable her to hang on at all, here.

She should concentrate on the development of the barn.

Two days later, a container of gravel strains up the road to Latchworthy Farm, dumps its load.

Jane sees, it isn't going to be a lawn, in front of Chris Gilbey's house.

These are the changes wrought in her old place, which signal to her, now, every time she comes down to the front yard, which is mostly to greet Miss Egan, the Post Lady.

The two women discuss the changes: the old Devon Longhouse they used to sit in, empty, the electricity ripped out, the patch of gravel in front now, the hummocky spoil.

Written crookedly over the mounds of earth are the broken lines of the old fence which used to encompass Chris Gilbey's property; attached to a limb of the fence is the typewritten square of paper from the Dartmoor National Park, wrapped in a plastic seal, like a flag, waving.

CHRIS GILBEY SAYS, 'I'm fetching my two boys this afternoon, for their exeat. Come and meet them, will you?'

It takes a moment to sink in: *he has children, sons.*

She has to say, 'All right, yes.'

'I'll pick up some food at the store in Gidford, what's it called, White's, and I'd be thrilled if you'd come and eat a spot of supper with us this evening, meet Jamie and Alan . . .'

She pauses, draws in a breath, still shocked at the idea of children around the place.

He adds emphatically, 'Only if you like, obviously.'

Her heart sinks, she doesn't want to go, yet she agrees, 'OK, then', because it's her job to get on with him, for her own sake.

He exclaims, 'Great!'

When he turns to go, she notices how his fine, mousy hair drops straight at the back, the ends gathered in points, like artists' brushes arranged on his collar.

JANE HAULS BACK at the progress of the day: she wishes time to pass slower because she doesn't want this invitation, it's not her thing to eat 'a spot of supper' with anyone, let alone him; it's a nightmare.

She clears the dung from the stables, leans over the gate, watches her two baby calves; she thinks how fine they look, the new energy spasms in their young bodies, gives them this curious habit: they flip, suddenly, or dive headlong for no reason, pull up after three paces, then look around for the next imaginary piece of action.

For ages, she stands by the vegetable garden and wonders – again – whether or not to give it up. She likes the idea but rarely eats vegetables herself, most of the produce is given to the Post Lady or the stock, it's not worth the trouble.

Unseen, she watches Todd disappear into the shed he's borrowing off her. Todd is in a long-term sulk; she can't mind it, it's like he's hibernating to forget her, she knows he'll come out of it.

Instead, she worries about this invitation: could she have said no?

Around 4.30, she bangs about in the yard, it's the afternoon feed: to the horses their oats, sugarbeet, hay, water, night-time rugs; to the chickens their scraps, the scatter of pellets, some gravel; to the dogs their dried meat, a bone to chew on, tonight.

Roo gobbles his medicine, unknowing.

She tempts out the farm cat, Louis; he makes a rare appearance to accept the scrap of rib.

Trailed by the dogs, Jane heads into the caravan. The expensive book given her by Chris Gilbey idles on the shelf. She looks through it: pictures of grand houses, the cuts of land arranged into squares, rectangles, the formal beauty, heavily tended. She couldn't do such a garden, even if she had the time or the desire to do so, but his giving her the book tells

184

her he'd like to make such a place for himself; she'll agree happily to look over his garden from her barn when he's finished.

She swaps her clothes around, pulls a brush through her hair, stands over the sink. She soaks a flannel in the hottest water she can bear, buries her face in it, suffers the heat for the reward, she's refreshed.

She scrubs her hands carefully, works at the seams of her fingernails; if she had a mirror here, she'd look into it.

She wonders about Chris Gilbey: with his two sons here, no mother, it's a certainty he's divorced, or he could be a widower. Did he kill his wife?

At seven, the torch is a white rod of light, it waves in the darkness between the caravan and the house; Jane follows the circle of light, heads through the cold air for 'a spot of supper'.

She's full of dread, angry at having to go through with this but, if she's to keep him in check, she should watch over him.

She's rubbed with strangeness, now – her old house is the same, but different, her feet crunch on gravel. Through the kitchen window, where she'd previously had her cluttered table, she can't see past a number of candles which burn on the windowsill, it's like a religious shrine in there; she recognises, yes, the candles are of the type known as church candles – long-lasting, expensive.

Now she faces up to the front door: this isn't her old beaten-up aluminium frame any more, he's replaced it with an oak one, the door cut halfway in the manner of a stable door, the top panel glazed with clear laminate glass. Through it, she can see a shadowy, unfamiliar place, blank, without furniture; the only light comes from the candles in the kitchen.

She knocks. The two boys pull open the door; the red setters Joey and Max push between them, smiling. Shadows cross the boys' faces; both are flaxen haired, unsmiling, serious. Incongruously, they're wearing rubber boots indoors, something's wrong with the floor.

She judges, they might be more scared of her than she is of them.

She says cheerfully, 'Hello', and they mumble back at her; both have dimples.

Chris Gilbey appears, greets her, puts a hand on the taller one's head: 'This is Alan.'

'Hello Alan.'

Then he transplants his hand to the smaller boy, a replica of his brother but finer built '... and this is Jamie.'

'Hello Jamie.'

Jamie shouts, 'Hello!' then rocks from foot to foot, glances at his brother for confirmation it was funny – how loud he said that! – and sure enough, both of them fall together, laugh, then fight like cubs.

Chris Gilbey talks to Jane over the top of their noise: 'Come in, don't bother to wipe your feet.' His laugh is the brief hiss, through his teeth.

'Christ,' says Jane accusingly, 'what's happened to my floor?' because she steps through on to gravel.

Chris Gilbey grins. 'What's wrong with wanting floors to be more or less level? You lived on a hill, going down to the bathroom, I was running to catch up with myself, coming back up to the kitchen, I was out of breath from the climb.'

When she closes the door behind her, Jane notices the well-engineered click, the precision with which it closes. In the candlelit gloom she surveys the building site of her old house and she's amazed: the concrete floors in the kitchen, hall, living room have been broken up, taken away, ground level is lower.

'Plus,' adds Chris Gilbey, 'I'm engineering an inch or two of extra height.'

The two boys are already in the kitchen, their high-pitched voices exclaim in excitement, the red setters run back and forth. The church candles are arranged on both windowsills, a portable gas heater sits crookedly, all three panels blazing.

A new table, its legs still wrapped in protective cardboard, is in the middle, surrounded by fold-out canvas chairs.

The boys kneel, pore over the table, twiddle pencils.

She notices the dogs have a quilted basket each, arranged around a corner of the room.

Chris Gilbey points at a shop-bought pie on an upturned cardboard box; next to it is a sheaf of paper plates decorated in a gaudy floral pattern and a column of plastic cups. He asks, 'Ham and egg, OK?'

'Fine.'

He points again: 'And Rioja.'

Tilted against the wall, their bottom ends screwed into the rubble to prevent them falling over, are two open bottles. Jane repeats, 'Fine', then adds, 'Whatever that is.'

He explains, 'Spanish.'

Then he turns to his sons, his voice drops to its quietest level. She remembers, he has these tricks he plays with his speech.

'Jamie, Alan,' he murmurs, 'if you clear this stuff away, you might receive something to eat and drink.'

They jump up immediately, scrabble at the pens and paper, race to clear the table.

So now, she realises with dread, they are going to have to find something to say to one another.

THE NEXT TIME Jane hears Chris Gilbey's special, low voice is

187

later on, after the meal. They've finished the ham and egg pie, drunk several glasses of wine each, the candles are half an inch lower, the red setters are slumped in their baskets.

The two boys have disappeared upstairs to play in their room, leaving rubber boots incongruously parked at the foot of the stairs, which themselves float some inches above the level of the hardcore.

Chris Gilbey has lit a cigarette.

The wine sings in Jane's head. She feels loose, adrift from her work, less fixed to this place; she views herself from a distance, out of place, unhappy.

Then this low voice comes at her and Chris Gilbey's gaze steadies, observant, as he murmurs, 'There's something I want to put to you.'

She blinks away tears; fuelled by the alcohol, she is surprised to find strong emotions aroused in her, for no good reason.

She wants to escape.

The voice continues, 'I'm not sure whether you're going to like it or not, but I want you to give me an honest reaction.' He emphasises, 'This won't happen, unless you want it to.'

She's certain, now, that it's going to be bad news, it's what she's been dreading, she'll hear something she won't like and, vehemently, she doesn't want the disappointment, not right now.

She thinks, Get a grip, *keep him in his box.*

She nods. 'Go on then, honest reaction coming up.'

In reply he kicks off with just two words: 'The ruin.'

'What about it?'

He continues, 'I've got hold of an old photograph of it', and he ducks sideways, trots out of the room; his feet crunch on the ballast underfoot, his fold-out canvas chair is left awry.

Upstairs, she hears a thump of feet: the two boys shout.

Chris Gilbey comes back with his soft blue bag; he separates the handles, paws through it, 'Ah . . . '

He pulls out a Xeroxed enlargement of a photograph, lays it on the table in front of her. She recognises the house she was brought up in and she loves it immediately with the same strength as she did then: she played in and out of its rooms, on the front steps, she broke the glass in one of the Gothic-shaped windows when she threw a stone further than she believed she could, Miss Egan, a young woman then, took her midday meal with them, she once found her father asleep at the bottom of the stairs, she can remember the exact smell and excitement of catching her first fish, the tumble of the latch on the garden shed, lichen on the step, there was the broken doll's house and the soft toy called Yellow Dog . . .

It's like a grief, tearing at her, how long she's been up here, fighting the *fucking* weather, sometimes she wishes she could let the place go, but she's held by it, yet, most compelling about this photograph, to her eyes, rather than her bedroom window or the branch from which hung the swing, are the changes wrought over time. She's seen them for herself of course but to have the bald evidence put in front of her, proof of how the place used to be, confuses her; it's almost magical – the distance the place has travelled.

Yet she's the same, only older.

She points out to Chris Gilbey the trees, look, there was a stand of ancient monkey-puzzles, now cut down, the drive looped in a circle around the giant beech tree, instead of running up one side of it to the front yard, the cottage in which they're now sitting was a wing, only, to the much larger house . . .

Then, Chris Gilbey taps the picture. 'I'd quite like to rebuild it.'

Jane feels a surge of drunken astonishment.

He asks, 'What d'you think?'

She exclaims, 'Why?'

He shrugs. 'I'd just like to rebuild it.'

She practically cries, 'You're joking.'

'All right, probably joking, but I might apply for planning permission anyway, see what happens.'

Jane feels immediate, raw jealousy. It was her place, where she was born.

She thinks, He must have *so much money*.

He repeats his question, 'What d'you think?'

'Great, go for it' – she can hear her own strangled, slurred voice.

Chris Gilbey grins. 'You never know, might happen.'

'. . . Incredible . . .' She shakes her head, because yes, it's bad news.

AT THREE IN the morning, Jane is still drunk when she oversees a Belted Galloway, Swallow, give birth to a strange, mauve-coloured calf which she christens Nightingale.

THE SNOW IS driven horizontally; scarcely given the chance to settle, it's swept over the rough terrain by the wind until it finds shelter behind the boulders or the walls, where the sheep also huddle, backs turned to protect themselves.

The moor is painted white by the storm with visibility down to a hundred yards.

Jane wears full-on bad-weather gear: a set of waterproofs, fur-lined leather cap buttoned under her chin, balaclava, goggles.

As she ploughs over the terrain the bag of cake bumps against her knees, she can hear only her own breath inside her head and the blow of the storm, they mingle as one – the storm's fury, her will to survive.

She knows the hollows, the nooks and corners where her sheep will find shelter and she visits three locations, to find a scattering in each. The sheep are unmoved by the storm: the rectangular slots of their eyes are calm, unexcited, whereas Jane can feel her whole body and face set for the battle against the weather, but these heavily pregnant animals, guarded by impenetrable, waxed-woollen coats, accept its worst on-slaught. One or two will die but this is accepted.

She nods the neck of the bag here, there; piles of cake are left in the spots clearest of snow unchurned by their feet, smaller boulders become table tops for the extra, rough-weather rations delivered to wherever they choose to bide the storm.

Then Jane's eye is caught by a semicircle of white on the ground some distance away. The shape is unusual: a perfect oval line, dusted with snow. Her first thought is, It's a boulder.

Even as she heads over she knows, suddenly, it can't be; the snow would be blown clean off a boulder that shape. It's a cow on its side, the snow caught, held by the fur.

Jane's back is pushed hard by the blizzard. She plunges on, arrives at the animal's head to recognise Elizabeth.

Jane kneels, checks for vital signs: breath, the state of her eye. She sees the wet nose flex, crinkle – the animal's alive, conscious but in pain, back legs wedged underneath a rock: she's lain down, worked herself into the trap somehow, so now she can't pull her legs free.

Jane goes to the other end, kneels in the snow; the wind is in her face, she's glad to have the perspex goggles to protect her

191

eyes, and she can see the cow is in the middle of calving – a snout, two paws are there.

The thought of the animal stuck, unable to open her legs during the birth – Jane is swept by a sudden wave of pity.

She carves snow away from the animal's back end even as more snow is driven into the area by the relentless wind.

She examines the nose of the calf protruding from the cow and she's puzzled at first but then realises the calf is missing an ear, plus, a clove of one foot is chewed, it's a bloody mess, the end of its tongue is bitten off. A fox has been driven by hunger, attracted to the smell from the cast animal; it's eaten at the calf even as the mother tried to expel it.

Jane hauls at the boulder trapping the cow's rear legs, she tries to tilt it in every direction but she's unable.

She runs back for the tractor; but when she returns to the scene, it proves impossible to purchase enough drag on the rock, the shape's wrong. The ropes slip off, time and again. She's in and out of the cab ten times.

Instead, she fixes the rope to the cow's neck, and drags the cow clear, risking damage to her rear limbs, but Elizabeth is free.

Before Jane has time to think, the calf slithers out, alive but weakened.

True to form, the mother's anything but grateful; instead wildly aggressive – shocked.

Jane has a battle of wills with her: Jane wants to lift the calf into the linkbox, take her into the farm. Meanwhile the cow barges around, sliding through the snow, trying to prevent her calf from being taken.

Jane shouts, swears, waves her arms. She dives for cover in the linkbox every time the cow stumbles towards her in panicky, desperate anger.

She needs someone else there, to help distract the cow, but

she battles on and in between hopping in and out of the linkbox, she manages to pull the newborn calf closer; finally she heaves it on board the loader, drives it clear.

The mother follows, anxious, blinded by the storm.

JANE CALLS THE calf Pedro; he survives.

His missing tongue means he can't suckle; Jane has to run this wild, traumatised cow into a crush to take her milk off her, pour it down Pedro's throat for him.

He walks with a limp, looks like he's been in a fight with a bear, but he learns to eat and within two weeks, starts to gain weight.

JANE GLIMPSES THE bright red livery of a Royal Mail van.

She's immediately sidetracked down to the front yard and out scrambles Dick, Gidford's traditionally cheerful Irish postman; he plants the letters in her hand.

Jane asks, 'Where's Miss Egan?'

'Poorly, I'm afraid!' he calls, already back in his van. 'Her hip, apparently, isn't it, operation and everything.'

Jane diverts to the barn, squats next to the new telephone which is already scratched and battered from its life in this building site. She dials Miss Egan's number; there's no reply.

So: later that morning Jane scoops up the double handful of mail from the Milkvit box, tucks the letters into an inside pocket.

She goes out to the stable yard, gathers saddle and bridle. A couple of minutes later, she's on Lady, across the moor in the direction of Scaur Hill. The patches of snow mark out the colder, driest spots.

Lady nods along in an easy canter, barely breaks her stride at the Wallabrook, sends up a spray of glittering water, Jane sees a fan of miniature fish suddenly strike out from beneath them, slivers of dark brown.

She rounds the top of Scaur Hill, reins Lady briefly to look back at her own tongue of land which inserts, like an interloper, on to the moor.

Then she presses Lady forward.

The other side of Scaur Hill dips to a further boundary between the downlands and Dartmoor, with several small-holdings such as hers butted against it; she's in a line, she recognises, more favoured than those on the western perime-ter of the moor, because more sheltered.

She dips lower, takes the first gateway off Scaur Hill, which leads to a square car-park area, fed by a single-track lane. A few yards down on the right-hand side Jane swings Lady into a gateway, heralded by a cacophony of barking. The Post Lady's shack is the same as ever.

Jane unhooks the latch from the gate. Lady saunters through, intrigued by this unusual journey.

Jane dismounts; the various dogs already accept her, quieten. She ties off Lady's reins, folds the long end into the cheekstrap, puts up the stirrups, lets her go. Lady wanders off to graze the hedgerow.

The Post Lady's shack is called Rhiannon – although there isn't a sign to say so – and it reminds Jane of a children's book illustration of the cottage made from cake, biscuits and gingerbread discovered by Hansel and Gretel.

The front yard is given over to dogs; a chain runs from a tree to a nail driven into the side of the wooden shack, several leads hang from it, the fierce collie now runs around the back of the shack to escape from her.

Jane stoops to go into the dilapidated wooden porch. She notices the same litter of broken garden equipment, the chair, still unused.

She knocks, but hears nothing. She pushes at the door, it tilts dangerously: one of the hinges is broken. She puts her other hand to it, lifts it cleanly, sets it closed behind her.

A trio of basset hounds look up at her mournfully; the old mongrel is stationed in the middle of the room. As usual, a dozen or more bowls and saucers decorate the floor and there are two chickens parading on the table.

To one side rests the Post Lady's bicycle, but without the bag in its red and blue livery, which normally sits in the front basket.

Jane calls out, 'Miss Egan?'

There's a feeble reply from above.

Jane carries on up the rickety staircase, where she's greeted by more dogs. She braves a terrier with rasping breath and bulging eyes.

There's only one room upstairs so it isn't difficult to find Miss Egan, lying in bed; her face is the same, with the brown lines drawn in her skin, the heavily lidded eyes, the vegetable nose, but her hair is loose, brushed so each fibre separates from its neighbour. As a consequence, she looks larger.

Miss Egan points at her throat, whispers, 'Sorry, not much of a voice, but all right, long as I don't shout.'

A roll-up burns unevenly in her fingers.

Jane sits on the edge of the bed. 'I thought it was your hip.'

'Hip as well,' answers the Post Lady, 'actually, hip mostly, wouldn't be in bed, otherwise, it's been a bit ropy for some time, but I've had to wait, to become an emergency.'

'They've given you a slot, now, though?'

'Next week. Apparently I should be good as new, after,

195

except, they've given away my round, you know.'

'I thought so,' replies Jane. 'Dick came up in a van, this morning.'

'Dick's all right,' replies Miss Egan, 'he's good fun,' and then she whispers, 'God knows they kept me going for long enough, the bike was on its last legs, and so was I.'

Jane nods; she was about to retrieve the bundle of letters from her inside pocket, but realises now it would be the wrong thing, to pretend to carry on as though nothing has happened.

Miss Egan says, 'D'you know, they've let me keep it, the bike?'

'Did they?'

'Wasn't that kind? I thought so, I really did, you know what these people can be like, it's the property of this organisation, all that type of thing, and I've grown used to that old machine.'

Jane smiles. 'I should think you have.'

'Anyway, just the pension, now,' adds Miss Egan, 'so it's tighten-the-belt time.' She lifts her hand to explain: 'Back to the roll-ups.'

Jane says, 'You don't have to talk, you know, if you don't want to spoil your voice, I can just sit for a while, or go downstairs, make myself useful.'

The Post Lady pats her hand, 'I know, I know, don't worry, I feel comfortable.' Her whisper breaks into a normal voice, then back again: 'So, you can do your own mail, at last.'

'I'm out of the habit,' argues Jane; 'anyway, who'll eat my vegetables, if you don't?'

'Sell them,' suggests Miss Egan. 'Put a little table outside your gate, like the woman at Discombe. The tourists will buy them.'

At the back of her mind, Jane thinks maybe she can employ

Miss Egan, ask her to do the farm accounts, something, anyway.

Miss Egan nods. 'I'll be better, you'll see, I'm not done with, yet.'

On Miss Egan's side of the conversation, they talk about the operation, how she's afraid they'll replace the wrong hip joint, so she'll write on herself with a marker pen: on the good side she'll write NOT THIS ONE, on the bad side she'll write YES, THIS ONE.

On Jane's part, she describes Chris Gilbey's plan to rebuild the old house, how she must be jealous, because she's angry, she hopes the Dartmoor National Park refuses permission, she doesn't want anything to do with it, which is unfair.

Then, they say their goodbyes. Miss Egan's dogs trail Jane to the door, dejected.

Outside, Lady is finished with the hedgerow, she's around the back of the dogs' kennels. Jane walks her into more open ground, mounts and heads up the lane; from here she can see the back of the same Scaur Hill which rises on the other side of the valley from her own End Field. When she tops the hill, the farm is the same tongue of land as ever, well tended, worked over, home.

WHEN IT'S DARK, she thinks, Down the pub.

In winter, the pubs in Gidford are close-knit, strung-out parties which last from November to March, the seats warmed by the same people, for much of the time. One or two affairs cross over, rivalries remain undecided, marriages are dug deeper or the bottom drops out of them.

The darts pitch in the Cross Keys is Jane's area; Todd and his biker cronies hog the bench in the other window.

Jamie, the son of the hotel family at Beaworthy, tries to annoy people, entices the same few victims to his corner of the bar.

The proprietors, ex-policeman Jim and his wife Peggy Mortimer, take turns behind the taps or among the punters, it's a tacit agreement between them, it's good for business to mingle.

This year the Gidford Amateur Operatic Singers choose the Cross Keys to surface in, on Thursday evenings, after rehearsals; they stick to the quieter side of the pub, next to the restaurant area, answer good-naturedly to various taunts about 'warblers'.

Jim Mortimer automatically takes charge of the initiative to help Miss Egan, he pulls a piece of paper off his delivery pad, turns it over; in his slow, deliberate hand he writes along the top 'Miss Egan'. He murmurs to Jane, 'Let's just get the names, then we'll sort it.' To kick off, he writes 'Jane Reeves', 'Jim and Peggy Mortimer', then he pins it on the wall at the end of the bar, in plain view. He twists a length of string around the end of the biro, squeezes a lump of Blu-Tack on to it and more is thumbed on to the wall next to the note, so the pen can hang there, ready for use; in the same way began the rota to clear the new sports field.

Jane has her regulation three pints, spread over the evening.

Todd crowds her, he drinks considerably more. To begin with he's friendly: he gives an update on the Infernal Machine he's building in the shed, he asks after the farm, he tells her about the contract job he's got at Leastone.

Then, as he drinks more, he becomes remote, aloof. Towards closing time he's morose, his eyes follow her.

Jamie tilts on his stool, rants against the hunt saboteurs, 'They say it's *cruel*, have they any idea? Nature is cruel, do they want to hire a scientist to dissect a lamb that's had its neck torn out, measure the adrenalin, to see if the fox is cruel, because it *is* . . . ' – he waves a finger – 'Which does the fox prefer, has anyone asked, to be chased by a bunch of hounds or by a hairy-arsed farmer with a shotgun or a trap or a bag of poison? Which is better, more natural?'

Jane barges through the closing-time throng, to ask Peter Davey the usual question.

It's difficult to look at Peter Davey in the flesh. One side of his face is mangled, scarred: a mare came at him in the stable, pinned him in a corner, he was lucky its top set of teeth skated over his eye socket and gripped instead on his cheekbone, otherwise he'd have lost the sight in one eye.

'Peter.'

'Hello, Jane.'

His wife is deaf, so Jane nods, waves; the ever-cheerful Mrs Davey returns the signal.

Her husband has this habit: he parks her in here while he goes to seek out the horse-folk who drink in the hotel, then he returns to pick her up.

Jane asks Peter, 'How's things?' She notices how the line of his collar is sharp – perfectly clean and pressed – against the leathery skin of his neck, his woollen tie is immaculate, he's well looked after.

Everyone should have a wife, Jane thinks.

Then she asks for the umpteenth time, 'Will you tell me yet?' and Peter Davey returns her smile, he mimes 'No!' because Jane's always wanted to know – why would he, of all people, have sold her a horse for half its value?

JANE BOUGHT LADY over eight years ago; she'd inherited the farm from her father, barely escaped from the whole business of probate, mortgage, preparing the business plan, when Peter Davey had telephoned and for a moment the line had been silent, before this voice said, 'I've got a horse for you.'

She hadn't put out that she was looking for one, but Peter Davey assumed she'd come and look; and she did, because Peter Davey, according to her father, had the keenest eye that had ever opened, for a horse.

So he took her into his yard and showed her this bay seven-year-old mare, half thoroughbred, sixteen-one hands.

If she'd seen her in a sale ring, she'd never have dreamt of buying an animal like this for the moor – one of those spindly legs would have gone into a hole or been caught between two rocks, snapped in half – but since it was Peter Davey who was offering her, she couldn't question his judgement. He knew exactly where she lived, who she was, he was near the moor himself, if he said this mare had enough common sense to run safely across broken, rock-strewn ground, it was true, she could.

Peter Davey walked Lady up and down his yard for Jane to look at. She saw how the action of the horse was all straight lines – no dishing of the feet, no cow-hocked stiffness in the rear limbs, all the circles could be drawn, all the triangles met up; then Jane rode her around a field for ten minutes and she was hooked, she came back wearing a big smile, shaking her head at the idea she could allow herself this prize, but she almost certainly wouldn't be able to afford her.

Then he mentioned this low, low figure.

She asked, 'Why you giving her to me?'

Peter Davey replied, 'Your father would have known', and with his death only a few months past, Jane felt tears jump from her eyes.

She judged the price was half what the animal was worth. She paid it without question.

As she left, Peter Davey smiled, it's stood in her memory, since: the smile switched on slowly, lasted for a long time, like it was a gift from this serious man who never gave much away, the moment lasted for a long time and Peter Davey had laughed – or at least, it was a long 'haaaaa' – which, combined with his squeezing her arm, shaking her hand goodbye, was enough to set her up with a feeling that keeping her father's farm, trying to make a go of it, would be the best move she'd ever made.

'Oh yes,' added Peter Davey, when Jane turned up with the trailer in his yard, 'she likes to round up the chickens, for some reason, if you've a mind to let her.'

For years Peter Davey's refused to say why he was unaccountably taken with this charitable impulse; it's beyond a joke.

Jane smiles, punches his shoulder, makes her way back to her bench behind the dartboard.

The next time she visits the bar, Jim Mortimer has the sweat wrung from his forehead, he says, 'Guess what?'

'What?' she asks.

'Know what I call this?' He taps the list they've put up for Miss Egan.

'No.'

'A hip list.'

They collect six names, aim for fourteen people to look after her, in shifts.

Jane braves the weather, steers a course over the rainswept, soggy upland, over the Wallabrook and beyond, to where evidence of tin mining disrupts the soil, the stones bear the teeth marks of chisels where they were shaped, used to support entrances to mine shafts, as well as to head the graves of the miners.

Lady takes to the new task with alacrity, she enjoys the mountaineering, practically, which sees them up and down – the horizon appears, disappears – like a boat tossed on a storm. For two or three days horse and rider make this detour through the ripped terrain.

Half buried in the peat soil, she finds what she hopes will be two suitable stones. If she could drag them out to have a look, she'd know for certain. She scrabbles with her hands to determine their shape, but she'll have to risk it.

Then there's the day of reckoning: she borrows the hydraulic grab from Leigh and Sons, who are contracted to put the lintels in, once she's got them on site.

Outside the back gate the expanse of the moor faces her, she engages four-wheel-drive, advances slowly, steadily over the rough ground, the vehicle pitches this way and that, the hydraulic arm a long finger curled in front of her.

She sets the manual throttle, takes her feet off the pedals to give a steady ride. It contravenes National Park rules – Dartmoor's licensed stock-keepers are allowed to move stones, but no one should drive a motor vehicle on to the moor to collect them – but she trusts no one will sneak.

It takes an hour to pull out the stones, the scarred metal finger moves clumsily with her unfamiliar handling of the hydraulics, but it pinches with unlikely strength.

She measures to gauge whether they're suitable, finds one is perhaps too fat at one end, but it can be chiselled into shape.

So in turn, she drives them before her. She can't imagine

their weight: two oil drums filled with concrete counterbalance the rear of the vehicle.

In all, it takes a day to escort the two lintels to the front of the barn. They look like two ordinary stones, but already she knows their every nook, cranny, chisel mark, their gravity.

As it happens, Chris Gilbey appears, drawn from his carcass of a house by the sound of the vehicle. 'Boy,' he exclaims and kneels to stroke the somnolent rocks, while she thinks, Hands off.

The builders, Leigh and Sons, send a team of six men with Kangos; to pack in the lintels, knock out the granite from beneath them, fit the woodwork, make good, will take a week's work.

Given she's plumped for hardwood frames and double glazing, the two downstairs windows might be the most expensive part of this barn conversion.

In fact, it takes them two days just to make big enough holes in the wall to fit the cross members through, to take the weight of the walls while space is made for the lintels to be fitted.

The lintels themselves are hoisted by the hydraulic grab; and now, they can get to work – this is to open the eyes of the barn.

AN OCEANIC STORM brews on the day that Leigh and Sons clear up, leave the site.

Jane, Roo and Billy are safe inside, out of the weather. Jane gazes out of the new windows, the acrid smell of fresh cement in her nostrils.

The wind and rain are tamed by the double layer of glass, unlike in her old house across the yard: its windows always let in the weather around the edges, the glass rattled, flexed with each gust of wind, but in here, it's quiet.

Jane touches a finger against the new putty – and she's enthralled.

Christ, she can see for miles, it's a spiritual thing: here, where she stands, is the spot to be, for all well-being, and the rest will fall into place. She feels the tension empty from her overworked frame as if a plug had been pulled out at her roots, she stands light as air, poised . . .

ROO WANDERS HERE and there.

Jane calls him, her own voice sounds strange; the acoustics of the barn have been revised by the apertures cut into the walls, sealed with glass.

She wishes everything else were ready; she'd sleep here, celebrate the inauguration of these windows.

It's a strange quiet now in this familiar building site which she's been a slave to for two months, except, the rain drills on the tiled roof, Billy pants lightly, at her heel, Roo lies down, groans with contentment.

It's not long till lambing.

MINUTES LATER, ON their way back to the caravan, Billy and Roo trot ahead of her, noses turned into the wind and rain. Roo's legs stagger at the impact, both dogs' coats are ruffled, their ears turned inside out by the storm.

Jane finishes the evening chores, feeds Billy and Roo.

Inside the caravan, she changes into dry clothes. Hungry, she tries some tinned Mexican refried beans but they smell worse than the dog food so she abandons them in favour of a lump of cheese.

She empties and restacks the drier with her wet clothes, ready to take their turn on the day after tomorrow. She shakes out her bedding, folds it and strip-washes at the tiny sink, brushes her teeth; the panel of heat from the wall is enough to singe her hair if she stands too close.

Suddenly, she asks the dogs out loud, 'Why can't we?'

Blasted by the electric heat, the dogs look at her, tongues slide back and forth in their mouths.

Immediately she knows it's the right thing to do.

So she pushes bedding into four plastic bin-liners, clasps hold of the torch, summons Billy, Roo, who look surprised to be asked to go outside at this point in their routine, nevertheless they stir, to accompany her.

All three leave the caravan, hurry past the rainswept farm buildings, trot down the stable yard under the curious stares of Lady and Tuppence; the light illuminates stripes of rain, glittering with splashes from the gutter above.

Jane hurries through the gate at the bottom of the yard, then with some trepidation approaches their future home.

She spares one hand to turn the handle, pushes at the blue-painted door with her foot, so they're safely out of the rain.

The eye of the torch moves over the walls; under its scrutiny, the building feels cold, they're unwelcome, there isn't the sense of a home in the making, instead it's a building site again – hostile.

She finds the light switch; now the single bulb burns overhead.

Jane talks to the dogs, to keep up her spirits, but they remain puzzled, disconcerted.

She has to shrug off the sense that this is a premature arrival; instead she sets about arranging the sleeping bag and the dog-duvet on the raised platform at the far end of the barn, while the dogs watch her from below.

She calls Billy; he scrambles up the steps, she clicks her fingers over the dog-duvet, soothes him until he lies. Then she coaxes Roo and settles both dogs together; they look embarrassed.

She switches off the overhead bulb, returns by torchlight, climbs fully dressed into her sleeping bag. Her calming the dogs has worked for herself, too; she retrieves the sense that this is a good idea.

With the torch off, they're in utter blackness, she can see nothing, hears only the dogs' breath and the rain on the roof, yet the windows are an extraordinary presence: more than the plumbing and the wiring they transform the place, allow a vision of its future.

Silently, she asks the inspector to come soon, so the 13-amp ring main can be switched on; should she telephone?

Alone, in the dark, she chases the work, tries to imagine when it might happen, how soon before lambing time.

Then it occurs to her: it's nearly a year since Michael Peddlar came on his farm visit, she should remind herself, she's answered all her problems, since then. She has the farm all squared off financially, tonight she tries out the barn conversion, she has the windows done.

It's warm inside her bag. As she drifts towards sleep, she tries to second-guess the future but it's impossible – an empty space.

Tomorrow's work runs through her mind, a line of tasks: the lame Scots ewes, castrate the calf, jack up the roof in the sheep shed and replace the rotten upright, Jed's bloody discharge.

So: Jane sleeps in her barn.

EARLY SPRING SUNSHINE shows itself, newly minted, bright, it casts long shadows because the sun still tracks low in the sky. The breeze turns on and off whimsically, surprises them with its sudden strength.

Jane and Chris Gilbey walk side by side up the stable yard.

'Hey, old man,' Jane greets Tuppence, her father's retired mount.

She draws back the bolt on his stable, notes his ear flicker in surprise – she has a stranger with her and what's more, the stranger has a saddle and bridle over his arm.

She adds, 'Yes, you, come on', and flips the rug from his back, sets to grooming him with a dandy-brush. His belly is a deep curve, compared with the neat, tucked-up abdomen of Lady.

She remembers from old times the patches of dark hair shaped like pebbles which decorate his back. This horse had a mouth of iron, in his day.

She tacks him up, while Chris Gilbey leans against the stable door; there's his cheerful, squirrel-like smile: 'Looks like a pretty wild beast.'

Tuppence is leaden footed, immobile; Jane leans over to brush the mud from his legs and grunts, 'If you fall off him, you'd have just as easily fallen out of your armchair.'

'Give me the chair any day, less humiliating.' His laugh is a brief puff, a hiss of breath.

She'll never like him; but she has to make sure they can get along.

Jane moves on to Lady's stall.

Around the yard, the pair of red setters, Joey and Max, thrill to the new, complicated scents; Billy follows their tails, aggressive, Jane glimpses his top lip peel back, tremble, the incisors pure white, while Roo watches them from his favourite position on the straw bales banked behind the stables.

When Jane shoots the bolt on Lady's stall, Lady wheels around, impatient; Jane follows. She drops the reins over her ears; Lady grabs at the bit with her mouth, anxious to be off. Jane settles the saddle, tightens the girth, draws her outside and the setters bark, spring around her, too close, innocent of the danger.

Lady flings her head up, but stands motionless, looks for the next thing to happen.

When Jane takes Tuppence from his stable, he moves with his slow, stiff gait; he knows there's nothing new out here, even if he is wearing his work gear again. He and Roo are the farm's two pensioners, yet they still have a good enough life.

Chris Gilbey buttons his coat; the riding hat dangles from his elbow, he looks excited, bright-eyed.

She says cheerfully, 'Let's be having you then.'

Chris Gilbey pulls the helmet from his arm, lowers it quickly on his head, pushes out his chin, fiddles with the buckle, asks, 'Do I look as daft as I feel?'

'Yes.' It's a small triumph, that she really means it.

'Thought so, never mind.'

He steps alongside Tuppence: 'OK. What do I do?'

Jane remembers from before his willingness to learn. She yanks down the stirrup, holds it for him. 'Left foot in there.'

'Hold on to the mane?'

'Yup.'

'Seen it in the movies.'

'This won't hurt him.' Jane tugs at Tuppence's mane; 'not if you take a decent handful.'

Then she crosses to the other side, coaches him from across Tuppence's withers: 'OK, put your weight into the iron, swing your other leg across.'

She hangs off the stirrup leather on her side, to prevent the saddle from slipping. 'OK, go.'

She can see the top of his hat as he looks down, steps away from the side of the horse, then with surprising agility lifts himself up, throws a leg across Tuppence's loins and with a bump he arrives in the saddle.

'You're up, you're there, well done.'

He grins, looks down at the ground on both sides. 'Always wanted to be a cowboy.'

Jane positions the ball of his foot across the stirrup, then holds his ankle, gives his leg a pat. 'There you go, perfect English seat.'

He twists his body, uncomfortable, snorts ironically, 'Oh, easy.'

She goes to Tuppence's head, takes a length of baler twine from her pocket, passes it through the snaffle to tie it on the other side, which leaves the end trailing.

Tuppence stands, mute, uninterested; the bristles around his mouth brush against her hand, his lip flops open, shut – she remembers this exact mouth pulling like a train, dragging her at a gallop over the moor, on the few occasions when she dared borrow him from her father.

Jane mounts Lady, passes by Tuppence's head to pick up the string; then she leads him off.

As Tuppence winds around to follow, Jane catches an incredulous expression on Chris Gilbey's face. She points out, 'There you are, you're going for a ride ... '

They progress at a snail's pace down the passageway out to the moor. Chris Gilbey grins all the while, leans at an angle. Tuppence walks sedately, head at half mast; Jane has to check Lady regularly, to keep the string from being pulled out of her hand.

Jane reads her watch: ten o'clock, she'll lose maybe an hour, it's worth it.

They pass through the gate on to the moor. Chris Gilbey lets go of Tuppence's mane, lifts a clenched fist in the air. 'I can do it,' he claims.

They ride out in the early spring sunshine, one of them confident, upright, fitted to the horse like a growth in the saddle, the other insecure, planted there for the first time, tilting to the right. Around them, like a tide of grey, the black-face ewes move away, heavily pregnant, about to drop.

The setters charge, cavaliers both of them; the sheep break into a run and Jane feels a blush of anger at the setters, at their owner as well. Ahead of Chris Gilbey she shouts at them, 'Joey, Max', then he calls them also, but his voice is like an echo, diluted, without the anger.

In their own time the setters peel off, unconcerned.

Jane winds back her anger. They ride on.

Dartmoor encompasses the two figures: a landscape weathered, fallen, worn out, broken-toothed, scarred, browbeaten by years of just this: last summer's heat followed by a scouring winter followed now by this blowy, cold spring; tomorrow's frost will bite into the same cracks started in the drought and then eroded by the winter's rain.

Chris Gilbey looks around him intently, small eyes fixed to the horizon, he loves it, he leans both hands on Tuppence's withers, calls out, 'Fantastic!'

Their horses nod along companionably.

Jane asks Chris about his family; she learns he was married but is now divorced, Alan and Jamie attend boarding school, he hosts them on various exeats and for part of the school holidays, he has a brother in Canada, a sister in Beckenham, Kent.

Jane wants to ask what he does for a living, but stalls, sure it is something that neither of them could be proud of, otherwise he'd have mentioned it by now.

They ride along at a snail's pace, their horses connected by the orange baler twine.

They swing uphill to Caistor, the sun is low, their shadows mingle on the rough terrain, the shoulder surmounted by the head of rock.

They stop, survey the ground swept from their feet, cuts of land fitted like a puzzle, seamed with rivers, fractured by escarpments, the decorative tors.

Jane points here, there: 'Hut circles, hundreds of them, swarms of people settled on the side of this hill, sort of a round stone wall with a porch stone, rough thatch rooves, turf piled on top.' She points at the boundary of the farm – 'My wall, apparently, was made out of stones which they'd already used, thousands of years ago, to make their houses.'

From his questions, she can tell where his interest lies: he asks what their concerns were, how flint was more valuable than gold, what games they played, how money passed back and forth, ownerships decided.

Jane leads Chris Gilbey home an hour after they started out. They amble up the front drive, neatly pass between their respective dwellings: Jane's barn on the left, Chris' house on the right ...

They pass through the gate, into the stable yard. Jane dismounts from Lady, throws a rug over her horse's loins.

She coaches Chris Gilbey's dismount.

Safe on the ground, he unclips his helmet, scratches his scalp. 'Ahhhh,' he smiles at her, pleased with the ride. 'Incredible, huh?'

She shows him how to unbuckle the girth, rub Tuppence down.

He casts the rug himself, he learns quickly, deftly, to stitch up the buckle.

She pats Tuppence's flank. 'Ride him all you like, whenever; he's retired, but it's good for him to work a little bit, just saddle him up.'

'Thanks, I will.' He touches her elbow. She has to stop herself, her instinct was to move away.

She wonders if it's worth it, the politics of this, probably not ...

NIGHT FALLS THICK and black at 6 p.m. From beneath the horizon, sunlight strikes a solitary twist of cloud, casts it gold, it resembles a lick of treacle, luminescent in the dark sky.

A WEEK LATER, Chris Gilbey drives from London to Park House, near Moreton, on a whim, furious.

He doesn't know what he's going to do or say but he eats up the M4 at over 100 m.p.h., the M5 flashes past in an hour. He arrives with sweat-soaked linen crumpled behind his knees, his damp shirt clings around his lower back, only to be told it's lunchtime, Mr John Bernard is out.

Chris Gilbey is brilliant with anger; lucid, effective sentences bite at the receptionist, criticise the National Park, demand more information.

She doesn't know where he is, she really can't help him.

He paces in the car park. Should he wait? No, he'll walk through all the pubs in Moreton until he finds Mr John Bernard.

He climbs back into the car, starts the engine and then he

reads a sign, black lettering on white, fixed to the wall inches in front of the Saab's nose. RESERVED, JOHN BERNARD.

Chris Gilbey sees red. He thinks, Too right, reserved. He clunks the gearbox into first, lets in the clutch – bang, he smashes the sign.

The damage to the car's worth it.

As he pulls back, he's pleased to see the sign's split, unreadable.

He sweeps into a reverse turn and thinks, Calm, icy calm. This little wanker, Mr John Bernard, took it on himself to refuse outline planning permission for rebuilding the house – but there is still the appeal.

THEN JANE PUTS her head down and aims into the black hole – lambing.

Bang on target, the first of April, the first three are strong, healthy males, a happy result, done with by 7.30 in the evening.

Later, she watches the television which rests on an upturned bucket in the corner, hooked up to a car battery which can be recharged off the hydroelectric power. She reminds herself: patience, she will be up twice a night for the next month – at least – to check the lambing barns, the nearby fields; this is a long-distance race, she'll need stamina and courage to face up to the work, the rollercoaster of disappointment followed by elation followed by despair.

Two days later she has seven single lambs, three doubles, one triple; one lamb shares the barn with her because its mother died.

The following night she's weakened, loses three lambs all in a row, one of which she had to pull out of the womb in pieces,

213

limb by limb, yet probably, even after all that work, the ewe will die.

On Sunday, 5 April, the earth is bitten by a cold frost and two more singles are born, so perfectly, with such ease as to cause her to linger for a while, watch their whiteness against the hoary frost, enjoy the victory of such scraps of life over the cold, hard ground.

Come dusk, she tramps around the fields with her bag full of rechargeable batteries and at various points she stops, switches on the motley collection of transistor radios which are hidden in the hedges, hung on fence-posts.

She replaces the batteries if necessary.

This absurd measure is to drive away foxes and on the return walk her farm crackles with unlikely pop music, talk shows come at her from every direction, difficult modern scores frighten her like fantastical accompaniments to horror films, the moor a giant presence which broods silently beyond the boundary wall. It fills her with a sense of magic and it also distils her purpose: to live here, work the farm, rub along OK with her neighbour.

By 20 April she's brought crowds of ewes and lambs into the lower barn because it threatens rain. She finishes the horses, feeds the dogs, goes inside at around six to find the bottle-fed lamb has died and she feels the blame. This forlorn, bloated scrap, the life drawn out of it, lies in the bottom of the cardboard box and she curses the time, the effort wasted in feeding it four times a day. She picks up the corpse by its back legs, carries it to the muck heap. In the dark, she digs a hole in the manure, drops it in, back-fills the hole, all the while telling herself she shouldn't do it like this; Chris Gilbey's dogs are likely to dig it up.

The next morning she takes a sharp knife, cuts neatly around the neck and limbs of another dead lamb, pulls the

214

skin off like it's cellophane wrapping; then she ties the skin around an orphan so the bereaved mother will recognise the smell, adopt it as her own.

She pens the orphan and the bereaved ewe together, watches as the anxious mother bleats, tests the infant, worries it for several minutes, pushes it with her nose, swinging around unhelpfully every time the lamb tries to suckle.

Jane returns an hour later to watch the lamb duck its head, extend its nose, walk under the curtain of wool obscuring the ewe's teats and now its tail wags furiously with satisfaction, it drops to its knees to continue, the mother stands rock steady, grinds her teeth, staring at Jane.

Success – the trick has worked, Jane feels a rush of pride.

Remorselessly, lambing proceeds despite terrible weather; every morning Jane stuffs cheese and raisins in her pockets: a supply of energy. At times she scoops a handful of rolled oats from the horses' feed-tub, knocks it back, her mouth dry instantly.

On 1 May she finds a mystery lamb which has been picked up on the moor by a walker, deposited inside her field with a sodden note tied around its neck; they thought they'd found an abandoned child, but ewes often park their lambs in sheltered spots while they wander further afield to graze.

On 4 May she finds a ram dead in the field for no apparent reason. Also, she calls the helicopter out for a schoolkid training for the Ten Tors Expedition who suffered an asthma attack on Watern Tor and lost sufficient core temperature to sink into hypothermia.

For a while, the arrival of lambs slows to a trickle. She moves them from field to field, indoors or outdoors, according to the weather.

Her fingers are stained with iodine.

215

Then, it starts again with a vengeance: she's up three nights in a row and suddenly has three orphans living in the barn with her, so she's back up to four bottle-feeds each day and they mess the floor with careless enthusiasm. Roo and Billy have a constant, electric fascination with them, but the lambs ignore the dogs, they're arrogant in their search for anything to eat.

On Sunday, 12 May she makes a fire in the End Field and burns carcasses.

In the afternoon she slaughters the lamb suffering from swayback and while she's engaged in the nastier duties of farming she commits an act of vengeance, somewhat, by also killing four out of the five cockerels who've been fighting, creating havoc in the stable yard over the last month or two – before they get to kill themselves.

The fourteenth of May breaks sunny with scattered showers; Jane turns out forty-five sheep with their lambs on to the moor and it's the babies' first taste of the open landscape. Initially they're daunted by the far-flung horizon, they hang back, but after this brief pause to read the enormity of their new world they jump imaginary hurdles, feel the early sun on their backs, play.

When she goes in, she runs her first bath this week, undresses, sinks through the slightly chill layer of bubbles into the hot water underneath and she soaks, lies motionless in the corner of the cavernous barn.

She counts the unpredictable rhythm of the faulty tap as it meanders up and down its barely audible range of gurgling noises.

Everything in here echoes, the space is still new; she's not used to it.

She climbs out. Heated through by the bath, dressed in

clean clothes, her eyes prick with an unexpected emotion because it's over: the buildings are in a mess, gates are broken, fences hurriedly tied up with string, there's a general detritus everywhere which will take weeks to clear up. She herself is still windblown, unable to sleep properly from so many broken nights, her fingers are stained purple from the disinfectant spray used on the umbilical cords, she's exhausted, she hasn't eaten, the inside of the barn is more of a bomb site than it was before, yet she's come out the other side of it all with the Scotch blackfaces having returned 80 per cent which, for the breed, is a good result.

From the grey-faces the crop is 130 per cent – again, acceptable.

Then, it gladdens her to ride out on a spring day with the sun squinting over Caistor Rock, see lambs dotting the fields, whiter than their mothers' white, new life scattered across the farm and surrounding moor.

She can forget the deaths: this year's horror stories are laid on top of those from previous years, trodden into the cyclical, non-linear shape of her life, each week, each month writes over the same time as last year – and she has years of experience: mutations, creatures with two heads or only three legs, dead in the womb, which she's had to pull out piece by rotten stinking piece to save the mother, the foxes and their callous, multiple murders, the crows with their appetite for eyes – all these things lose their horror, become the round of her life, a successful life.

She dismantles the temporary enclosures, slings them on the flatbed hooked to the tractor. As she trundles sedately from gateway to gateway, she counts each small, snowy-white creature with four legs, a good appetite and growing and playing, as a member of her family.

217

JANE SITS IN the lee of the wall, her back to the granite.

It's early June, night falls slowly. She watches the sun lower demurely towards the long, jagged line of the horizon; it casts the gorse-dotted slopes in black relief against the pink-and-pearl coloured sky.

There's the distant, unintelligible sound of the radios fixed at various points around the fields, they interfere with the natural quiet, provide an incongruous background noise of voices, music jumbled together. It's as if she were on the balcony of a crowded city tenement block.

Across her knees lies Todd's newly renovated 12-bore, because for the third evening in a row, she's waiting for Chris Gilbey's dogs.

Jane pictures the routine: he feeds Joey and Max, the red setters, at around 6 p.m.; he lets them out for a final run at around 8 p.m.; from the house to the End Field takes five minutes, if they aren't distracted.

So: they'll arrive any time now, or not at all, and if not, she'll walk home with nothing to prove they've been worrying her sheep.

She waits.

On her left is the moor, visible through the five straps of the gate; in front is the End Field, where half a dozen lambs play King of the Castle. They gambol over a small promontory where the wall has slipped, sent a spillage of rocks and earth into the field; brothers, sisters and cousins try to knock each other from this miniature piece of high ground until it's their turn to be bounced.

The dusk hastens; still she waits.

From time to time she takes a nip at a flask.

Sleep threatens her vigil – a leaden fatigue drags at her eyes, her head nods dangerously low.

Then, they're there, as if working to a timetable; they leap

218

the boundary wall, graceful as deer, they barely touch the top of it, a dab of their paws only, to make sure they're clear. As always, they smile happily, this is a great night out, their long feathered tails wag from side to side like a form of propulsion.

Between the wall and the fence now, they scout around for some moments in the mystical shadow cast by the conifers in the windbreak. They're probably nagged by the smell of a fox; their paws crack on the bed of pine needles, twigs.

The ewes have already started to move away; nervous, they look in the dogs' direction, stamp their front feet, turn and face up to the danger with worried rattles in their throats before they move further off.

The lambs take no notice; irresponsible, disobedient, they continue to play on their hillock in the fading light.

Now the dogs finish in the windbreak, find their entrance into the fields, they scrape their long backs under the wire, back legs buckling so they can squeeze through, tongues loll from their mouths.

They lope easily over the ground. It's a beautiful sight, the copper of their coats, caught in the last reflections of the sun in the sky, against the bright green spring grass.

The sheep scatter.

Jane rises, draws the cartridge from her pocket; she breaks the gun, drops the charge in the barrel; it slips from her grip with a well-engineered *thunk*.

She closes the gun, holds it in both hands, watches as the setters gather pace, head for where the group of lambs scatter wildly in all directions, now, from their castle, finally awake to the alarms called by their mothers.

The dogs run as a pair, with the same purpose: they fix on a victim, course after it, twist and turn as it runs, bleats, seeks an escape.

Jane watches this down the barrel of her gun, she keeps the

stock pulled tight into her shoulder, aimed a fraction ahead of the front runner.

The lamb makes a straight gallop across open ground. The dogs catch up, bowl the lamb over – it cartwheels, all four legs describe a circle before it hits the ground, twists back to leap on its feet. The dogs have turned, catch it now before it even knows which way up it's facing.

Jane takes up the pressure on the trigger, anger like a short circuit to a well of aggression against the dogs but, more potently, their owner, who should have listened.

She watches as the lamb all but disappears beneath the waving tails of the red setters. Instinctively, they bite on its neck. When the lamb ceases to move, the dogs leave off, they've had their fun, they're not hungry – it's not long since they were fed.

Jane lowers the gun. She walks towards the dogs who now cast around, smelling the blood; they cover the patch of grass, scent back and forth. When they see Jane, they bound towards her happily, beg for praise, their smiles self-congratulatory. They're curious about the gun – interested because they're bred to work with them. She notices tufts of lamb's wool tacked to their jaws, here, there.

Jane doesn't say a word, doesn't scold them or recognise them; instead she takes a loop of baler twine from her pocket, cuts it in two, runs the string through their collars; they walk with her happily enough, although surprised at the new routine.

She takes the shortest distance to the fence, ties them against it tight enough to prevent them from twisting around to chew their way through the string, but low enough to allow them to lie down.

When she walks away, they start to bark, pull against the tethers, mystified.

Jane steels herself to go and check the lamb. She looks down on a scrap of wool, bone and nervous energy, now killed off; there's no outward sign of a wound, but here and there sparks of red stand on the oily wool, the angry, violent colour conspicuous in the thickening dusk.

Jane checks under its front leg, for a pulse, but there's none. She can feel the life drawn from it, as if it were her own.

JANE PICKS UP the gun, breaks it, withdraws the cartridge.

She climbs into the Defender: it's a sorry occasion, the christening of this G-reg Land Rover, to bring her on this expedition.

She leaves the dogs tied to the fence, drives back, gate after gate.

Fifteen minutes later, she's in the barn.

The only surviving bottle-fed lamb sleeps in his box, the *tic-tac* of his hooves on the concrete floor silent at last.

She's hauling back on her anger. It won't profit her, to lose her temper with Chris Gilbey when she tells him. She doesn't want to veer off the straight and narrow; neighbourly relations are at stake, *but, keep him in his box*.

She ferrets a glass from the washing-up bowl on the floor near the hot tap, pours herself a nip of the Glenarat cask-strength whisky, a present won from Chris Gilbey because she started living in the barn ahead of his moving into the house. It's strong enough to set her mouth on fire the moment it touches.

She wishes Chris Gilbey had listened to her. Why couldn't he have?

She aches not to have to walk over, tell him, lever their strained relationship further apart.

221

She climbs to her feet, goes to the door. Every time she pulls it open, she imagines her old house there, rebuilt from the ruin – that's if he bothers to appeal.

So: jealousy doesn't help.

He has to realise . . .

A different vehicle stands in front of the house at the moment: a burgundy, all-terrain Mitsubishi. She wonders what happened to the Saab.

Jane's boots crunch on the gravel; she can see now that this landscaping puts in place the first part of a loop which will restore the roundabout at the foot of the giant beech tree, if the big house is rebuilt.

Now she can look into her old kitchen: the usual candles sit on the windowsill, the flames multiplied further in the various stainless steel saucepans, temporarily suspended on a loop of string. The quantity of boxes and discarded packaging makes the place look like Santa's grotto.

She can hear music: an operatic voice climbs through the notes, accompanied by a feverish orchestral excitement.

She takes the brand new, black-iron door knocker, drops it against the stop; she notices it's shaped like a fox's tail. Inside, the music stops abruptly.

There's a pause, then he pulls the door open, he blinks, realises immediately: 'My dogs.'

He ducks, puts on boots, swears under his breath, '*Fuck, fuck, fuck.*'

He asks, 'Where are they?'

'In the End Field, I left them there, tied to the fence, so you could do the scolding.'

They climb into the Defender, he doesn't even comment on the new vehicle. She pulls the starter button; the diesel engine clatters into life.

Chris Gilbey swears again, 'Fuck, why didn't I listen to you . . . '

They lurch forwards. He asks in a steady, calm voice, 'Were they chasing sheep?'

She nods. 'Yes.'

They go through the stable yard, beyond into the fields. The Defender's engine grinds steadily as they bounce along, its headlights show the grass as coloured grey. They drive in silence.

Chris Gilbey – she's pleased to see – leaps out before the Defender stops, to open the gates.

When they reach the End Field, the headlights pick out the two red setters, Joey and Max, who eagerly welcome their arrival.

She thinks, Now he'll know.

Chris Gilbey looks at her, unembarrassed, but accepting the blame. 'This is my fault, more than theirs.'

She watches as he goes to the dogs, his figure ghostly white in the headlights. He doesn't greet Joey and Max or answer their manic demands for affection, merely scolds them, then unties the string.

The dogs jump free, delighted.

Chris Gilbey calls them angrily, takes them by their collars. His stiff, two-legged gait contrasts with the dogs' fluency, energy, youth.

He leads the dogs to the back door of the vehicle, incites them to jump up, which they do, glad to be in human company after their bizarre confinement.

Jane and Chris Gilbey climb back into their seats, their movements identically matched, the doors close together – *slam*.

She grips the steering wheel, because it isn't over yet. She says, 'I want to show you something else.'

She engages drive, swings the Defender around in a circle until the headlights pick up the forlorn figure of the dead lamb, brilliant white except for its black socks and ears.

The engine ticks over steadily.

He says quietly, 'Shit', his face blank. Behind them, in the back of the vehicle, the red setters pant happily, pad about their new cell.

Chris Gilbey is white with anger; in the minimal light from the Defender's instrument panel, she can see the fine points of hair tremble on his collar. He asks, 'Wait here a moment will you?'

He hops out, goes around to the back, takes both dogs by their collars.

Jane hears them wince: he is rough, they know something's wrong.

Next, Jane sees his figure walk in the lights of the Defender, the dogs reluctant, digging in their toes.

He reaches the lamb and commands one dog to sit; the other he pulls by the scruff, plants its nose into the corpse of the lamb. His mouth moves and she hears angry words; his hand comes down once, twice, on the animal's rump. The red setter shrinks from him, yelps. He then takes enough time to make the first dog sit, stay ... before he punishes the second one.

Then it's over.

Jane gets out, meets him halfway; she explains, 'I'll just go and dump the body.'

He nods curtly. 'OK.'

She feels a blush of guilt, putting him through this, then it's replaced by anger: it's his own fault.

She walks to the lamb, picks it up by the back legs, carries it to the fence, lobs it into the windbreak, where it lands with a thud; by morning, it will have been partly eaten, within a week or two it will have disappeared, a litter of wool and bones the only marker.

Jane climbs back into the vehicle and they set off for home.

As they trundle back over the fields, Chris Gilbey continues his apology; he is not embarrassed or weak, merely accepts his fault, works to retrieve himself.

Jane holds her tongue, she wants to let the event sink in. This is her victory.

CHRIS GILBEY LEADS the way indoors to her old house; as before, Jane is awed by the strangeness of it, she notices new concrete floors, pink plaster rises halfway up the walls, a litter of cardboard boxes is piled in the hall, the chimney breast has been opened out with a new granite lintel bearing the weight, fitted tight into it is a brand new, cream-and-green Aga.

If he's out to rebuild the ruin, what's this going to be, the servants' quarters?

Chris Gilbey sits at the beechwood, square table; she notices the cardboard has gone, it has green legs. He was a regular visitor to Exeter's January sales, then.

Already, he unfolds a chequebook. Perversely, she's embarrassed, as if this were her fault.

As he smooths back the cover he asks, 'I can never remember what day it is.'

She answers, 'The fourth of June.'

He bends for a while, to write the date, her name – and then he looks up, gives her the familiar, beady look. Without preamble he asks, 'How much d'you reckon a lamb will fetch when you take it to market, eventually?'

She mentions the standard amount, which, since the onset

of the BSE crisis in beef, rose by a third before it dropped back by a quarter.

Chris Gilbey concentrates on the cheque; his pen dips to write. Then he stops, looks up again and asks, 'How many lambs have you lost this year?'

'In total, so far, I'd say a dozen.'

Chris Gilbey replies, 'I'm going to play God', then he adds, 'bring them back to life, economically speaking.'

Even as he scribbles his signature, Jane understands; when he holds out the cheque for her to take, she protests.

He cuts her off: 'I want to cover your losses, wholesale.'

She's incredulous. 'That's crazy, just because − ' but he insists, 'Go on.'

'I'm not taking that.'

The cheque wriggles again, 'You are.'

She replies, utterly certain, 'I am not.'

His elbows rest on the table; he tugs at both ends of the cheque, looks at it, then at her.

He fixes her with his calculating gaze; his teeth appear, rest on his bottom lip.

An age passes.

He unblinkingly considers the stalemate. Then his voice drops in volume; Jane has to strain to hear, although his gaze remains steadily fixed on her. 'Listen,' he murmurs, 'I have made a quite serious mistake. I don't often make a mistake, I certainly don't like making them.'

She wants to slap him, knock him off whatever cloud he's sitting on; it should be enough for him to be an ordinary human being, instead of playing at this higher form of gamesmanship. He's out to turn this around, make it his triumph instead of his mistake.

Then he delivers each word carefully but quietly: 'I don't *just* want to retrieve lost ground, I want to make progress.'

226

He waits, looks for her response.

'It's all right,' she insists, 'it's good enough for me, your writing out the cheque here and now, I wish everyone who ran over an animal on the road would do the same, you've more than made up for it . . . '

Suddenly she's certain it's true: with this offer of substantial extra payment he's out to make her feel like *she's* the criminal, the one who's profited unreasonably.

He gazes at her steadily. 'Make me a happy man, take it . . .' He holds out the cheque.

Jane suggests, 'Tell you what.'

'What?'

'I've had three lambs die, from either foxes or dogs . . . '

Chris Gilbey understands, even before she's finished. 'I get you.' He tears up the cheque, starts to write another and he adds, 'Given they might well have been my dogs who were responsible, it's a good reckoning.'

He holds out the revised cheque: 'Except, call it four lambs' worth, it's been a good year.'

She can't believe it: this man can't take losing, whatever the game is.

She takes it.

'Done?' he asks.

'Done.'

Jane thinks, Still my victory.

THE FRONT DOOR of the barn is open, sunlight streams in, liquid honey in colour, to reveal motes of dust and pollen swimming in the viscous air. The heat which has had Jane working in her underwear most of the day is unfelt in here;

227

the thick walls and double-glazed windows give the barn the coolness of a cellar.

The door to the back is also open, to create a through movement of air, and out here a line of Jane's washing hangs stiff, square, dried in double-quick time; the sun sucked out the moisture in minutes.

Roo stands in the middle of the undeveloped, open-plan interior of the barn; aimlessly he looks into the corners, shifts around a half-circle, his nose twitches.

Jane kneels to pet him. His coat has even more lustre, now, it's glossy, plus there's another improvement: he asks for his food, comes to find her at teatime, wears his enquiring look, as he used to, rather than waiting for it to be pushed under his nose.

Yesterday, she saw him make an attempt to engage in play. Billy made his usual pass: a growl, a nip at Roo's ear to encourage him to romp as they used to. Roo gave a hop, twisted his head closer to the ground, invited Billy to carry on, for the first time in ages. Billy didn't notice – he'd already passed by – but Jane saw.

She strokes behind his ears, gazes into the familiar eyes which hold wisdom, instinctive knowledge. How much younger will the drugs make him – next, he'll be a puppy.

After his petting Roo wanders outside into the sunshine, lies down, huff, puff, he gives his usual groan.

If she looks at what happened last year with a narrow view, she had to sell her house to pay for Roo's drugs; it takes her breath away. To have kept him alive, she has to box and cox with Chris Gilbey, now.

Jane thinks, Move on. The line of tasks is bolted on to the front of her life, the same but different: push the windfall branches off the rooves of the stables, wire-brush the corrugated iron ready to be painted, Bounty's calf is weak; she has

228

to arrange for a calf-feeder, take the milk from Bounty, she has to hive off the calf called Ambrosia, who's scouring.

Tomorrow will be dry, sunny.

JANE HEADS FOR the horizon, Lady blowing on the uphill slope, the meadow pipits and skylarks singing on the wing, conspicuous in their looped flight but impossible to trace when they come to ground – silent, invisible.

Ahead, Billy ranges easily over the rough ground, delighted with the expedition. It's too long and hot a haul for old Roo; even with the new youthfulness granted him, he knew to stay behind.

Jane heads past the deserted ruin of Cleave Farm, sidetracks the barely discernible remains of Browne's House – a square keep or two marked by little more than a six-inch rise in the level of turf, a trio of stones just hanging together. This Farmer Browne – he was like a storybook character – brought his young wife up here three hundred years ago, to keep her from the eyes of strangers. It was the right place to come.

She tops the hill, gains a new horizon. She pulls her binoculars from inside her coat; the twin circles occlude as she adjusts the eyepieces.

There's a cow missing.

She scans back and forth; the moor runs past – a jumble of rock-strewn slopes, an inland cliff, a valley, an upland bog, the cradle for a river.

Nothing.

She heads into the high plateau which sits like a plate in the middle of Dartmoor. The names are legendary: Cut Hill, Fox Tor Mire, Cranmere Pool.

She heads north-west, the sun risen behind her, just to one

side; Jane can feel it warm the back of her neck under her crash helmet. As the heat of the day is slowly dialled upwards by this yellow furnace behind her, the peaty smell of the country mixes with the scent of the horse, familiar to her from her two-hour rides every morning to find the cows, because they stray for miles in summer, given the sudden, luxurious fodder available on the moor.

Cranmere Pool. Lady now walks with some trepidation. The peat is sliced across with crevasses as deep as two men, where the waterlogged soil has dried out, shrunk, torn itself open to reveal flashes of white, smooth bedrock at the bottom. Jane wheels Lady around them.

This place used to be a lake, then the lake slowly filled with vegetable matter, became a bog; thataway, a terrier was sent down after a fox, somewhere on the lip of the pool, the terrier scraped, dug, got itself stuck, the men took shovels to dig out the terrier, they tapped into the pool and within a couple of months the water drained out.

So now it's a seasonal morass, wet in winter, dry in summer.

The next time Jane lifts her binoculars, she's on the edge of Langton Scarp; the cow is stuck in the cradle bog, below.

Jane murmurs, 'There.'

She takes up Lady's reins; the leather is slippery with sweat, she shortens their length to keep closer contact with Lady's mouth and prepares for the steep descent. Lady smells the urgency, worries the bit with her teeth, lifts her nose to pull the reins free but then accepts Jane's control.

The slope falls beneath them, crowded with boulders, tufts of gorse. With each jump, Lady grunts, the impact travels up her front legs, into her chest but this is her only complaint; she remains sure-footed, correctly gathered under Jane's weight.

230

Together they bounce down the treacherous slope like a kicked football. The dog pours after her.

At the shore of the mire, Jane dismounts, unclips her chinstrap, drops the crash helmet on the ground. She unfastens the ropes from the back of the saddle, dandles them off one arm.

She calls Billy near, commands him to sit; his thin frame trembles with excitement at the unusual adventure.

Now: she'll drop a pair of ropes around the cow's head.

Jane heads into the mire, the ropes hung over one arm. She reads the signs: this bog is the same as prevail on most of the upland plateaux in the middle of Dartmoor, when shallow basins of granite filled with water sat in extensive, stagnant lakes and, as with Cranmere Pool, the lakes clogged with waterweed, sedge grass, bogbean, which rotted to become vast tracts of peat bog. Unlike when she faces up to the quaking bogs, Jane can't see any sign of the patchwork of brilliant green carpets of moss stitched together with seams of rushes; the moss will hold a man's weight but to venture on to it is akin to walking on a bowl of rice pudding – the skin ripples away as the liquid absorbs the impact, underneath is a peaty mire, prevented from draining into nearby rivers by banks of gravel or condensed vegetation.

This has been a dropping summer – wet. Jane knows to stick to the hillocks, any knob of land which can support the smallest growth of heather or rushes will carry her weight.

She angles back and forth, heads towards her cow, while behind her she hears Billy's cry, and now she's close enough to see the disturbed bed where the cow has floundered for days, churned up a morass; with each lunge to escape, she's dug a hole for herself to lie in, deeper. Her long periods of rest have allowed the peat to settle close around her limbs, making each new effort more tiring.

231

In an arc determined by the length of her neck, the reach of her tongue, every blade of vegetation has disappeared and her mouth is black from where she's chewed the wet peat for its moisture; without food or drink, the cow has lost the will to live, now she's resting her head on the ground, for all the world like she wants to be here, this is her place, it's comfortable.

Jane pauses to catch her breath, decide on tactics.

Behind her Billy's bark ceases, which leaves only the calls of tiny birds.

It's unlikely she'll become trapped, but the possibility scares her, she's alone on this remote upland, helpless, only the dumb animals to witness any disaster. However, it isn't quicksand; the weight-to-volume ratio isn't on the side of the bogs where bipeds are concerned. They can take off your boots, give you a sticky hour or so, but it's the heavy quadrupeds – cows, ponies – who become locked.

She removes her boots, socks, trousers. She picks up her ropes, finds the ends, in each one makes a loop, ties them off with a reef knot. Then she approaches her cow.

The silt is cool, refreshes her feet; she sinks to her knees and so leans on her hands to crawl forward, her weight distributed evenly, quickly she breaks through and she's black to her thighs and elbows.

The cow lifts its head to observe her, its eyes widen for a moment, display the whites, like a warning, but obscured by the crowd of flies which home in on the sticky liquid expelled from the corners. Her tail lies on the ground like a discarded rope, except it twitches back and forth. Her spine rises above the ground like a black ridge, almost part of the bog itself.

This life and death situation is peaceful: the sun stares unmoved, the meadow pipits and skylarks continue their singing in flight, a kestrel tracks a rising air current, sheep are pinned to the far slope, Lady stands, her reins tied up.

Jane waits to make her final approach until the cow's nose sinks to the ground again; her show of interest dies.

Jane clambers through the peat, stations herself close enough to reach its head but only at full stretch.

Then she unhooks one of the ropes, keeps the built loop in one hand while she flings the other end away from her, towards Lady.

Now she'll arrange the rope behind the ears of this cow, where it can pull safely against the cranial ridge at the back of the neck – she'll have to work her way closer.

The peat sucks at her bare legs; it takes all her strength to drag them clear, make a step.

She fights her way to the cow's shoulder, then escapes from the mud by climbing on to the cow's back as though to ride it out.

The truth is, if it starts to thrash around, she's safer astride the animal than anywhere else.

The cow's hide burns in the sun, the hair is gritty and coarse under her as she settles. A groan escapes from the cow, perhaps at the indignity of having someone climb on its back; it blows roughly at the ground, whereas Jane's breath comes fast, light – she's anxious at the emergency, her naked legs are vulnerable.

Then she leans forward on to its neck, dangles the loop in front of its nose, catches it, reels it in. So: she takes the second rope. In the same way, she leans down the cow's neck, to hook the rope under its chin. As she does so, the cow grunts, throws up its head, Jane tilts to one side, swears in alarm, her arms and legs tighten around the animal's neck but she stays put in order to take advantage of the cow's head lifting to drop the noose neatly under its jaw.

Then, with the cow's second heave, Jane's weight is compromised too much; she's thrown into the mud on its left-hand side.

She hits the ground already struggling to pull herself clear and, like an alarm, she can hear Billy's worried cry repeat from the edge of the mire.

The cow now dredges up its last reserves of energy to try and walk out; as its head weaves back and forth it catches Jane in the shoulder, pushes her sideways.

The second blow crashes into her middle back, knocks the breath from her body.

Her legs are stuck, she wants to stay upright yet at the same time she has to avoid the blows from behind.

The cow's head is a heavy, blunt instrument wielded on the end of a powerful neck as it repeatedly thumps into her back – she can feel the bony eye socket against her ribcage, her spine, her ribs again, as the cow keeps up a furious bellow, scared of its slow death.

Moments later, the attack finishes.

Billy keeps up his alarm cry, dashes back and forth, tries a foot here and there, sinks in the mud, then withdraws.

Lady is grazing.

Still pegged halfway down the scarp is the scattering of sheep. She watches them from the corner of her eye.

The cow looks daft, with its mantle of ropes.

Billy falls silent, staring, his tail waves tentatively.

Jane pulls one leg clear, then the other. She feels the bruises on her back, her hip, a knife-like pain catches her ribs.

She walks on her knees, ploughs on, she reaches the tussock where her clothes wait, hauls herself on and for a while she sits, catches her breath.

The cow rests, forlorn.

Jane takes stock: she's covered in black mud; she can taste it in her mouth, the sun dries it on her face – the skin tightens.

Jane takes her shirt off, uses it to wipe the mud off, even works the cotton between her toes, rubs at the grittiest particles, leaves herself clean enough to put on her trousers, socks, the leather Doc Marten boots she wears in summer, then she opens out the shirt, rubs it against the lone clump of heather which shares her tussock, finally spreads it in the sun to dry.

For a short while, she lets the sun warm her bruised frame, her closed eyes are circles of pink, the sun is that strong; consciously she tells herself to relax, find out if she herself is all right, she gives herself permission, she's more important than the cow.

To this end, she circumnavigates her internal organs, visits each hurt to judge whether there's a broken rib or damage to her back. She tests her vertebrae, teasing the pain to find its boundaries, its severity.

The rib surprises her with an unpredictable stabbing which is as likely to happen when she's still as when she's twisting or bending, it paralyses her for seconds at a time.

Jane heads back, slowly, picks up the tails of the ropes as she goes.

When she's reunited with Billy at the edge of the bog, he gives her a furious licking, dashes back and forth like a mad thing, pleased. Pain tweaks her nerves, spoils her response, halts her breath, while Billy spins like a muck-spreader to throw off the black glue that's stuck to all four legs and his underside.

'Right.'

Jane taps the toes of her boots against the firm ground, watches the wet peat slide off – the smell is similar to charcoal, but with an undertow of ammonia.

She tugs at Lady's head.

Reluctantly, with a backward lean of her ears, Lady agrees to turn around.

Jane unbuckles the saddle, rests it on its horn, then removes the girth entirely. She uses a sheet knot to fix the end of one rope to the girth, just behind the buckle, then walks it around the front of Lady, picks up the other rope, ties it, leaving enough to toss over Lady's withers, fix it to the other side, prevent the girth from dropping to the ground.

So it's like a harness, the girth across Lady's heart.

She encourages her horse to step forward, take up the slack; now the ropes are taut from her flanks to the head of the cow.

Jane takes Lady's bridle, makes a gentle click in the back of the throat, to encourage her to walk forward.

It's the wrong horse, wrong ropes, everything wrong about this – she wishes she had a tractor.

Lady takes a pace, feels the drag behind her, she sashays sideways, then steadies.

Jane clicks her forwards again.

Behind her, Jane can see the cow's muzzle stretch, her eyes roll to the whites, trying to see what's happening.

Jane drives Lady more strongly, watches her foreleg cock against the solid ground, the hoof cutting in, taking the strain.

She urges, 'Come on, Lady.'

There's a solid drag on the rope; Jane takes her sideways a few paces, gives her some ground to cover so she can work up an appetite for progress.

She wants to twist the cow's weight further out of the bog – like unscrewing it. She arcs Lady back and forth, pushes her forwards; the cow's neck is stretched to breaking, following Lady's drag on the ropes.

Billy barks at the goings-on; Jane hopes the noise will frighten the cow further.

The enormous strength of the horse, even one as finely built as Lady, should be enough, if only the cow would help herself.

Jane suddenly leaves go of Lady's bridle, follows the twin ropes back down to where the mire begins and as she walks, anger rises in her breast at the dumb animal's attitude; red faced, she shouts across the bog, 'Come on you dumb piece of cow shit, work for it!'

She burns with determination.

Driven by Billy's insane cry, she walks back to Lady, brings down the flat of her hand hard on the horse's rump: 'Gee up!'

Lady snorts, bounces forwards; the ropes whip tight.

Jane leans, hauls on the bridle.

The cow plays on the end of the line, suddenly, like a wounded bear.

Jane sees Lady's legs quiver, step forward; for a moment she thinks the impetus will end, and she shouts – more at herself or the situation – 'Come *on!*'

She brings her hand down again on Lady's rump, twice, drives her on, then leans on the bridle. She tries to see past Lady to the cow, but instead notices Lady's hocks buckle underneath her as she drives the whole apparatus – herself, ropes, cow – forwards.

Jane shouts, 'Yeeeeess!'

The cow sleighs out of the hole she's dug for herself – and then lies inert on a ridge of firmer land within the mire.

Jane thinks, Success.

Lady trembles. Billy watches, ears pricked.

Jane's temper calms.

Then euphoria steals over her as the exhausted animal's tongue snakes out, a pink muscle, curls around a swatch of bog cotton grass and eats.

In a while the cow will stand; all that'll remain is to guide her out of the area, move her to some water.

Jane soothes Lady's head, wipes the sweat from her neck and flanks; soon, they'll ride home.

Sure enough, minutes later, the cow heaves herself to her feet, still up to her belly in peat.

Jane then handles Lady's bridle, walks her forwards and to the side, pulling the cow towards the soggy but passable path.

The cow plunges, is snagged several times, but the team pushes on until she sits unconcerned, ungrateful, on the edge of the mire, as if nothing had happened.

Soon, she'll seek water, push on back to the herd.

Jane unclips the makeshift harness from around Lady's shoulders, pokes the sheet knots apart. She buckles the girth back on to the saddle, coils the ropes between her thumb and elbow, tacks Lady up. They ride home under the dispassionate, yellow eye of the sun; the gravity of the landscape holds down a clear blue sky.

JANE'S DETERMINED TO make it all right, between herself and Chris Gilbey, because now the setters are always cooped up, he only takes them out on the lead.

She wants to try and make it neighbourly between them, so she offers to take the boys for a ride on Tuppence – what worked for the father might do all right for the sons.

Around five o'clock, when the heat of the day has passed but before the midges begin to bite, Jane prepares.

She doesn't bother with a saddle, so that both children can ride back to back; she gives the older one, Alan, a leg-up and he sits facing forwards. Chris Gilbey lifts Jamie, plants him facing Tuppence's tail.

The boys are delighted, Jane notices their first smiles.

They're on their way.

They amble through the Top Field; Chris Gilbey leads Tuppence, Jane walks alongside to catch hold of them if they should begin to fall.

The boys smile, chatter.

Then, out of nowhere, a military jet flies over so low they can see the whites of the pilot's eyes, taste the paraffin fuel. The sound wave drums into the ground – shock.

The boys scream, Jane flinches, Chris Gilbey ducks involuntarily, hisses a curse between his teeth, then turns to shout at the plane, 'I'll have that pilot's *ass!*'

Yet, Tuppence doesn't move a muscle.

Afterwards, they laugh in astonishment at that.

When the jet had passed over, Jane noticed the same thing as before: the ends of Chris Gilbey's sandy hair, a neat ring of points around his collar, trembled, for a moment or two, in anger.

She knows, one day, she'll face that.

THEN, WITHOUT WARNING, Todd emerges from his long hibernation, in triumph – the Infernal Machine is ready.

The Top Field was the first to be mown – razed to a stubble, suddenly of a yellow colour, the underside of the grass revealed, anaemic from lack of light, it will turn green again within a week or two, but now there's a sufficient number of the large-size, round bales of silage – and Todd fetches Jane.

He shouts down the yard, 'The Infernal Machine . . . !'

As it turns out, Chris Gilbey and his two sons are there as well; the whole party follows Todd as he blasts around the bottom of the wood store in the enormous four-wheel-drive

Fiat tractor, reverses smartly to address the entrance to the shed . . .

There is a cheerful, carnival atmosphere, the boys follow the tractor purposefully as if they were the farmers and Todd an employee.

Chris Gilbey wears a sunhat, dark glasses, his sandals click against the soles of his feet.

The roar of the Fiat drops to a steady tickover.

Todd jumps from the cab; his long hair parachutes, briefly, then, walking his headbanger walk, he nods into the darkened shed and shouts, 'Let's go, then.'

Jamie runs to catch up.

As Jane approaches, she can hear Todd giving the boys tasks, to include them, as he fishes low enough with the hydraulics to pick up the little trailer . . .

'What's it do?' asks Jamie.

'Wait and see.'

'It's an engine,' reports Alan.

'An engine?' answers Todd. 'This ain't no engine, this here's an *artistic creation.*'

Chris Gilbey snorts with amusement.

Jamie's struck by it; he repeats after Todd, 'An artistic creation!'

Todd swings into the tractor cab, the Fiat's tickover jumps. The children flee.

The whole assembly is pulled from the shed: its first outing.

Todd keeps an eye on the variables: the children held at a safe distance, the upright jinked unconventionally sideways to snare him, the height of the lean-to in front of the shed. The power steering gives him a quick, precise exit; he roars off around the wood store back the other way. The machine jumps erratically behind the Fiat on its custom-made trailer.

Jane, Chris Gilbey, Alan and Jamie follow the Fiat as it rolls through the cow yard, into the Top Field; it curves left, then runs backwards.

By the time the others have caught up, the machine is in position, uncoupled. It looks like something out of a *Mad Max* movie.

Todd, his long hair flouncing, primes the diesel.

The boys clamour with questions – what does it do, what bit is that for?

Chris Gilbey lets them run on; he stays behind with Jane.

Todd says, 'Now then', and the boys stand each side of him as he rests on his heels, so he's closer to their level. 'Pin back your earflaps and I'll tell you how it works.' He points at the block of cast aluminium at the rear of the trailer. 'Engine,' he says, 'cannibalised out of an old refrigeration unit', then his hand moves towards the front of the machine. 'And this one's the business end, the wrapping machine ... ' He pats a vertical column of black plastic: 'See this, what looks like a roll of extra-large bin-liners, here?'

The boys nod.

'This is plastic sheeting, you'll see those bales' – he points at the rolls of grass stationed nearby – 'you'll see them lot whipped around, meanwhile the plastic binds them up till they're airtight.'

Todd straightens, walks them around to the other side of the Infernal Machine, his hair floating in his wake.

Chris Gilbey and Jane stay a tactful yard or two shy of the boys, to give them the impression they're on their own with Todd. Jane wonders if it could always be like this – cheerful, sunny, uncomplicated.

'Now this,' says Todd, 'is the clever bit.' He holds on to a two-by-four upright, a mast. 'See on top there – ' Todd points – 'there's a light I grafted on to the top of the pole, taken from a breakdown rig', and he teases a thin pair of coloured wires

241

clipped to the mast: 'this is a remote control system, taken out of a set of electric garage doors, so's I can work it from inside the cab of the tractor there – ' he points to the Fiat.

'Now,' he marshals both boys off to one side, 'go back ten paces, don't move from this spot, and you'll see what happens' – Todd winks at Jane – 'stay put: remember we're in uncharted waters.'

Jane plays along, calls out, 'God knows what's going to happen, if Todd's had anything to do with it.'

'Exactly,' adds Todd, 'this is untried, untested technology, this is. You saw what happened to the space shuttle that time, stand well back is my advice.'

He winks at Jane again – and with her smile, he bounces back to the Fiat.

Jane edges closer to Chris Gilbey to explain: 'Before, it would have taken an extra tractor, just to sit there and drive the wrapping machine, so he's saved himself the use of one tractor, plus, with the remote control, he can pull off the whole operation without getting in and out of his cab.'

Then Todd's running towards them, he pushes a camera at Jane. 'Occasion not to be missed.'

Now, conscious of his four spectators, so driving with impressive speed and accuracy, Todd lowers the grab on the front of the tractor, embraces the first bale of fresh cut grass.

Jane's face is screwed up behind Todd's camera, ready.

Just as Todd lifts the bale, plants it on the bed of the wrapping machine, she takes the first picture. Through the viewfinder, she sees Todd's arm as he reaches up to where the remote control is clipped to his sun visor.

Immediately, the yellow light starts flashing at the top of the mast, the refrigeration unit climbs from tickover to its working speed, the automatic clutch bites, the bale of grass gathers speed, quickens its pirouette.

Jamie and Alan break free, gain a yard or two – with the noise from the Infernal Machine added to that of the Fiat, their mouths move in near soundless cries of excitement.

The black polyurethane is pulled from the reel, stretches around the bale's circumference. As it turns, a thump from the hydraulic piston shifts the bale around a notch at a time on the other axis.

Jane takes more pictures as the grass disappears under its PVC coat; the noise this close is deafening, they can't hear themselves speak.

This is Todd's success – and Jane prays that, yes, it always will be like this, a sense of progress, work, achievement – is it happiness?

With his shorts, his T-shirt, long curly hair, Todd really does look like a wild man.

Half a minute later, it's done, the knife drops on the PVC, the bed of the machine tilts, rolls the bale on to the ground, tightly encased in black plastic. Todd is ready to plant the second bale, afterwards grab the finished one, stack it on the hardcore.

Jane, Chris Gilbey and his sons stand in a line, to watch how the work goes.

THAT SAME EVENING, in the quiet, cool interior of her barn, Jane can't shake off the noise of the Infernal Machine.

She hears it, steadily ticking over, in her mind, as if it had somehow continued with a life of its own.

She shakes her head, but it's still there; perhaps standing so close has given her a temporary tinnitus, she thinks.

In every other respect, her hearing is normal: she can hear herself lever out the dog food for Billy and Roo, the tiny snap of the tablets as she breaks them into halves to make up Roo's intake of diuretic and painkiller.

There's the *dink* and scrape of the chipped enamel bowls as she sets them down some distance apart on the concrete floor.

She presses her hands to the sides of her head; the noise disappears, almost.

She can hear her own breath.

She lets go – and pulls open the back door to go into the yard, catch the last of the sun before it disappears behind the stand of trees and the outbuildings.

The noise persists; it's louder. She guesses, then, that Todd must have returned to adjust the Infernal Machine ready for the ongoing harvest, tomorrow.

She wants to see him: it was his success, today, he worked with spirit, ingenuity.

From her back yard, she climbs easily over the fence into the paddock behind the stables which also, further along, encloses the sheep pens.

She cuts across, climbs in and out of fenced enclosures, until she's completed her short cut to the Top Field.

As she goes, the noise stays with her, yet she can see from some distance away that the Infernal Machine stands idle, the tractor is parked up, there's no sign of Todd.

The noise is more distant.

She turns in different directions, but it's difficult to tell where the sound's coming from; it seems to issue from the pile of wrapped bales, from the side of the stock barn . . . she's listening to echoes.

She returns via the more conventional route: through the stable yard. The stables themselves are empty; the horses enjoy the nights outdoors.

Jane notices the noise is louder.

Near the bottom of the stable yard, she knows it's true: the dull, methodical drumming of a diesel engine comes from in or around Chris Gilbey's house.

She recognises, with a lurch, this new sensation that comes whenever she thinks of his name: it's like being lifted then swiftly dropped by a wave of disappointment, dislike.

She arrives at the patch of land behind his house; for some time now it's sported a small shed angled into its furthest corner and this would be to house the gas or oil tanks, she presumed, but now she stops, looks to where the sound unmistakably comes from, inside the shed – because she knows what's happened: it's a diesel generator, to give him electrical power.

JANE PASSES THROUGH the gate which divides the stable yard from the front yard, then she walks along the edge of the gravel.

She stops at the path which leads to her old house, glances in the window – and there's proof: a five-amp flex hangs from the ceiling; on the end of it is a naked lightbulb.

She glimpses the two boys, Jamie and Alan, bat back and forth, unaware of her. She can see their mouths move continuously although she can't hear what they're saying; it's like a repeat performance of their antics when they shouted unheard to celebrate the triumph of the Infernal Machine.

The electric light momentarily brightens their flaxen hair.

Jane feels a blush of anger crawl from her neck up.

JANE RETURNS TO her half-built barn conversion.

The dogs welcome her; she feels herself sway in disbelief.

It's a warm night: she sits in her familiar armchair dressed only in a T-shirt and shorts; her Doc Marten boots are dusty, worn, planted squarely on the concrete floor.

She listens to the generator; how loud is it?

Not very, is the answer, but it doesn't have to be, she'll never grow used to it.

This is the end.

What will it take, legal action? She'll have to tread carefully; isn't it true, it's a difficult thing, complaining about noise pollution? She recalls stories from the television, of bitter arguments lasting for years, people had to keep notebooks, buy a meter that measured decibels ...

Yet, it's not that loud.

But he must have got planning permission?

She glances around the unfitted interior of the barn: there's been a hiatus in its development, she's waiting for some drawings which she commissioned from the architect in Exeter, Elizabeth Jennings.

She fetches a cup of cider, drains it almost in one go.

JANE SWITCHES ON the television and turns up the volume: a shaved head talks earnestly, a Negro girl wriggles to music on a purple stage, pinned by coloured lights.

She watches for an hour.

Then she slowly thumbs down the volume button, until underneath the sound of the television, she hears again the faint roll of the generator.

So: it wasn't a bad dream.

When does it stop? When he's turned off the last light, gone to bed?

She pictures Chris Gilbey upstairs in her old room – and drinks more water, to sober up.

Then she's charged with a sudden energy, she has to escape, right now.

Roo lies at her feet; she bends to pet him, aggressively pulls at his age-weary body to encourage him back to life; she calls, 'Come on, come on ... '

Billy doesn't need help, he's there already, licking at Roo's face, his front legs dance in agitation.

Jane switches off the television, pulls on a coat, opens the front door into darkness and strides down the moonlit drive; the dogs scout ahead, surprised.

Roo's tail windmills as he runs, stiffly.

The night air is chill; to answer it, she hurries, stirs her circulation.

She comes out from under the tunnel of greenery overhanging the drive, across the cattle-grid, over the bridge.

The stream empties through this neck of the moor with a sinister, tickling noise at night.

A harvest moon shows the way.

Caistor Rock is a black shape against the blue-ink sky dotted with stars, the ground rolls in front of her, lumpy with gorse, as she follows the path between white, staring boulders, up towards the giant granite plug.

Billy bounces ahead, while Roo walks stodgily at her heel, now it's uphill.

Bats trip blindly through the air, radar bouncing in all directions, as they pass to and from the deserted tin mine drilled into the side of the hill which they've made their home. Come October, they'll hibernate.

Jane walks herself into the situation: he's installed a generator, the first thing is to find out if he has permission, then what she can do about it.

247

One answer is to pay enough to bring a mains supply up here.

Yet, she smells danger, with Chris Gilbey, real danger. This could escalate so fast, turn hateful, there's a lack of gravity holding her on the ground, suddenly, it's worrying, she's light-headed, could lose her temper in an instant. Is she over-reacting?

She makes a detour: escorted by her two dogs, she swings to the right, the slope easier now as she only just broaches the contour line.

She heads into the dark mass of sky and landscape: a moonlit summer night.

She tracks along the narrow sheep path towards the prehistoric stone row which lines up outside the corner of her farm: it points, broken-toothed, towards Langstone, a half-mile over the horizon.

She's drunk, full of a sense of portent, her nerves jump at the prospect of visiting this ghostly place, at night, in the shrouded landscape, but she coaches herself not to mind: the long-lived souls who she might believe throng hereabouts are benign to her.

At the top of the stone row, she drops purposefully into the bottom of the kistvaen, sits on the lip, hands folded in her lap.

Still for a moment, she concentrates on finding the noise of the generator – and receives it, even from this far away, it's a murmur . . . She stubs her toe into the ground, to eclipse the noise.

This prehistoric site was only intended for the interment of ashes, merely an indentation lined with rocks . . . and her feet rest on the granite floor, rounded toecaps almost touching the other side. A small heather plant grows between the stones.

She asks for guidance but none comes.

To her right, twin rows of menhirs form a processional

route, but only for summer hikers now, rather than those illiterate, hide-wearing savages who were trying to hide the burnt remains of their dead, covering them with stones so they'd never return.

She pushes herself to her feet, climbs out of the kistvaen.

As she heads up the hill towards Caistor, her breath becomes louder.

Sheep gleam like white flags in the dark, they move on invisible legs, away from the dogs.

Jane thinks, We're their predators.

When she reaches Caistor, she dawdles around the base of the rock.

At night, the monolithic, unchanging stature of the tor asserts itself without fuss; it's not that it doesn't alter, the changes to its bulk are constant but only emphasise how long its position, its character have remained unchanged.

Jane wants to remain true to herself, equally.

Yet, change has to be a constant visitor at one's side; if not dramatic or instantaneous, then wearing as a trickle of water digs a trench, over the years, in the ground it lies on.

The wind – over centuries funnelled just as it is now – moved gravel and dust in a small circle which wore a small depression into a softer patch of granite on the top of Caistor; frost action created heavier, more corrosive debris which in turn ground the depression deeper, into a rain-filled hole which might drown a child.

Maybe in just such a way – slowly, organically as it were – she ought to let any changes at Latchworthy grow. There's no worry, is there, she'll get used to the noise, or they'll bring up the mains supply.

Can she keep her calm?

For one reason or another, she can't get Chris Gilbey out of her head. It's not only what he does, but the way that he does it, with manipulation, deceit, not talking to her . . . she'll never like him.

She veers to the side of Caistor, finds her way between two massive ledges of rock. She reaches the point where they scissor together, so lifts herself up, the arms of her coat rub as she leaps, clambers around the three or four folds of granite; there's the scrape of Billy's nails on the bare rock.

Hand over hand, she claws her way to the top of the granite outcrop.

Billy joins her; Roo is unable.

From this point, by moonlight, the moor surrounds her, deep, unspoilt. The dark sky caps it.

She drops to a sitting position on the rock surface, rests an elbow on one knee, her other arm around Billy who sits adjacent.

Her breath eases; then silence folds her closer. It's akin to vertigo, the sense that the world has an edge which she might fall off, an obscurity that is indefinable, bottomless.

The view takes her breath away.

She listens deep into this silence and hears nothing – but also, sees no sign.

Now SHE'S PAYING hand over fist for the vet.

O'Bryan comes back with the X-rays of Lady's leg, it'll be a conservative treatment programme, maybe some ultrasound, prevent any sort of stress on that quarter, no running, no situations in which she might put her feet down wrong, complete rest, zero excitement . . .

Jane feels unreasonable anger at Lady – only for a moment – because it's easy to blame the horse for being injured.

She thinks, It's to escape from the blame herself.

The image springs to mind as clearly as in a slowed-down TV picture: her hand came down on Lady's rump, the horse jumped forward, the ropes whipped tight – then Jane glimpsed it: Lady's hock quivered ...

'Strained tendons,' says O'Bryan, 'are buggers.'

He settles on a wide stance, to pull her foot forward, off the ground.

Lady grunts, staggers to maintain her balance on three legs.

O'Bryan probes with his fingers, then replaces the foot carefully.

Lady remains poised, keeps the weight off the sore leg.

'As you know ... ' begins O'Bryan, straightening and placing three fingers on the inside of his forearm, 'there are three tendons, and if one is torn or ruptured, the other two are more vulnerable.'

They walk back to the yard.

So: one step forward, two steps back.

Jane is nonplussed.

After the vet has gone, she walks away to escape from the noise of the diesel generator.

THE FOLLOWING DAY, a cow is walking around in circles.

Jane administers the appropriate injection of minerals, but two doses later the cow is still cornering as if she's on a racetrack.

YET THE SUMMER is still here, visits its lazy, somnolent magic

251

on the place, especially in the last few hours of the day, after the heat but before the midges come out at sundown.

At 5.30 in the afternoon, Todd and Jane reach the Wallabrook; they're sharing Tuppence because Lady is still lame.

At this spot, some five years ago, Mick brought out the JCB, scooped earth from the bottom of the stream to make a pool deep enough for swimming.

Todd stares; this is rich, to have a pond in the middle of a wild moorland stream which is deep enough to dive into. He strips off, dives in head first, arms straight but legs curled back, his heavy frame displacing all the water, it seems, then he comes up for air, gleeful, already at the other bank.

Jane slips off Tuppence's back, strips to her costume and walks in.

They call to one another when they find the warm spots which move through the current; patches of water have been heated during the day, having settled around sun-baked boulders further upstream.

Todd's head sits on the surface of the water. 'Not so cold as you'd think.'

The lavender-coloured dragonflies helicopter back and forth, gaudy flying machines which work the banks of the slim, deep passage of water.

Billy snaps at them.

Then Jane walks out, goes to Tuppence; she leads the old horse into the brook at the head of the pool, turns him downstream.

She calls, 'Out the way, coming through', and jumps on his back.

Todd's floating head asks in disbelief, 'You're never?' The wet hair clinging to his beefy shoulders gives him the look of a Trojan warrior.

'Out the way.'

Todd drifts towards the bank while Jane clicks Tuppence forward, he knows what's up, he's going for a swim.

After three paces, the water level rises to his hocks; a pace further on, the underside of his belly. Jane feels the chill water around her ankles.

She pushes him on, reined to the centre of the stream.

Tuppence sinks gracefully. His tail floats, he pokes out his nose.

Now the water rushes up Jane's thighs, covers her midriff; she and Tuppence are swimming. It's a curious, bouncing motion, his legs treadle beneath him, Jane clings on to his mane, her seat loosened; the turbulence of the water lifts her off.

At the sight of her, Billy is up to his usual trick: he dashes up and down the bank, alternately barking madly then biting the earth, ripping off chunks, before running for a new position.

Roo watches calmly, seated.

Then Tuppence is rising again: his feet hit the bottom, his back reappears, his stomach, legs, dripping wet.

She rides him on to the bank, then dismounts, gives him a reward, rubs behind his ears, takes his bridle off.

She slips back into the water and Todd's floating head is there, he asks, 'Ride me, then?' and it's easy for her to take his hand, squeeze it, run on to his shoulders and they embrace, she wraps her legs around his hips.

Jane feels a lift of pride, she lays a hand along his chin; the other she runs down his back.

They kiss.

It's like the end of the journey, she has herself back in possession, after the troubles of last year, she can take a mate.

So: it's the beginning, a renewal.

While they make love, the dogs lie panting in the late sun.

253

AFTERWARDS, THEY GATHER up their clothes, the dogs; Jane loops Tuppence's reins on her arm.

They choose a random sheep path to take them home, facing into the sun which lingers behind a distant Caistor.

Yet, as they come closer, there's the noise of the generator, like a warning.

JANE FIXES A rope to Lady's head-collar, switches back the bolt, encourages her from the stable.

She's improving, less lame, and Jane takes her number one horse for these gentle walks, as entertainment.

She heads into the Top Field. They stroll past the mountain of big-bale silage, walking over newly mown grass: the wheel marks made by the Fiat decorate the ground in kaleidoscopic patterns.

Lady limps beside her.

Jane watches carefully, judges: yes, definitely better, but it'll be a slow haul.

She reaches the topmost corner of the field where the concrete water tanks are placed, swings right, tracks inside the windbreak.

Lady has loosened up a bit, Jane sees her ears flicker: back, then forth.

A dozen yards further on, Lady flings up her head, stops dead, ears pricked forwards. She's seen something; Jane can't discern what. She encourages Lady forwards again, Lady's stride is more dainty, now; her neck swings from side to side, her head stays high.

Jane soothes her.

Moments later, Lady stops again, takes one step shy of the

windbreak; Jane herself is sure she caught a flash of something in there, the colour red winked in the corner of her eye, she must avoid this, immediately turn and take Lady home.

She stares at the windbreak but sees nothing. Lady snores on long, outward breaths, scenting, fearful.

Carefully, Jane guides Lady into the turn for home.

Yet even as they do this, Lady bounces, Jane has to hurry to keep up, holds her elbow against Lady's shoulder to keep herself out of the way of Lady's front feet, then Lady dives, her weight falls on her extended fetlocks, her head lowers, Jane knows what's coming.

Lady shies sideways, away from the windbreak, Jane's on the wrong side, in the way. She tries to run around the front but then Lady jumps forward, so now Jane is knocked by Lady's oncoming neck, falls under her chest, is trampled.

As she goes down, there's the noise and fright of the accident: the horse's strained breath, the thud of hooves, the uncoordinated click of metal hooves striking . . .

Jane notices two things at once – in the windbreak there's a human figure, a red top, a blue leg angled from behind one tree to gain the hiding place offered by another.

Close by, in the same instant, she sees Lady's off rear foot imprint itself on her bare thigh, there's a sudden, agonising pressure as she momentarily bears the weight of the horse and as Lady gallops off Jane looks down to see the neat, exact imprint: a red, angry bruise, a smear of mud, it's a horseshoe, facing down, the good luck pours out.

JANE EXPECTS TO see Lady fleeing across the field; instead she is only a hundred yards away, face on to the windbreak, her eyes peeled to the whites, her ears talking like mad, her nostrils are rolled out with fear, pain.

She's carrying her rear leg, can't stand on it.

Jane curses.

SHE TESTS HER weight on the leg, finds it's OK, not broken.

She takes the bad leg with her down the gentle gradient of the Top Field, winces at the bolt of pain which meets every step.

The farm is spread out below her.

She heads down through the stable yard, into her barn, eases herself into a sitting position, leans against the wall, reaches for the dusty, scratched phone; the vet's number is one she knows by heart.

She knows also, it's nine-year-old Jamie, Chris Gilbey's son, who is wearing a bright red T-shirt, blue jeans, today.

He was hiding in the windbreak, spooked her horse.

O'BRYAN, THE VET, races almost from the other side of the county, but he doesn't need long to make up his mind. Almost as soon as he's arrived, he's gone.

Only minutes later, Peter Davey rolls into the yard in the battered Daihatsu four-wheel-drive, clambers from the cab. Jane marks his spindly, long-legged frame, underneath his left eye the rind of scar tissue like a rope across his cheekbone, the jaw on the same side misshapen.

'Jane.'

They shake hands. 'Good of you to come. This is Todd.'

256

'Pleased to meet you.'

The trio walk up to the Top Field where Lady stands in the same spot: close by is a sheaf of hay, water, a feed bucket.

Todd stands off to one side, while Peter Davey inspects this same horse that he sold Jane for half its worth all those years ago; but now it's a different story, Lady's eye is dulled with pain, the gloss has gone from her coat within hours, she rests the swollen leg. When Jane attaches a rope to her head-collar, her nose comes up, her eyes roll, she makes a groan of complaint at being asked to walk forwards, refuses to budge, even with the painkillers coursing through her bloodstream, now.

Peter Davey runs his hand down both her hind legs; in the one which trembles he strokes at the swelling, measures the heat.

Jane unclips the rope. Lady stands there, doesn't move.

'Nothing you can do,' Peter Davey admits.

Jane agrees, she was told that.

'Who is the vet, O'Bryan?'

'Yes.'

'He's good.'

Jane feels powerless, a sense of injustice invades her, but she knows that for a man who's rarely seen off his own place, Peter Davey's visit is a gesture, means something. She thanks him.

'Thanks for nothing,' he replies, 'it's a sad day.'

There's silence, a while passes, a grace note. Angels pass overhead.

So: they head off back down the field.

Jane looks back when she turns to close the gate behind her: Lady is in the same position, looking over her shoulder.

Jane leads Todd and Peter Davey down to the stable yard.

THEY'RE IN THE tack room. The noise of the generator is a steady, even tone, underscoring these events.

Peter Davey tests his clean-shaven chin with his fingertips.

Todd leans against the door, puts his hands on his hips for a moment, then drops them.

Peter Davey pulls out a half-burnt cigar from a tin.

'You know, before your father died, I forget, now, how long ago, me and him bred what we knew was a fairly good point-to-point prospect, and we had a bit of a scam over it, we over-watered her before every race so as to slow her down, so we kept the odds better for ourselves, that is, until the last race of the season, then we put our shirts on her, and cleaned up.'

He pauses for a while.

'Any road, that one there, Lady, she was our next prospect, your father's and mine,' he explains, 'so your father owned half of her anyway, a fact not known to the world at large. Then your old man went and died, and I was left with half his horse, and no one to know. So I called you up and forced you to buy her for half her value.'

So Jane gets her long-awaited answer, as to why he sold her for so little.

Peter Davey goes on: 'We shared a bit of everything, me and your father, so your taking this horse was only fair, if you like, because she was a secret held, between me and him.' He points upwards.

When Peter Davey leaves her yard, there's the handshake, but there isn't the smile that she enjoyed before: when she bought Lady off him, she remembers, he hung on to her hand for ever it seemed, while he exhaled this 'Ahhh', a sound of goodwill, accompanied by that long smile.

Now, in its place, Peter Davey wears a mute expression, he's quick to separate, climb back in the Daihatsu, all legs and arms, his Adam's apple bobs up and down as he sucks at the lifeless cigar parked between his lips.

JANE CHECKS THE action, cocks the spring with some difficulty, feels the thump of the metal in the heel of her hand as the bolt leaps forward to the end of its travel. It's working.

From here, they can see the full sweep of the moor, Lady has a sight of the open landscape.

She scouts in her pocket for the handful of nuts.

Billy and Roo wander around, Todd stands off to one side; their shadows are yards long, now.

Jane murmurs a trickle of kind words as Lady briefly raises her head, accepts the nuts.

Jane runs out of terms of affection.

A nerve in Lady's rump jags with pain, her ears are limp, set neither forwards nor back, unmoving.

The dogs meander back and forth, question what's happening. Todd keeps his distance.

For a while Jane waits, soothes her horse, thinks of the work she's done, the years they've enjoyed together, adventures on this range of wilderness.

The tranquil, dusky horizon marks the precipitous slope beneath Wotton Tor which Lady would carelessly take her down. Grey Weathers is like a triptych on the western horizon; hidden further up the fold of the valley is the abandoned Cleave Farm where she always rides on Christmas Day and always makes a mental note, puts down a marker for herself, to judge how time comes around again, for her horse, her dogs, the farm a year older each time, sometimes in the freezing rain or snow, sometimes in chill winter sunshine with skies so blue it might be summer, if it weren't for her

shoulders hunched against the cold, the gloves on her hands
... now it won't happen again, with this horse.

She scratches beneath Lady's forelock; now she lifts the tip
of the bolt gun between Lady's eyes, presses harder, aims
exactly into the whorl of white hair, the star between Lady's
eyes, pauses for a moment.

Three things happen at once: a loud crack empties into the
sky, the recoil jumps against her hand, and in the same instant
the horse that she's ridden for the last eight years drops like a
stone, cleanly, as though a string holding her up has suddenly
been cut.

Todd stirs, shifts his weight.

A sigh is pressed from Lady; but then she's utterly still,
deadweight, her blood will settle.

The dogs, having fled at the sound of the concussion, now
return, ears cocked, inquisitive.

Jane thinks, Their lives aren't scored on the landscape –
hers, Lady's – as she used to think, they've merely overlaid
these acres for a while, indistinctly, before someone else will
come along to replace them.

The discharged bolt gun dangles from Jane's right hand; she
checks an impulse to throw it away.

JANE SPENDS THREE nights in a row in the Cross Keys public
house. She wears a brave face, mentions nothing of her loss
unless someone else does first, she jokes at the dartboard and
the pool table, leans her elbows on the bar, smiles at other
people's stories, puts down her money, buys the round,
drinks her share.

Todd drives the Mini Cooper home.

It was Jamie, Chris Gilbey's youngest, who spooked her horse. Jane wonders whether to talk to him, if she can hold on to her feelings.

The next day she scoops up Jamie in the stable yard, takes him off, away from his brother.

He looks distant, worried; it reads as arrogance.

Jane asks, 'Was it you, hid in the trees?'

The colour drains from his face, his mouth turns down at the edges, he lifts the back of his hand to obscure his face. Jane picks it off, keeps talking, 'Listen, was it you, hid in the trees?'

The boy gulps air, tries to bluff that he's not about to cry. Jane holds his arms in like he might up and fly, she shakes him, just an inch or two. 'You were there, weren't you?'

Jamie's mouth is still pressed closed, he dares to look at her only occasionally.

She advises him, 'You can admit to it. It was an accident.' She can feel him heave, still, with his smothered cry, but as she holds him, he calms; the movements lessen.

When she lets him go, he runs away, scared.

By the end of the week they're all gone, father and sons, it's the end of the summer holidays, there's no car, the noise of the generator is not so much quiet, as it were, just waiting for their return.

The work demands to be done: insistent, steady, a matter of life and death.

Although, Jane might believe she hauls on the line of chores, hand over hand, to keep herself sane in the aftermath of Lady's death.

At dawn she rides Tuppence out to find the herd. The air is light, intoxicating, but there's a mad atmosphere on the moor:

261

the side of Fraser's Hill is on fire, the smoke palls on the horizon.

A heifer, Joyful, behaves oddly, crosses and recrosses the stream in some unexplained, lonely panic.

Two steers are trapped in the newtake, they run up and down the wall to find a way out.

The sign on her back gate, PRIVATE, has split in two.

She sees a Charollais bull, where no bulls are allowed.

When she catches up with her herd, they all stand motionless as though waiting for something; none is bulling.

Jane rides back to the farm where the dent from Lady's corpse is still visible in the grass, as well as the vehicle tracks from when the body was collected by the Mid-Devon Hunt kennels.

She stays away, scythes the bracken which is trying to take over the End Field, her leg aches as her arms swipe forwards, *forwards*.

THE POST LADY sits; Jane takes the chair opposite.

Miss Egan sifts the paper envelopes, the kitchen knife a thin oblong of reflected light next to her.

Jane idly examines the surface of the kitchen table; the sun throws each imperfection into relief. She remembers, the chickens walk around on it.

The last time she came here, she was riding Lady.

Jane watches Miss Egan's fingers, adept at sliding the letters from the envelopes, her protuberant brown eyes scan the lines quickly.

The Real Meat Company confirms it can't agree to qualify her farm as organic – not as yet – because she treats her animals with prescribed drugs, she's given them mineral licks, the sheep have been fed on non-organic supplement.

The irony is, without a mortgage around her neck, now she can probably afford the luxury of converting, wear the extra cost of organic feed, the increased loss of animals due to the restricted veterinary care.

A handwritten note from a neighbour gives her notice that the field she's proposed renting to bring on her calves is only available until May: she'll either have to sell short or find extra keep.

She enjoys the stability of the new money, such a setback can't cripple her any more, there isn't the sense of impending financial ruin that she suffered last year, at the arrival of the mail. Even the flow of the letters themselves has dwindled.

The older woman picks at the next envelope, holds it ready, a large-size A4.

'From the Dartmoor National Park,' she begins, then stops, frowns, unfurls a plan.

Together, they lean over it.

JANE BECOMES INTENT, focused.

Her stance changes, she grips the edge of the table as if she has to hold fast, she leans closer to the plan.

Frowns are engraved on both their faces.

Jane uses the envelope as a straight-edge, she lays it over the drawing.

The older lady checks the date on the top of the page, then she sifts through the letters, to find a similar envelope, posted months earlier.

Jane bats back and forth around Miss Egan's kitchen, unable to sit.

263

Unknowing, Tuppence waits in the yard.

WHEN JANE ARRIVES back at the farm, she turns Tuppence into his field, dumps the tack, fetches out the Mini Cooper, bumps down the drive.

She wants the truth of the matter, first hand.

She races off the moor, down the lanes through Gidford; a few miles out the other side, she comes to a T-junction, turns right, takes the main road towards Newton Abbot. She grips the steering wheel with both hands, holds the engine to its furthest sticking point, the front-wheel-drive pulls her around the corners, full speed; she only eases the accelerator when a steep incline means she would choke the engine.

Just outside Newton Abbot, she turns into the driveway of an establishment run by the Dartmoor National Park. She's been here before; but this time she hardly notices the grand old house, office for the DNP's planning department.

She walks in, gives herself half an hour before she has to return to the farm.

Immediately, the planning officer comes down to meet her – a male, bald, with bright blue eyes set slightly down at the outer edges, which gives his face a naturally comic expression: John Bernard.

Jane explains what's happened: she's just received notice of the appeal, the rebuilding of the house at Latchworthy Farm, near Gidford . . .

John Bernard listens, the blue eyes sharpen, yes, it's his case, there's the appeal, she's the only neighbour.

Jane explains how Chris Gilbey told her he was going to rebuild the house, they talked about it, but she didn't know he was going to bring it out, extend it forwards, so far.

Jane feels hot, flushed, her jaw aches from talk, she's inexperienced at this.

She repeats, still amazed, it's like an eclipse: Chris Gilbey is trying to take for himself a *clear, fifty-mile view across the Devon plain*.

JANE AND TODD are slumped in the two armchairs. Each holds a beer. They're not consciously looking, but at the focus of the two chairs are the Harley-Davidson and the Husqvarna, driven in through the barn doors, out of the rain.

Finally, they've spoken about the irony of the situation: that if they'd got together last year, maybe Jane wouldn't have needed to have sold up. They might have formed a partnership. He could have come in with her, paid a bit of rent, she needn't have given the place over to Chris Gilbey.

She has to hang on to the memory, that she didn't want it to feel like she might have sold herself to Todd, back then. It wasn't false pride, more that they would have been going into a relationship on the wrong foot. This is better, their coming together without any financial bearing on the situation.

Yet, it's worse.

Jane remembers with disbelief the early months of this year, January and February – in those days, she was crowded with optimism, work carried her forward, she had new wealth, which instantly dissolved the intense, nervous irritation of her financial predicament, Chris Gilbey had barely arrived, she had thought she could contain the situation, turn it into a likeable, neighbourly relationship – but now, bad news has crept up behind her, she's turned around, here it is, a blank wall, it faces everything off, both in terms of the farm and of her own interior life, which for so many years has been uncomplicated, steady.

Jane's bewildered; she has never experienced such bottled-up emotion, combined with a sense of impending doom.

She counts it as bitter, unfair, that Todd has to walk in on this, instead of easy, unfettered happiness.

JANE AND TODD walk the outskirts of the farm.

She thinks, I'm bumping against the boundaries like the maddened calf born from Puzzle, last year.

It's windless, but the air is heavy with autumn moisture, as thick as it can be without turning into fog – static, rich weather.

Time stands still, idle.

Trees let go of the first leaves, a jay ducks its head – the only evident movement a comical one, as it decides which branch, next.

Billy scouts ahead; following on their heels is Roo.

They walk for some minutes, gain the highest point on the farm: standing on the matched pair of concrete tanks which provide the farm's water supply.

Dartmoor is behind, to the left, to the right; in front lies the farm: enclosed fields, a wooded valley, the river – a loop of cultivated land holding out against the wild.

The same as ever, the green, gently rolling downlands of the mid-Devon plain reach as far as Exmoor, fifty miles away, sighted in the V-shape made by Scaur Hill on the one side, Caistor on the other, the same as the view from her barn which Chris Gilbey intends to eclipse.

The sky is a featureless pearl grey, opalescent.

Jane counts the animals: Belted Galloway cows, Scotch sheep, grey-face sheep, chickens, dogs seated beneath them, only one old horse; Todd at her side, now.

The lack of movement gives the landscape the look of a painting: the feed barn with its adjacent pile of plastic-wrapped silage bales, the stand of beech trees, the backdrop of the moor.

Jane feels her inbred response, to get back to work: worm the ewe lambs, sort the broken-mouthed, move Harry the ram to the Stable Field, after the second cut of silage begin to spread manure.

A moment later, the impulse passes.

They climb down from the water tanks, walk along the side of the windbreak. Their breath, the clump of their rubber boots, is loud in the expectant landscape.

Here Lady fell. Then, past the spot where her father died, his hand tucked inside his coat, *Like this*.

They move steadily forward, the dogs run ahead.

The gates stand open or shut, according to a map drawn by her alone, as she goes about her daily work.

They follow the inside fence of the windbreak; the unnatural quiet allows them to hear Roo's pant, as well as each crack of a twig under Billy's feet as he explores.

They cross the top of each field, the pasture mown but grown anew.

A gate is tricky to open – Jane's pet hate. She thinks, How quickly this place would fall into disrepair, if no one cared.

They make a detour, scramble over the fence into the windbreak itself, something Jane's not done for years, since it's become such a thicket, the lower branches of the pine trees deprived of light, so dying off.

Todd unshoulders his coat, lays it down.

They don't undress, but sit on the coat, like it's a picnic. He's bear-like, a Viking, she's a suitably strong bride.

When they make love, his shoulder moves at her chin.

She closes her eyes.

She has the sense of the grass growing quicker; the wild animals and the birds are miraculous.

Billy and Roo stand, watch, no longer surprised at this ritual.

AFTERWARDS, AS THEY stoop among the low branches, every now and again they come across the skeleton of a dead lamb or sheep, gnawed clean by carrion hunters, the crows or foxes, the fur strewn for yards around.

Parallel with the End Field, they climb out of the windbreak, head downhill, pick their way through the trees, over the boulders, the ground falls away sharply beneath them now and it's soothing, the sound of the river working at the foot of the valley.

They cross the pipe carrying water to the electricity generator, a straight line among the tumbled mass of foliage, the roots bared, torn by storm waters pouring off the higher land.

Jane was overawed at the destruction down here, after the 1987 hurricane, which saw a dozen trees blown over, not to mention the crushed fences, a barn destroyed.

They reach the river, clamber among the rocks; the water is still low after the drought of the previous two years so they can make their way over the dry humps of boulders, some of them big as motor cars, which have been discovered by the youthful, erosive power of the water.

During the hurricane, Jane tells Todd, a boulder fell from the ridge of ground above, pushed one unlucky sheep in the river, pinned it to the bottom of the stream, so it drowned, a silent, unobserved death. She noticed it only weeks later when she came to see if she might retrieve lumber.

They comment on the mystified but enthusiastic dogs, wondering at the drugs in Roo, what they've done, exactly, to engineer this renewed vigour.

They beat a path through the woods to the electricity generator shed. Jane retrieves the key from its hiding place, unlocks it.

Here is electricity, power.

If she tries to bring the mains supply up here, which means paying for the last two miles of cable, she'll be rid of Chris Gilbey's diesel generator, but also this shed will inevitably be closed down, fall into disrepair, a silent ghost of her father's good idea, to be discovered anew, marvelled at, some time in the twenty-first century perhaps: look, this old building contains an ancient machine.

Yet, still virile now, it shames her with its steady, uncomplicated roar, almost free of cost.

In the gloomy interior, the rush of water and the drumming of the dynamo fill their ears, until Todd winds the valve closed.

There's silence. Jane performs the routine service, then Todd winds the valve open, releases the water pressure. They stand close, allow the noise to vibrate through their bones – Jane tries to draw it in as a permanent memory.

Roo and Billy pant at her feet, eye her anxiously.

They lock up, hide the key, plod back up the hill.

Here, she tells Todd, is where she first caught sight of Chris Gilbey as he trespassed on her field.

There – he swung over the stile, heading away from her.

Now she has to face him, at the appeal hearing.

ON THE DAY of the appeal, they rise to a sun weakened by high, grey cloud cover, the same stillness dawdles over the farm that she's used to, there's no cock-crow.

When Todd opens the door, the dogs run out: Billy scatters, barks for no reason, Roo hot on his tail.

Jane and Todd linger in the front area between the barn and the house. She remarks, there's still no sign of Chris Gilbey.

Yet his absence, even, tightens her nerves.

She walks up the yard, visits Tuppence who is his usual self: slow moving, steady, unconcerned, his foreleg lifts, knocks once against the door, a standard request to be let out, while she changes his night rug for day, turns him loose.

She goes back to the barn, doesn't trust Todd's watch, he telephones the speaking clock to be sure of the time.

She looks out clean clothes, brushes her teeth: such practical attempts to appear respectable are probably worth counting on.

They sit together in the makeshift kitchen area, count the moments.

Roo sits with them; his nails click on the bare concrete.

They watch time pass.

The appeal will be heard at eleven, it's a fifteen-minute drive to Gidford, so they'll leave at half past.

She soaks her face with a hot flannel, pulls her fingers through her hair, instead of a hairbrush.

She tries on a coat, then takes it off again despite his protests.

She chooses the Defender, for the drive down. When she tries to fit the strip of toothed metal into the ignition, her fingers shake. Todd climbs in next to her.

The diesel engine settles immediately, gives its familiar rattle when cold.

She takes off, the chunky vehicle slow but powerful.

She bounces out of the driveway on to the unfenced, single-track road which crosses the moor, and the presence of the farm leaves her, like a skin sloughed by the cattle-grid; she's left with this sense of nakedness.

The Defender fills the width of the lane, carries them over the second cattle-grid, takes them off the moor, between the hedges, now, which hold back the cultivated fields – down-country.

Jane bowls into Gidford as if her life depended on it; then in the town square she comes to a halt, reverses into a space.

She's nervous, makes a mistake: she pushes over a moped belonging to the ironmonger's son. Todd picks it up, pulls it on to its stand, then they go into the Cross Keys.

In the pub, Jane stares across a pint of cider, the background noise passes her by, she fights off the feeling of inadequacy, what will she say?

Half of her wants Todd there, the other half, no.

In the event, she leaves her glass, leaves Todd behind. The autumn sunlight blinds her as she heads over to Endecott House, alone.

THE ENTRANCE TO Endecott House is a medieval arch holding up a deep, musty porch; Jane walks through, squeezes past a knot of elderly ladies who check the notices posted on the board.

Her eyes adjust to the gloomy interior. Inside, there are rows of chairs laid out – around fifty – for the audience to witness the appeal, which will be heard around a pair of trestle tables which have been set against each other in a T shape.

Up there, at the moment, Chris Gilbey sits alone.

271

Jane stares for a moment, registers that it's really him, this isn't a dream.

For several moments she watches: he has a slim pile of papers in front of him, he smiles, leans forward, talks politely over the table to his adversary from the Dartmoor National Park, John Bernard, who is taking up a position opposite him, across the table, plus he has someone at his side, probably a lawyer.

This good-humoured conversation gives Jane the measure of Chris Gilbey's confidence in this action he's brought: it's a confidence, she recognises, that he'd be able to summon anyway whether warranted or not, a necessary part of the costume.

So they are the plaintiff and the defence, in this mock-trial: Chris Gilbey versus the Dartmoor National Park.

Her gaze moves on.

At the centre of the T sits a man whom Jane doesn't recognise. He has grey hair dressed in plentiful waves, black spectacles, a dark suit: he has an imposing, theatrical presence, while beside him sits a thinner, younger man, who's arranging papers likewise; their heads are together, the younger man points, words drop inaudibly from the corner of his mouth.

Jane wanders in, there are knots of people, plus one or two others sitting down already. She nods to John, Kathy, Mr Stanton, Robin Cook from Barton, Jamie, the middle-aged son of the family who run the hotel down at Beaworthy, it's no surprise to come across Miss Egan – Jane knew the Post Lady would be here, frail, tilted to one side, but full of energy, life, she wears the same clothes.

Jane greets these people, while at the same time she's distracted, glances always at Chris Gilbey.

Now there's a general movement: everyone sits.

In silent agreement, Jane and Miss Egan are next to each other.

A hush falls on the room.

The Independent Planning Inspector remains seated, so his introductory address is informal; in a matter-of-fact tone he outlines the situation, it's something he says every day of his life. He's charged by the Department of the Environment to adjudicate a planning application made by Mr Gilbey to the Dartmoor National Park, for the proposed rebuilding and extension of a derelict property at Latchworthy Farm; he'll listen to Mr Gilbey's presentation first, afterwards, the Dartmoor National Park will give their grounds for refusing to grant planning permission, and after he's heard both sides of the story, he'll invite members of the public to ask questions or to make statements either in support of or against the project, so to that end, he invites Mr Gilbey to start.

Chris Gilbey stands, fingers the notes on the table in front of him.

Jane recognises the special, low voice; she can sense everyone lean forward, strain to hear.

'First, I have to say something – that to arrive here, in this beautiful place, was one of the proudest moments of my life; to feel a part of it, to be lucky enough to own a portion of it under my feet, is awesome, but hand in hand with that sense of respect for the place I've never been more conscious of a sense of responsibility towards it . . . '

His gaze strays over the public, seated to his left; he catches Jane's eye.

She feels stuck, she suppresses the impulse to acknowledge him – but his calculating look appears briefly, to be replaced by open friendliness and he makes a small signal – because he can't know whether she's for or against him.

273

Jane listens as he introduces his proposal; his tone of enthusiasm builds, now.

The speech is long-winded, thorough, conversational. He campaigns on two issues – the first is that he is proud to restore the place to its former grandeur: he brings up affectionate, anecdotal details concerning the old house which stood there, not so long ago, he mourns its loss.

Jane is cold with anger.

Then he leaves the table to stand adjacent to the flip-chart; from here, he uses the drawings seen by Jane in the offices of the Dartmoor National Park to illustrate the proposed new building. He compares it favourably to an enlargement of the photograph of the old house.

The Independent Planning Officer makes notes on the papers in front of him; Jane imagines they're affirmative, yes, yes.

Chris Gilbey's second purpose, Jane realises now, is to reinforce the benefits which the proposed building programme will offer to the local population – jobs will become available, both directly and indirectly, substantial orders will be placed with local contractors and suppliers, he will contribute to the local economy.

It's half an hour later when Chris Gilbey winds up his address: 'I've invested in property, before, yes, but I'm not a property speculator. I've no intention of making a fast buck, then leaving. I want to build a life for myself, raise my two sons here, and in doing so, I want to invest substantially in the restoration of this property, which will inevitably impact favourably on the corporate well-being of Gidford.'

He glances here and there, to see his message hit the mark; then he sits.

The Independent Planning Inspector gives no sign of being impressed. 'Now we'll hear from Mr John Bernard, from the

Dartmoor National Park, and from Mr Harris, his legal representative.'

When Jane took her HGV tests, the invigilators had this same studiously uninvolved air, it's trained into them, she guesses.

It's Mr Harris, the lawyer for the Dartmoor National Park, who rises to his feet. He has a different style of address, he simply talks, there's no sense of a grand soliloquy to the public, he has facts and figures, mostly concerning the traffic flow up and down the lane from Gidford to Latchworthy, as well as details of a handful of other unsuccessful applications in the area ...

It sounds precious little – cars per hour, number of households *en route*, the number of designated pass spaces. It's dry stuff.

Then, only at the last minute, he makes the point which Jane's been waiting for: that the planning permission for rebuilding the ruin was transferred to her barn – a planning permission which she herself has taken up for a building which now seems to have its view ruined, shortened by fifty miles, if Chris Gilbey's proposed new building is allowed. He makes this point in such an offhand way that it seems doubly powerful to Jane, the unfairness of it made greater because of the deadpan delivery – but that might be how it appears only to her. Certainly, if the judgement's made on the skill and personality of the two speakers, the National Park would have lost already – Chris Gilbey has painted a portrait of himself, of his character and motives, which she knows is wrong.

She can't bear it: anger flutters in her breast, she's dismayed at the idea he'll win the appeal.

With his dry, disengaged voice, the Independent Planning Officer checks his watch, moves on. 'It's now ten to one o'clock. May I suggest we adjourn for lunch, and reconvene here at 2 p.m. sharp for anyone to ask questions or make statements.'

Jane finds herself on her feet. 'Excuse me.'

The Independent Planning Officer pauses, looks at her over the top of his black-framed glasses. 'Yes?'

Her knees shake, she tries to lock them, tenses her legs, keeps her hands behind her back: 'Jane Reeves, Latchworthy Farm,' her voice stumbles on. 'I can't spare any more time, not this afternoon. I was wondering if I can have a say, now?'

'Go ahead.'

Jane avoids Chris Gilbey's eye. She stares at the Independent Planning Officer from the Department of the Environment, her mouth dries, she feels sweat pressed from her skin, she leaps at the first thing that comes to her mind, as if it will save her: 'He is a property speculator, and if I'd known that from the start, I'd never have sold it to him.'

A hush falls on the room. Everyone was preparing to pack up and go for lunch but now they're like statues, no one speaks.

Jane plunges on, her voice a shout in the sudden quiet, her words clumsy, unformed.

Then she looks at Chris Gilbey: he's facing away from her, his fine, straight hair shines under the overhead lights, the tip of each point stands on his collar, shaking.

The space he occupied in her, almost like fear, a dread, empties now, suddenly, and refills with determination.

SHE DESCRIBES HOW she first saw him trespass on her fields, and the story from then until now. In her account, she manages to include unsubstantiated allegations she heard from John Bernard, that Chris Gilbey had burned down a

Grade II listed façade in Norwich. She's on her feet for fifteen minutes.

When she sits down, there's an immediate murmur of approval. Jamie from Beaworthy gives a solitary round of applause.

Jane is breathless, a headache grips her forehead, she wants to leave.

Unmoved, the Independent Planning Officer is once again calling to adjourn for lunch. It's a strangely pedestrian atmosphere. She feels as if she's been fighting for her life.

Jane stands again, joins the circle of people winding around the chairs in a clockwise direction, in order to leave the room.

As she shuffles forward, she becomes aware that Chris Gilbey is heading around the opposite way, they're both making for the door and are pegged equally distant in their respective lines, unable to escape each other.

When he arrives at the door first, he waits, holds out his hand: 'After you.' His animosity is contained but she can feel its heat, see it, plainly; his graciousness is for the benefit of the Independent Planning Officer.

Jane steps into the murky porch, the outdoors a bright picture ahead: a sun-washed street, parked cars glint, people walking.

Then, behind her, Jane hears the word 'Cunt.'

She doesn't believe it, but then it comes again, Chris Gilbey is calling her a cunt, and this time it acts as a switch: a red mist of anger colours her view, she turns and he's there, facing her, she wraps a hand around his face, she walks back with him towards the wall, the frail figure easy for her to push off balance, his legs tangle with hers, his arms try to claw himself free.

She pushes Chris Gilbey against the granite wall of the porch; the shock enters his sharp blue eyes. She feels his teeth, his saliva against her hand which adds to her anger, she tilts his head against the wall – thump – then anger tracks through her nervous system, comes out in an involuntary spasm: in spite of his vigorous resistance she bangs his head against the wall harder, a third time and the report is a remote, dull thud, as if builders next door dropped a hammer. His small, clever eyes roll, show briefly white, then close. He slides to the floor.

Jane recovers her equanimity immediately, in front of the queue of startled people. She's surprised to hear words come from her own mouth, 'Sorry everyone.'

She arranges Chris Gilbey on his front, turns his head sideways, makes sure his airway is clear, places one arm beside his head, the other curled down to his hip.

Then she leaves.

JANE TRIUMPHS AGAINST Chris Gilbey's appeal. It's posted as usual in the local press. When notice of his failure comes through, Chris Gilbey's car was seen drawn up outside the newsagent's shop.

Now it's local folklore: as soon as the newsagent unlocked the door, apparently, Chris Gilbey walked in, bought up the entire stock of the local paper, the *Western Morning News*, with no explanation.

Everyone knows, it's like in that film, Chris Gilbey's effort to prevent local people seeing the article, the grounds on which he was refused, as well as the fact reported, that the plaintiff bringing the appeal was assaulted and concussed by a woman farmer.

It was an overwrought effort to prevent everyone in the area from hearing about his humiliation – Jane enjoys hearing that word, yes, his humiliation – except now he ensures the story is told over and over in Gidford's half-dozen pubs, for the rest of time.

He hasn't been seen since.

At Latchworthy, a FOR SALE sign has gone up opposite Jane's barn.

Together, she and Todd are drawing up plans for Todd to purchase it. To maintain income, he'll have to avoid selling machinery in an attempt to raise capital. It'll have to be a 95 per cent mortgage. Jane will lend him 3 per cent, plus stand as guarantor. He'll use the Stable Field as an equipment park.

The final irony was that the FOR SALE sign interrupted Jane's view, until she told David Fowles to move it.

NOVEMBER 11 – HARRY the ram is required to go to work, yet the proud stamp of his foot is no more, he won't stand: it's a mag deficiency or a viral infection.

Whatever, Jane has to lift him because he's threatened by bedsores, now, his manly face has worn thin, his testicles hang like gourds, a nuisance, but all this effort is aimed at encouraging their eventual performance.

Jane plumps for making a sling.

She rummages through a trunk for an old nylon sheet, then shoulders open the door to the workshop to lift the block and tackle from where it lingers for years at a time on a nail against the back wall.

She finds Harry in the same position, his nose on the ground, his back end offered as if for target practice.

Jane drags the block and tackle up a ladder to hook it over the beam. From this height, Harry looks like an accident victim, ready to be taken away.

She pushes a corner of the yellow sheet under his bony

sternum, hops over to the other side to pull on it; she hauls once, twice – the sheet is halfway through.

She straightens it under him so it reaches from his elbows to the crook of his groin, see-saws him backwards and forwards a time or two, a further indignity.

Now the yellow sheet is evenly spread, it floats from under him, Harry the ram is garlanded in yellow, his back legs hooked over the straw bale, his weight squashed on to his front quarters, it's as if he's been trained to adopt such a position, decorative enough for the harvest festival or the Gidford Show Procession of Floats.

Jane ties double sheet-bend knots, to fix him to the lifting gear. She takes the rope which snakes up to the rafter, begins to haul on it. The mathematics of the pulley block account for the easy work.

Harry is lifted inch by inch, he's suspended, the weight taken off the sore spots. His feet dangle uselessly.

Jane eases the rope by fractions until his toes are on the ground, then she ties off the rope.

She takes Harry's jaw in her hands; the density of the bone, the width of his brow, the depth of his skull surprise her, after dealing with the more diminutive ewes for so much of the time. She says, 'Buck up, Harry.'

The oblong slots in the middle of his eyes – again so much bigger than in the ewes – are mute, an expressionless, animal depth with only a pure life in them – built on instinct.

The next morning, she sidetracks from the usual chores to check Harry's condition. His water's half gone, he's eaten every scrap of hay, it can't be all bad news.

She takes the bottle of penicillin from the cranny in the wall, the hypodermic from her pocket, draws off 10 ml and bangs her fist three times on his rump; the third time she deftly wraps the needle in her fist, in it goes, she drives the plunger home, pats the top of his head, 'Come on Harry, stand up.'

Yet, he won't give up his holidays easily. It's two whole days before he's walking around again.

On 16 November, Jane shakes the cobwebs out of the ram's harness, levers out the old block of dye with a screwdriver to replace it with a square of bright red; with this emblem blazing in the middle of his chest she leads him out to the Stone Field.

Occasionally he digs his toes in, refuses to move, but she pushes him on.

He walks with swaggering self-confidence.

Jane thinks, Better late than never.

Yet, his arrival is greeted with a deafening lack of interest from the blackface ewes; one or two of them spare him an incurious glance, but there's no show of welcome or affection.

Jane slips the halter from over the ram's ears, says, 'Go get 'em, Harry.'

Harry struts for a pace or two, his testicles bang against his hocks, his ears are forward, he looks keen; for a moment Jane thinks he might paint the field red while she watches.

Then he puts his head down, eats grass.

As ever, she'll have to wait to see what the score is.

Just then, she hears the double-thump of Todd's Harley climbing the driveway, the powerful torque delivering him safely, again.

So much of farming, Jane thinks, involves waiting, while working to prevent a disaster somewhere else.